ONE LAWLESS NIGHT

Greedy for as many memories of her as he could take away with him, Matthew made the evening last as long as he could.

He walked her back to the hotel slowly. It was late; the night was dark. Stars blinked gloriously in the sky, blind to every unhappiness on earth. Their conversation had changed in the past hour, from boisterous to happy to contented.

Matthew stopped at her door and pulled his hat off his head.

"That was . . . a real good meal."

"Yes, it was wonderful. Thank you, Matthew."

"You're welcome. Enjoyed it." He bent and kissed her cheek. " 'Night, Ettie. Sweet dreams."

A half hour later, a very soft knock fell on her door.

She pulled her wrapper on and went to open it; Matthew, standing in the hallway, stared back at her, his blue eyes intent.

"I want to stay with you tonight," he said quietly.

Her heart began to pound in her ears. She had never felt more sure of anything in her life, or more frightened of anything, either.

"Yes," she whispered, stretching one hand toward him. "That's what I want, too."

By Mary Spencer

Fire and Water
The Coming Home Place
The Vow

Available from HarperPaperbacks

Fire and Water

⋈ MARY SPENCER ⋈

HarperPaperbacks
A Division of HarperCollinsPublishers

HarperPaperbacks *A Division of* HarperCollins*Publishers*
        10 East 53rd Street, New York, N.Y. 10022

Copyright © 1995 by Mary Spencer Liming
All rights reserved. No part of this book may be used or
reproduced in any manner whatsoever without written
permission of the publisher, except in the case of brief
quotations embodied in critical articles and reviews. For
information address HarperCollins*Publishers,*
10 East 53rd Street, New York, N.Y. 10022.

Cover illustration by Aleta Jenks

First printing: April 1995

Printed in the United States of America

HarperPaperbacks, HarperMonogram, and colophon are
trademarks of HarperCollins*Publishers*

❖ 10 9 8 7 6 5 4 3 2 1

This book is dedicated to my mother, Judy Spencer, who always believed I could be a writer, and who, when I was confined to bed rest for the last three months of my first pregnancy, came one day bearing a legal-sized pad of paper and a sharpened pencil, both of which she thrust at me with a one-word command: *"Write."*
This book is also dedicated to my father, Peter Spencer, from whom I inherited straight teeth, a bad back, and a love for corny jokes.
Thanks, Mom and Dad, for everything. I love you both very much.

Special thanks go to Ms. G. Faye Allen and to my two great-uncles, Alton E. McQueen and Morris N. McQueen, for their invaluable help and support, and also to my cousin by marriage John Sullivan, without whom Matthew Kagan would have been faceless. Thanks for letting me take all those pictures of you, John!

For Thou, O God, hast proved us; Thou hast tried us, as silver is tried. . . . Thou hast caused men to ride over our heads; we went through fire and through water, but Thou hast brought us out into a place of abundance.

Psalm 66, verses 10 and 12

Prologue

Washington, D.C., November, 1893

Five minutes. That was the most David Call knew he had to live.

He could hear the footsteps on the stairs, heavy boots running up after him. He could hear the shouts. Not too loud. Angry, but not too loud. It was late, and the men who'd come to kill him wouldn't make the mistake of waking any neighbors.

Five minutes. It wasn't much, but it was all he had. It would have to be enough.

His hands and body shaking badly, he stumbled inside his bedroom and slammed the door. They were close. So close he could hear them right there on the landing. His fingers slipped on the key as he desperately tried to turn it . . . slipped again; a hand on the outside grasped the handle just as the key turned fully.

He fell against the wall, staring as the knob twisted

in vain. A fist struck the door, and one of them shouted, "Call!"

Sweat poured off his forehead; his teeth chattered in his mouth.

"It won't make any difference, Call!" Another fist slammed on the wood, making the hinges squeal.

He was going to die. He knew that. There was nothing he could do now, even if he wished it. It was Mariette he must think of. *Mariette.*

His wobbling knees nearly gave way when he tried to walk to his desk; the shouts, the violent twisting of the doorknob, magnified his fear. But he thought . . . *Mariette* . . . and made his legs work.

She would want him to be strong. He had done all of this for her, to prove himself worthy. Now, in the last few minutes of his life, he would do what he must, and he would do it right.

Dropping into the chair, trying to ignore the threats of the men in the hallway, he pulled his opened journal toward him. He'd already chosen the poem; he'd searched it out long ago, though he never believed he would need it. If he had, he would have finished the matter before. He must finish it now, while he had life left.

Lesson Plan, November 5th, 1893: McGuffey's Alternate Third. Page 176. Two . . . four . . . six. First is Capitals. Second is Letter S.

He wrote it as clearly as his shaking hand would allow.

"Call, you can't escape!" The door was going to give way soon. A man's body shoved at it, cracking the wood.

He was breathing through his mouth, afraid he would faint out of fear, too soon. He willed his hand to work harder.

Third is Donne, "A Valediction: Forbidding Mourning."

This last gave him courage. His death poem, yes, but also his love poem for her. He wanted to write, *I love you, Mariette,* but couldn't. This was the only way he could say good-bye. There could be nothing of her in any of this. Only he and Anderson knew. . . . How he prayed Anderson would finish what they'd begun, that he would keep the vow they'd both made, that he would find a way—*please, God*—to keep Mariette safe.

They shoved at the door again. It splintered. He closed the journal, pushed it away, dropped his pen. They shoved once more, both men. The door broke almost in two.

David Call leaned back in his chair and closed his eyes.

Mariette.

He loved her so, with a passion he'd never been able to speak. He loved her, but he wondered, crazily, in these last moments of his life, if she would know how much. He had never told her in words; he hoped she would remember his actions. If she did, she would know. If she would only remember. . . .

With a loud crack, the door gave way completely. David Call looked at the men who were going to kill him and closed his eyes once more.

1

Sacramento, California, May, 1894

She had forgotten what California was like in the spring. Back east the weather would still be cool; in some places there might even be snow still melting from the winter. Here it was hot, more like summer than spring, and Sacramento itself was humid, the busy, swelling delta and river ways making it so, yet Mariette found it far from unpleasant. Humid it might be, but it couldn't compare to the swamplike misery of the District of Columbia. Why the early fathers of the United States had ever determined to set their capital in such a place, Mariette would never be able to fathom. She was glad to be quit of it and thankful to be home again after an absence of so many years. Now, as she made her way down Second Street, the sun noon-high and the sky clear and blue, she wished, achingly, that she could stay in this place where she'd spent most of her youth. That was impossible, of course. Her father had made it so.

The bell to the entryway of the Wells Fargo office jangled as she pushed open the door, and the clerk behind the counter greeted her at once. "Good morning, Mrs. Call."

"Good *afternoon*," Mariette corrected, smiling at the young man.

"Yes, ma'am," he replied good-naturedly, pulling a letter and a paper-wrapped package from beneath the counter. "It came at last. Arrived just an hour ago on the last stage."

"Oh, my!" Mariette couldn't keep the vivid relief she felt out of her voice. She'd waited so many months for this moment. "Is there any charge to pay, Mr. Sattler?"

"No, ma'am." He set the letter in the gloved hands that eagerly reached for it. "It was all paid for at the point of origination. This came with it." He pushed the package toward her. "It's all paid for, too."

"Thank you, Mr. Sattler," Mariette murmured, picking up the small package with curiosity. She hadn't expected Josiah Anderson to send her anything but the letter, yet it bore his name—Anderson—and so must have come from him as well.

She took both items to the office bench and sat, putting the package aside and tearing open the wrapping around the letter.

"Guess we won't be seeing you every day, now, since your letter came," young Mr. Sattler said, and Mariette, concentrating on the unfamiliar handwriting that greeted her eyes, answered distantly, "Yes."

Dear Mrs. Call,

I opened your letter to my brother only yester-day, and am sorry that it has taken so long for you to have a reply. I am certain you had no way of knowing this, having left Washington so soon after the regrettable death of your fine husband, but my dear brother also died last month, in a riding accident.

"No," Mariette whispered, squeezing her eyes shut against the words. The fingers that clutched the paper trembled, and a tide of emotion swelled over her . . . disbelief, horror. Fear. "Oh, no. Not Josiah."

"Is it bad news, Mrs. Call?" Mr. Sattler asked.

Mariette gave him no answer as she lowered her eyes to the letter once more.

I have only now been able to set aside my grief and attend to my brother's business matters, thus this delay in responding to your letter, for which I again apologize. I know what good friends your husband and Josiah were, indeed, I can think of no other man whom Josiah liked and respected more than he did Professor Call. He was deeply honored to work with him at the university, and was devastated when Professor Call died, as I'm sure you remember from the words he gave at your husband's funeral.

I'm afraid, Mrs. Call, that I haven't any knowl-edge of the project you mention in your letter, which Josiah had worked on with your husband. There were many such projects during their associ-ation, I recall, but this particular one is unfamiliar to me. Is it possible that someone at the university

*might know about it? Mr. Carteroy came with
some other gentlemen from the university after
Josiah's death and went through his study quite
thoroughly, removing everything they believed was
of value. If you wish it, I should be happy to visit
Mr. Carteroy and discover if he knows anything
about the project you are interested in.*

Mariette's lips tightened as she imagined how
amused Mr. Carteroy would be to receive such a visit.
Mariette didn't doubt for a moment that he and Elliot
Chambers's henchmen had indeed made a thorough
search of Josiah's study. They'd done the same thing
to David's on the night he died, but they'd left the
place a shambles. Had they had any better luck finding what they sought in poor Josiah's study, she wondered, or had the promising young professor died for
nothing?

*I did find, among my brother's things, a jour-
nal of your husband's which I thought you might
like to have. I do not know how Josiah came to
have it, but I'm certain he would want me to
return it to you, and so I have sent it along with
this letter. I wish I could have done more and
been of greater help.*

*I do hope, dear Mrs. Call, that all is well with
you, and that your decision to return to your
native state has proved a good and happy one.*

With all best wishes, I remain, sincerely yours,
Lucy Anderson

Mariette folded the letter and set it aside, unwilling
to think long on what its contents meant. She took up

the small package and unwrapped it, knowing before she was done what would greet her eyes.

David's strange little journal. He'd made notations in it every night, then tossed it aside without care. Mariette didn't even know what he'd written in it, though once or twice she'd caught words in passing and had thought he might be writing out lesson plans. With a faint smile she brought it to her nose to smell again the fragrant tobacco David had used and that had permeated all of his things. Tears ached in her eyes; she pressed her lips together and held them back.

"Are you all right, Mrs. Call?" Mr. Sattler asked, having watched her intently these past several minutes. "Was it what you were expecting?"

She barely heard him, and stared at the red leather-bound journal with sudden wonder. How had Josiah come to have it? He must have taken it the day after David died, when he came to the house to pay his respects. She'd been so distraught, but she could remember now that Josiah had insisted, quite firmly, that he must go into David's bedroom. And he had; Mariette hadn't cared about it, hadn't cared about anything then. He must have taken it, and she had forgotten all about it until this moment.

David's strange little journal.

She stared at it, and when understanding struck her at last it was with all the power of an explosion.

"Oh, my Lord!" she uttered.

"Are you all right, Mrs. Call?" the clerk repeated with real concern.

Mariette quickly stuffed the journal and the letter into her large purse.

"Yes," she said, standing and tugging the bag's drawstrings closed. "Thank you, Mr. Sattler. Good day."

Ignoring his protests, she pushed out of the building and onto the boardwalk. The bright sunlight seemed suddenly blinding. Mariette blinked against it and thought, as her shock subsided, that she must go home at once and have a look at David's journal and think everything through very carefully. Turning in the right direction, she was too distracted to see the men in front of her, and in her haste ran right into one of them.

"Whoa, there, Mrs. Call."

Mariette stepped back and looked at the man.

"You!" she cried in horrified disbelief. His hands were on her, on either side of her waist, and with disgust she pulled free. "How dare you!"

"Ma'am," the man replied pleasantly, smiling and tipping his hat. "It's a pleasure to see you again."

"A pleasure for *whom*, Mr. Quinn?" Mariette asked tightly, taking in his perfect, polished outfit with disdain. She hated him so much she could hardly contain the feeling. The gun she'd bought after David's death felt heavy in her bag. "Not for me, I assure you." She tried to walk around him, but he stepped in front of her.

"Now, don't run off, Mrs. Call. I only desire a moment of your time. Or rather, Mr. Chambers does."

Mariette looked into his handsome face, his smooth, smiling expression, and let herself enjoy the brief fantasy of what it might be like to put a bullet in that place between his big blue eyes.

"I haven't a moment to give," she said. "Not to you, sir, and certainly not to Mr. Chambers. You may tell him, with my compliments, that he may take himself to Hades. Now let me pass."

"That's not very friendly, ma'am," he chided. "Not

when Mr. Chambers asked me to come all the way to California just to see you."

Speechless, Mariette stared at him.

"Mr. Chambers has been purely heartsick that you haven't seen fit to let him call on you since you returned to Sacramento," he went on, reaching out a hand as if to take her elbow. "He was certain I might be able to persuade you otherwise." He gripped Mariette's upper arm so tightly that she made a small sound of distress. "There are some things a gentleman such as Mr. Chambers just can't bring himself to do, especially when a lady is involved, and then there are men like myself, who'll do just about anything"—his smile widened—"to anyone."

He wasn't any taller than Mariette and he wasn't very strong, needing little muscle for the kind of profession he pursued. The big, silent men standing behind him, however, more than made up for whatever Drew Quinn lacked.

With a determined effort Mariette wrenched her arm free.

"Don't touch me, you *murderer*!"

"And don't you be difficult, Mrs. Call, or you'll live to regret it. You come along quietly to see Mr. Chambers, now, and don't make a fuss."

Mariette made up her mind in less than a moment. She would do it. She had her gun; it was loaded. She would shoot him, here and now. He had killed David, and she would kill him. With both hands she began fumbling with the drawstrings on her bag, while Drew Quinn and his men watched the unexpected action with curiosity.

"Mrs. Call . . ." Quinn warned.

"Oh, be quiet!" she snapped, rummaging through

the contents of the bag, shoving David's journal aside. "This is difficult enough without you saying anything more, Mr. Quinn."

She found it at last. A Colt double-action .45-caliber revolver. It had been a heavy nuisance to carry around for the past three months, but the merchant she bought it from had assured her that, correctly aimed and fired, it would most certainly kill a man. Her fingers curled around the stock just as Drew Quinn reached out and grasped her arm again, so hard this time that she dropped everything—the gun, her purse—right onto the boardwalk.

"No more nonsense," Quinn said in an angry whisper. "Now pick up your bag and come along quietly, or I'll—"

"'S'cuse me." A big shadow fell over all of them. "Is there some problem here, ma'am?"

The shadow came from behind Mariette, but she could tell by the look on Quinn's face, by the looks on the faces of the other men as they stepped back, that whoever stood there was impressive. A dark scowl crossed Quinn's handsome features before he released her and stepped away as well.

Mariette found that she was shaking, and pressed one trembling hand against her stomach, where the realization that she'd just been about to kill a man had formed a knot. The shadow man moved closer, so tall and big that it felt as if a wall had walked up behind her.

"Ma'am," he said in a slow, lazy tone, "were these boys here botherin' you?"

She turned her head and looked at him, or rather, at his shoulders, which were what her eyes met until she craned her neck upward to see the giant's face.

He was one of the biggest men she'd ever seen, and was certainly a stranger to her. She never would have forgotten such a man if she'd seen him before. He was black haired and blue eyed beneath the brim of his hat; a thick mustache sat above the mouth that was, at present, set in a taut line of disapproval as he stared at Drew Quinn.

"Sir—" she began. But Drew Quinn interrupted quickly. "A disagreement, Marshal. That's all. No harm meant."

"That right?" the big man said, unamused. "Disagreement, huh? You always go yankin' women around like that when you have a disagreement, boy?"

Mariette glanced back at Quinn, who looked rather unsettled.

"Mrs. Call and I are old friends, Marshal," he replied, sending a chilly smile in Mariette's direction. "Isn't that right, ma'am?"

She couldn't think how to respond. Quinn had called the stranger a marshal, and as much as she longed to speak the truth, she didn't dare involve the law in any of this.

"It was a . . . disagreement, sir," she said at last, rubbing her arm in the place where Quinn had held it.

"You see, Marshal?" Quinn said easily. "Just a little disagreement. Nothing more."

The big man made a grunting sound and bent to pick up Mariette's bag.

"I'll tell you what, boy," he said to Quinn, "I don't care if it was a kiss on the hand." He shoved the bag at Mariette. "I ever see you or your friends treatin' a woman that way again, and you and me'll go have us a little talk in private. You understand what I'm sayin', now, don't you, boy?"

Quinn flushed deeply, and Mariette wondered if he'd ever been addressed in such a way before.

"Of course, Marshal. Completely." Quinn looked at Mariette. "Forgive me, Mrs. Call, if I've caused you any distress." He sounded a perfect gentleman. "It was purely unintentional, I assure you."

Mariette said nothing, only glared at him.

He tipped his hat. "It was a pleasure seeing you again, ma'am." He turned as if to leave, then stopped. "By the way, Mrs. Call, a friend of yours from back east asked me to give you his regards when next I saw you." Quinn's smile was perfect. "The very best regards, ma'am, from Professor Josiah Anderson. Good day, ma'am. Marshal."

2

Sacramento had always been one of his favorite cities, but Matthew was beginning to wonder if maybe he shouldn't have another think about that. The place certainly was turning out to be a curse for him this visit. If he'd known what he was getting himself into, he would've told his boss in Los Angeles what to do with his damned political favors, and Matthew himself never would have set one foot outside his own territory. But here he was, in Sacramento, and it was too late for him to turn tail and run.

The windows from the state supreme court offices in the B. F. Hastings Building offered a full view of Second Street. It was a good-looking city, no doubt about that. Nice wide streets, well thought out, plenty of boardwalk. Just what a city ought to look like, in his opinion. In the distance, Matthew could see the dome of the state capitol. It was a mighty fine building, one he'd set up against any other state capitol.

And just below, if he craned his neck a bit, he could see the place in front of this building where he'd just about lost his temper a half hour ago.

There were plenty of things that made Matthew madder than a wild pig with a wasp up its snout, but seeing a woman harassed was at the top of the list. Just recalling the way that lowlife fancy pants had manhandled that woman dressed in widow's weeds made his blood boil all over again. Mister Slick and his friends. They'd had her outnumbered all right, had been having a real good time intimidating her until he'd shown up. Matthew would have enjoyed knocking their noses into the backs of their heads, but the poor woman had been so pale and shaky that he hadn't wanted to upset her any more, and so he'd let them walk away.

He'd wanted to escort her to her home. He'd told her so, he remembered, or had started to tell her, but she'd mumbled a quick thank-you, grabbed her bag, and run off faster than he could think, and he'd found himself standing there on the boardwalk with nothing but the memory of a fine-looking woman with blond hair and big gray eyes and skin as perfect as fresh cream to keep him company.

Matthew rubbed his chin thoughtfully and called back an image of the man who'd been pestering her. There was no doubt he was trouble; Matthew'd seen so many criminals in his day that he could just about pick one out in his sleep. The question was, how much trouble was he? Matthew wouldn't have minded spending a few more days in town to find out the answer, or maybe even to take care of the problem personally, but all he had was this afternoon and tonight, and he doubted that'd be sufficient. Still, he didn't like the thought of that good-looking widow-woman being bothered again, especially by a slick, fancy-pants little—

A door behind him opened.

"Marshal Kagan?"

"Mmmm?" Matthew didn't even turn.

"Senator Hardesty will see you in Judge Byer's room, sir."

The whiskey was smooth, Matthew had to admit as he settled into the big easy chair Senator John Hardesty had offered him. A whole lot smoother than the situation was. The good senator, a short, balding man of great fame and wide influence, looked as if he'd just gotten over a deathly illness. Pale, sweating, and tense, he paced the room for several minutes as Matthew kept silent and watched. At last the man stopped, stood in one place, and contemplated the flowery carpet.

A long silence prevailed, while Matthew sipped his whiskey and began making a mental list of all the complaints he was going to give his boss when he finally got back to Los Angeles, the first of which was having to spend any amount of time with a politician who stared at carpets.

Just as Matthew took a long sip of whiskey, Senator Hardesty said, "Do you have any children, Marshal Kagan?"

Matthew nearly choked. He sat forward, sputtering whiskey all over and gasping for air.

"'Course I don't have any children!" he said when he could. "What kind of thing is that to ask a man?"

The senator lifted his head and regarded him with

interest. "It's a very common question," he replied. "A perfectly normal question."

"It's a damned nosy question, if you ask me," Matthew told him. "And, no, I don't have any children, leastways, none that I know of. I ain't even married, so I sure hope I don't have any kids I don't know about."

The senator nodded, drew in a breath, and released it loudly, then went to sit in the chair behind the big desk in the room. He looked, Matthew thought, thoroughly dejected, a man beaten to the ground and weary of life.

"You're a fortunate man, then, Marshal. A wise and fortunate man. You've been spared the greatest suffering a man can know."

Matthew gave a silent groan and closed his eyes. Lord! How long was this meeting going to last? If he'd wanted melodrama, he would've gone to the theater.

"My daughter," Senator Hardesty continued sadly, "has been the joy of my life. We've always been close, and even after she married, she and her husband lived near me in Washington, D.C. This is the first time we'll be parted, truly parted, since the day she was born." He looked at Matthew for sympathy. "I don't think you can appreciate how difficult it is for me to let her go, sir. I'm sure you can't appreciate it, never having had children of your own."

"Don't s'pose I can," Matthew agreed readily. "But Santa Ines ain't exactly the other end of the world, you know."

Senator Hardesty gave him a wan smile. "More than you know, it is, Marshal Kagan. I'm grateful that you'll be escorting her there, and that you'll keep an eye out for her safety. Mariette's been under a great deal of stress lately, since the untimely death of her husband. Of course, she's still grieving. I'll feel much easier knowing she's not making this long journey alone."

Matthew could think of nothing to say—nothing polite, anyway. Twenty years a lawman, and here he was, reduced to playing nursemaid to some spoiled senator's daughter.

"Marshal Brown recommended you highly, Marshal Kagan, and assured me that you're his most capable deputy. I'm certain Mariette will be safe in your company."

Matthew glared at the man and stood to refill his glass. "Marshal Brown is a paper-pushin' toe-kisser who got where he is by handin' out favors like this one," he said curtly. "He wouldn't know the meanin' of the word *capable* any better'n he knows how to load and shoot a gun. But I'll keep your daughter safe. Hell! I'd keep your pet dog safe if it meant getting back in my own territory again."

Senator Hardesty gave Matthew the kind of look that Matthew knew only too well—the one that warned he was just about pushing his limit. Matthew met the look directly as he settled into his chair once more.

"Marshal Brown isn't the only one who hands out favors in this state," the senator said with gentle menace. "I remember your grandfather very well from the days when I was an assemblyman here, Marshal Kagan. And your father. Your family's cattle ranch in the Santa Ines valley has prospered quite well over the years, I understand."

Matthew's eyes narrowed, and the senator's face relaxed.

"And, of course, there was your brother's divorce a few years ago, which I'm sure you'll recall I helped push along. An interesting situation, that divorce. The circumstances surrounding it were somewhat questionable, as I seem to remember, and required some . . . smoothing over."

"That whole mess was nothin' but a mistake," Matthew muttered. "And in case you didn't know, my brother and his wife got remarried."

"Yes, I did know." John Hardesty's benign smile widened so that his teeth showed. "I was glad to hear that all had turned out for the best. They've been happily wed for, is it two years now?"

"Three."

"Yes. That's right. And they've started a family, isn't that right? They have two young sons?"

Matthew looked at the man with contempt, understanding anew just why he hated politicians.

"Next you'll tell me what they had for supper last Tuesday," he said dryly.

Senator Hardesty laughed. "Of course not, sir. My observations are merely friendly, I assure you. I've simply a natural, friendly interest in a family with whom I've enjoyed a long association. And a natural worry for them, too. It would be such a shame, wouldn't it, if all that unpleasantness from the past were to somehow make itself known? Such a terrible, unhappy shame."

"I said I'd keep your daughter safe," Matthew said from gritted teeth. "What more do you want?"

Senator Hardesty leaned forward. "You make that promise too quickly, sir, as if accompanying Mariette were some kind of foolishness. But I love my daughter, and I want her watched over. *Constantly.* I want to make certain she arrives safely in Santa Ines, and I want you to understand that before I let her go tomorrow."

Matthew stared at the man for a silent half minute, then set his whiskey aside. "You got some things to tell me, I reckon, that I don't know about yet. Go ahead and put your cards on the table and we'll see what we come up with."

The senator paled, his bluster suddenly fled. "That's all there is. Nothing more. I only want to make sure Mariette's kept safe. Does it seem so strange to you that a father should want such a thing for his child?"

Matthew gave a sarcastic laugh. "Senator, there ain't all that much that could happen to your daughter on a trip like this, 'cept for maybe a little unwanted attention from some fellows on the train or some blisters on her rear from rattlin' around in the stagecoach. The porters on the train are always keepin' a watch out for women who travel alone. The blisters she'll have to live with.

"Now, I could understand it if you hired some lady companion to travel with your daughter, or maybe if you paid somebody you could trust to keep an eye on her, but to go to the trouble of havin' a federal marshal sent all the way out of his territory just to hold your little girl's hand down to Santa Ines . . . well, sir, I'll tell you straight out, that's a bit much. So you go on and explain what this is all about and we'll get along fine."

If it was possible, Senator Hardesty grew even paler. "There's nothing else to tell," he insisted. "Mariette is my only child. She's the daughter of a United States senator, a ready target for every manner of blackmailer."

Matthew gave him a look of utter disbelief. "Hah! That's the best joke I've heard all year. You think anybody'd go to the trouble of kidnappin' your daughter when they could buy your favors just as easy and probably a lot cheaper? Forget it, friend."

"Now, see here!"

"No, you see here," Matthew suggested angrily. "I've had enough. I didn't come all the way to Sacramento to listen to some overblown political jackass spout threats and nonsense at me. I'm here because you told that spineless boss of mine to send me up here. So all right. You wanted me"—he pointed a finger at the indignant man—"you got me. If you ain't satisfied with the merchandise, I'd be happier than a cock in a henhouse to pack my bags and go on home."

Senator Hardesty was an admirable opponent, Matthew discovered when the man's features smoothed over and he spoke his next words.

"There's no question of being dissatisfied, Marshal. You are exactly as I've been led to believe."

"All right, then," Matthew said, forcing a calm he didn't feel into his voice. "We'll just sit here and have us a nice little talk, and you'll answer my questions the way I want 'em answered, or I'll get up and leave town and your daughter can find her way to Santa Ines by her lonesome."

He probably shouldn't have been so hard on the old man, Matthew thought several hours later as he stretched in the small bed. Not that it had done him any good, of course. Senator Hardesty might be a weary, broken man, but he was still shrewd enough to keep his mouth shut about things that Matthew figured would be mighty interesting to hear. The man was a blank-faced liar, sure enough. Matthew wouldn't have wanted to meet him across a poker table, ever. There was a lot more to the situation than met the eye, but Senator Hardesty wasn't going to be the one to tell him what it was. All he wanted was his daughter kept safe. He'd said it so many times Matthew couldn't keep count. The trouble was, he never said what or who it was he wanted his daughter kept safe from.

"Emma, honey." He patted the bare arm of the woman who was sleeping against him, her head warm on his shoulder. "Come on and wake up, now. It's gettin' to be daylight and I've got to go."

She stirred, made a muffled sound of disagreement, and flopped her arm across his chest as if to make him stay.

Matthew chuckled and moved his fingers down to her waist to tickle her. "Come on, sugar. Get your lazy old self up. I'm going to be late at the depot if I don't get a move on."

"Matthew!" she protested sleepily. He kept tickling and she made a fist and whacked him. "Stop it or I'll kill you!"

He laughed and sat up while she rolled to her back and glared at him. "Just about killed me as it was, honey," he said, adding, with sober amazement, "My Lord, we broke your bed again."

"Every time you come to town, Matthew Kagan, I end up having to buy a new bed."

Matthew stretched and yawned, making a good deal of noise, and scratched his hairy chest, then stood and started searching out his clothes. "Sorry 'bout that, Emma. There's just somethin' 'bout you that makes me kinda reckless, I guess."

Emma sat up, wrapping herself in the sheet. "Don't you try to flatter me into thinking I'm the only one who has that effect on you, Matthew Kagan. On your grave your epitaph will read, 'Some men leave behind a string of broken hearts. Matthew Kagan left only broken beds.'"

Matthew grinned at her as he pulled on his pants. "Emma, you're a fine woman. Got a wit I could sharpen a knife on. Always said you was too smart to be a whore."

"Too smart not to be, you mean," she corrected, pushing auburn hair back from her pretty face. "I have the pleasure of entertaining men such as yourself, sir, and get paid for it, too. What other occupation could give me that?"

Buttoning his shirt, Matthew gave her a wry smile. "Now who's tryin' to flatter somebody up?" he teased, then said, more seriously, "Not every man who comes through that door is a gentleman, honey. You're going to get tired of havin' to put up with that kinda thing one of these days."

"Then I'll retire—when that day comes." When Matthew made no reply she finally said, "I'd retire this minute if I had something better to do."

"Would you, honey? What would you consider somethin' better?"

"Being a wife."

Matthew's smile, when he looked at her, was warm and gentle. "You'd make some man a good one, too, Emma. You surely would. Bet this town is full of men who'd like to have a woman like you for their own."

Her eyes held his steadily. "What about you, Matthew?"

He laughed and sat to pull his boots on. "Me? What would a sweet young gal like you want with an old man like me? You'll be needin' some young fella who can keep up with your . . . ah . . . energetic talents."

"You're not so old," she said, frowning.

"Older than you know, sweetheart. Old as sin. Wouldn't waste half a dollar tryin' to redeem my own self."

She gazed at the floor in silence, then asked, quietly, "Will you be back in Sacramento any time soon?"

Standing to strap on his gun belt, Matthew said, "Don't think so, honey. Don't think I'll be doing what I do much longer, or so my boss tells me, and I won't have much reason to travel up here. Reckon this'll be the last time you'll have to put up with me." He sat on the bed beside her, took one of her hands, and brought it to his mouth to kiss. "I'll miss you, Emma. We've had us some fine times together, and you're a good, sweet woman. Too good for this kind of work. I sure wish you'd get out before it eats all your sweetness up."

She touched his face with the tips of her fingers and shook her head.

Matthew put money on the bedside table, then bent to kiss her. When he lifted his head he looked into her sad face. "You take care of yourself, Emma. If you ever need some help from old Matthew Kagan, you know how to get in touch with me." Nodding toward the money, he said, "I left plenty for a new bed. Make sure to buy one that won't break so easy."

She gripped his arm. "Come back if you can. Please."

He kissed her again and left.

3

Tickets in hand, Mariette picked up her traveling case and walked toward a nearby bench to await the call for her train to be boarded. Her other luggage had been tagged and loaded already. There was nothing else to do.

She sat, put her bag down beside her, and looked at the tickets she held. This was the end, then, at last. Once she boarded that train there would no longer be anything familiar in her life: not her father or any of the homes she'd known or the life she'd lived for all of thirty-three years. And no David . . . nothing left of what she'd had with him, save the vow she'd made at his grave. All but that would be left behind once she boarded, and she would begin a new life in a place she'd never even heard of until she received the wire asking her to come and be the schoolteacher there.

Santa Ines.

It sounded barren and desolate. She'd never been

in the southern part of California. All desert, was
what she'd heard of it, and a lawless desert at that.
She didn't mind the lawless part; the vow she'd made
was unlawful, after all. But she wasn't sure if she
would like living in the desert.

"Mariette!"

She frowned at the sound of the unwelcome voice
but found, when she lifted her head, that her father
wasn't alone.

"I didn't want you to come," she said, standing,
looking not at her father but at the big man behind
him. She hadn't seen the man's badge the day before,
but now, as she looked at it, everything became perfectly clear. "Of course," she said. "I should have
realized yesterday that you were an angel on my
father's payroll."

The black-haired giant had been in the midst of
removing his hat and had been smiling widely at her,
but after a moment's hesitation he frowned and stuck
his hat back on his head.

"Mariette," her father said again, reaching out a
hand that Mariette recoiled from.

"I didn't want you to come," she repeated furiously. "How could you face me after what you've
done? I hate you!"

"I know you do, sweetheart, and I don't blame you.
But I keep thinking of when you were a little girl, of
how I could always make you laugh, and I . . .
Mariette," he pleaded, "you're my daughter."

"I wish you had remembered that," Mariette said,
"before David and I paid the price for your greed.
Now I want you to leave"—she looked at the scowling
giant behind her father—"and take your hired man
with you. He's given you plenty of service for your

money already." Then she added, with heartfelt disgust, "A federal marshal! You should be ashamed, sir, for selling away such a dignified office!"

"Now, just one minute, here," the big man began.

"This is Federal Deputy Marshal Matthew Kagan, Mariette," her father said quickly. "He'll be accompanying you to Santa Ines."

Mariette gaped at them as if they'd both sprouted horns. *"What?"*

"To keep you safe, sweetheart. Do you think I'd ever let you travel so far without protection?"

The porter began to call for boarding.

"You hypocrite!" Mariette uttered scathingly, full of wrath and indignation. "Keep him for your own protection, for I'll not have him!"

As she picked up her bag and tried to walk away, her father put out a staying hand.

"Mariette! Think of me what you will, but I regret what I've done! If I could only take it back, I swear to you I would! Can't you forgive me?"

She jerked free of his touch. "Not for as long as I can remember the way I found David that night." She held her traveling bag high, as if for protection. "Now leave me be. I want nothing to do with you or your henchmen."

"Mariette!"

She heard him calling her as she pushed her way onto one of the train's passenger cars. She chose a seat on the far side of the car, away from the depot's platform, shoving her bag beneath the cushioned bench chair and thrusting herself into the seat. She refused to look back toward where she knew he stood, and instead made her aching eyes gaze out the window at the river, which ran next to the depot.

"Mariette! I never meant it to happen! I swear it!"

He had moved to the open window opposite her, was begging to her through it. A huge lump was in Mariette's throat, her chest jerked sharply with each breath she drew; she felt almost desperate to get away. Pressing her lips together tightly, Mariette began to read the names of the ferries and barges that moved in front of her. If he dared to board the train, she told herself, she would have him tossed off. Senator and father or no, she would do it.

"Sweetheart . . . darling, please listen to me. . . ."

She would not listen to him. She had spent a lifetime listening and had found nothing good in it. He would go away in another moment, would stop making a spectacle of himself. He'd spent too many years gathering the power he now wielded to lose it by making such a distasteful scene.

"You know how much I cared for David. He was like my own son. I've grieved his death with my whole heart, and even more. Oh, Mariette, please!"

The tears fell hot on her face. She closed her eyes and shook her head and prayed for the train to go. Other passengers boarded, yet still he stood there, at that window, making a fool of himself.

"I—I wish you would remember how it used to be with us, Mariette. When it was just the two of us, after your mother died. Don't you remember, sweetheart? You were my whole life. You were the only thing I loved. Mariette, don't leave me like this!"

His voice had grown shrill and tearful. The train's engine had begun to make noise. Mariette felt suddenly confused, terrified. Why had he stood there so long . . . so long that the papers would hear of it all the way to Washington, D.C., and back? What was she doing on this train, leaving everything she'd ever known? She had a sick, dreamlike sensation that it was all so wrong, but that she'd never be able to move quickly enough to stop it.

She looked around wildly. The train was filled with people, every one of them staring at her and her father at the window, thrusting his face into the car and looking toward her with desperation.

"Mariette!"

The train began to move.

"Mariette!"

She put a hand to her mouth, turned her face.

"Mariette, please!"

The faces of the other passengers blurred. She heard him running alongside, calling her name, and she gazed at the blurry figures and thought, as his voice died away, that if they only knew the truth, they would never look at her with such condemnation.

Someone took the seat beside her and Mariette began to turn away, but a big hand came around her neck and turned her back, and a warm, strong arm moved about her shoulders, and Mariette suddenly found herself weeping into a giant's hard shoulder.

Well, this was just a dandy turn of events, Matthew thought irately as Mrs. Mariette Call pressed her face against his shirt and cried like her heart would never be whole again. The only reason he'd boarded the train in the first place was to give her a piece of his mind, which was just what she deserved after the way she'd insulted him. He'd been called plenty of low things in his day, but that . . . what she'd said . . . that was the worst. If some fella had dared to talk to him that way, the man would be eating his kneecaps right now and thanking God he was still alive to do it. But he'd stopped just inside the rail car and listened to her daddy pleading with her and had seen the way she looked, so full of pain it hurt just to watch. And when she'd started to cry . . . well, hell, he wasn't made of stone. He'd get around to setting her straight, sure enough. Just as soon as she stopped weeping, he would.

She lifted one arm all of a sudden and hugged him around the neck, pressing her face harder into him while she cried and cried. Matthew drew her close and ran a hand over her finely curved back.

"Well, that's all right, darlin'. You just go on and get it all out." He patted her shoulders gently. "That's all right now," he murmured again.

Everyone on the train was still staring, and Matthew lifted his head and demanded, "Ain't you busybodies got anything better to do?" They all at once looked away.

She cried for several more minutes, holding him, and Matthew patted her and spoke softly and looked out the window at the Sacramento River as the train rolled on. The river gave way to marshy fields after a while, with hundreds of water fingers veining through them, and then to neat farms and fields inhabited by cattle and other livestock. All the while Mariette Call held him, her tears subsiding, her warm, feminine body relaxing until she rested comfortably against him, and all the while Matthew held her and murmured, even when he knew she'd fallen asleep. He stared out the window at the passing scenery, telling himself sternly that holding Mariette Call wasn't different from holding any other woman, or even as good as it had been holding Emma the night before.

So it was something of a surprise to him, some time later, as the porter called out their arrival at Stockton, to feel so bereft when she suddenly came awake, and when she pushed out of his arms and sat upright and blinked confusedly.

Mariette Call, he decided in those few moments she took to gather her wits, was a handsomer woman than he'd had a chance to know the day before. She reminded him of a drawing he'd once seen, during his schooldays, of a young Queen Victoria—stately, pure, perfect.

Once her eyes focused on and recognized him, her smooth, goddess-statue face grew taut with disdain. She didn't lift her nose, but her voice sounded as imperious as if she had.

"Marshal Reagan, you smell like cheap perfume."

Matthew laughed and looked away, shaking his head and thinking that he'd remember those words for the rest of his life.

"It's Kagan," he said when he turned back to face her indignant, righteous expression. "Matthew Kagan, Mrs. Call, and I expect you to remember it."

"Please believe me, sir, when I tell you that I don't care what your name is. I want you to remove your-self from this seat at once, and when the train has arrived at Stockton I would like you to return to Sacramento and tell my father that I have refused your escort."

There was nothing more sure to make him stub-born. "Let's get us a few things straight right at the start," he said. "First off, there's nobody on God's earth can buy Matthew Kagan, or his badge, for any price, so you can just get that nonsense about your rich daddy payin' my way right out of your head. And second, escortin' some stuck-up senator's daughter down south sure ain't my idea of no honeymoon. The only reason I'm doing it is because the federal marshal I answer to gave me the choice between this duty or spendin' the next six months pushin' a pencil in Barstow."

"I'm flattered to be the lesser of two evils, sir," she said icily, "but I am perfectly capable of traveling without assistance. You may leave the train at this station and tell the marshal you work for that I have refused your protection."

The train began to slow and the porter called out their arrival at Stockton once more. Matthew folded his arms across his chest and gave Mariette Call a measured look.

"Your daddy been in politics a long time?" he asked.

The little muscles on one side of her face began to twitch. "All of my life."

He looked away and chuckled. "And you think the federal marshal in Los Angeles'll let me off that easy? You really think that, Mrs. Call?"

The train's whistle blew sharp and long, the brakes made a grinding sound. Mariette Call bent to gather her things, and even before the train came to a final stop she had stood and pushed past him and gone to sit in another seat in the back of the car. She was the first passenger off at the station, Matthew saw, when the porter called out their ten-minute stop.

4

She was stuck with the man, Mariette thought grimly when she reboarded the train ten minutes later and found him sitting in the seat she'd moved to. He looked comfortable, like one well used to the dreariness of traveling; he was so relaxed, in fact, that his enormous person took up well over half the seat's space.

"Have a nice time in Stockton?" he asked pleasantly.

His legs were stretched out over her traveling bag, making it impossible for Mariette simply to pick it up and move again. Seeing her glance at her bag, then back up at him again, the smile on his face widened, an open challenge.

She was stuck with the man.

"Would you mind making a little more room, Marshal?" she asked from clenched teeth.

His eyes wandered down her figure, to her hips,

where they lingered. "Don't s'pose you need all that much more room, do you, ma'am?"

The gun in her purse felt heavy to Mariette again, and she wondered what the other people on the train would think if she suddenly shot a fellow passenger.

She said to him, curtly, "I wonder, sir, in which sty you were raised."

He chuckled and scooted over. "I deserve that, I reckon. My sister by marriage is always givin' me grief over my bad manners." His smile grew dangerously charming. "'Fraid you'll just have to put up with it, Mrs. Call, for the next few days."

"Will I?" she asked, her body rigid as she sat.

"I guess you will." It was a statement of fact.

"We'll see about that."

He laughed again. "I guess we will."

The remaining seats in the car filled, with plenty of curious faces glancing surreptitiously at herself and the giant.

"I don't suppose," Marshal Kagan said conversationally as the train began its tugging motion, "that you saw who boarded the car in back of us at that stop with his two apes in tow?"

Mariette looked at him, at his tanned, calm, handsome face, and wondered how he could ask her such a thing.

"Of course I saw him," she said.

He looked back at her with eyebrows raised. "Wha'd'you mean, of course you saw him? You weren't expectin' him, were you?"

"What do *you* mean?" she demanded in turn. "Weren't you?"

"What's that supposed to mean?"

"Really, Marshal. You should know!"

The expression on his face could have melted a glacier. "I think you'd better tell me just what it is that we're talkin' about. Is that fella some gentleman friend of yours?" he demanded. "That what he's doing followin' you around?"

"Of course not!" Her stomach churned at the very thought. "I despise Drew Quinn!"

"Is that his name?"

Marshal Matthew Kagan was some kind of fiend, Mariette decided. A handsome, sadistic fiend. "You know full well it is!"

"Ma'am," he said tartly, leaning closer and looking quite angry, "I don't know it. I'm startin' to think I don't know nothin' about this whole mess, and that gives me a feelin' I'm not real fond of. You better tell me why that fella got on this train."

Leaning away from his imposing person, she said, "I assumed, sir, that since you work for my father . . . "

His expression became something terrible, so that Mariette actually felt afraid, and he leaned over her so far, gripping the arm rest, that he bent her backward. "Don't you *ever* say somethin' like that again," he warned. "I work for the United States government and no one else!"

"Yes, sir," she whispered obediently.

"Now, what's that man doing on this train?"

"Well," she said, as reasonably as she could with her back bent so far that she felt it might snap, "I imagine it's because he means to kill me."

If there was one thing Matthew hated more than just about anything else, it was that tingly sensation that shuddered up his spine when something unexpected happened. The reason he hated it, that feeling, was because every time he felt it, something bad followed, and he ended up doing the kinds of things that kept him awake for months afterward.

That unpleasant tingle was crawling up his spine right now, as he stared at Mariette Call. He told himself, in the few silent moments that passed, while the tingling spread across his shoulders and into the back of his head, that she was a senator's daughter, that her expression betrayed not the slightest bit of falseness, that she had beautiful, steady gray eyes, and that he was in a whole lot of a lot of trouble all of a sudden.

"I think you'd better explain yourself, ma'am," he said, easing away from her.

"I thought you knew," she said, pushing herself slowly upright, straightening her hat with one hand. "I truly did think so."

Matthew made no reply at first, but took a moment to glare at those folks in the car who were once again regarding them with undisguised curiosity.

"Well," he said, when every eye had finally turned away, "you thought wrong. Your daddy handed me a stack of lies, sure enough. I figured he would, but I ain't no mind reader. I can't tell what the truth is on my own."

"I certainly believe that my father lied to you," she admitted. "But I'm not certain how far ahead to begin. Perhaps it might be best—" Matthew saw how she struggled to find the right words. "Did he . . . did he tell you how my husband died?"

"Your husband's death was registered by the county coroner in D.C. as due to natural causes. That's what your daddy told me, Mrs. Call, that and the fact that you weren't home at the time the death occurred. You tell me how it is you think he died."

"I don't think, Marshal Kagan, I *know*. I was the one who found him that night, tortured and beaten like some kind of animal! My husband—!" She stopped with a sharp sob.

Matthew set his fingers over her arm and squeezed slightly. "You get ahold of yourself, now," he commanded in a low, stern voice. "We don't got any time for that kinda thing. You can go all to pieces later on if you want, but right now you just keep talkin'. Understand?"

Sniffing, wiping her eyes, she nodded.

"Good. Now, you say you found your husband that way, and it's plain you think he was murdered. All right," he said when she glared at him. "You *know* he was murdered. Was your daddy lyin' about that coroner's report, then?"

"No," she replied with taut fury. "He told you the truth. David's death was legally filed as due to natural causes." Her gray eyes were cold as steel. "Do you understand, Marshal Kagan, or need I explain it to you?"

No, he thought. She didn't need to spell it out. He hadn't spent the last twenty years doing what he did without learning a few unpleasant facts of life. Everything was suddenly crystal clear, at least as far as the good senator was concerned.

"Was it because your husband had turned on him? On your father? Was that why he was killed?" His lawman's mind rapidly turned the matter over again and before she could answer, he said, "No, that ain't it, is it? That don't explain why your daddy would haul me into this mess. If he'd wanted both of you dead, he would've fixed it back in D.C."

"My father isn't the one who had David killed,"

she said, "but he might as well have. He went along with Elliot Chambers's decision to question my husband on certain matters. Later, when David was dead, my father told me he never thought Chambers's men would kill him. He begged me to believe him, but still he used all his political influence to have the murder covered up. Can you imagine how I felt at my husband's funeral, Marshal? Knowing my father gave David over to those men and having to stand by and say nothing as he accepted condolences from his political cronies and told everyone that he had loved David as a son!"

Matthew gave a groan and rubbed a hand over his eyes. "Sweet mercy," he said with a weariness that he felt all the way to his bones. "Are you talkin' about the Elliot Chambers I think you're talkin' about? I don't s'pose, with my luck, there could be any other?"

"I doubt it," she replied. "One Elliot Chambers is surely enough for this world."

The way she said the man's name made Matthew's spine start tingling all over again.

"Your daddy was fool enough to get mixed up with Chambers, is that right? He did him the kind of favors and lookin' the other way that a man like Chambers needs to keep his illegal activities covered up?"

"I think so. Yes."

"And your husband got suspicious and was fool enough to go lookin' for information on one or both of 'em, and found it, didn't he?"

"My husband," she said with curt anger, "was not a fool, sir. He was a renowned and highly respected professor of mathematics. He was—"

"A *fool*," Matthew repeated, "who got himself killed playin' at somethin' he should have left alone."

"He was trying to do something about what he considered to be wrong and corrupt!" she protested. "No one has ever been able to find out enough about Chambers to stop him. There have only ever been rumors and whisperings. David thought perhaps, being so close to my father, he might be able to find something more real. Do you think he should have simply closed his eyes and pretended ignorance when he believed he could bring Chambers to justice?"

"What I think don't make any difference. Your husband's dead and gone, Mrs. Call, and when that last breath goes there ain't nothin' will make any difference anymore."

Her eyes filled with fury. "You certainly don't speak like a man who's sworn to defend and uphold the law, sir. My husband gave his life for the sake of a legal system he cherished, while you, a United States federal marshal, speak of such a sacrifice with contempt."

"Oh, my God," Matthew muttered irately. "What the hell would you know about sacrifice? For that matter, what the hell good did your husband's death do? He lost his life for somethin' he probably couldn't even begin to understand, to pull down a man too powerful to touch, and left you behind to fend for yourself. Was all that worth whatever he found out about?"

She looked away. "I don't know."

"You don't know?"

"I don't know what it was David discovered about my father and Elliot Chambers," she admitted softly. "He never—David never told me what he'd found. All I knew was that he and one of his associates, Josiah Anderson, thought they could find evidence

that Chambers was illegally importing goods into the
country. David never told me anything more about it.
After he was killed, my father admitted that
Chambers had discovered David had something on
him, and that he'd wanted David stopped before he
could do any damage. As I've told you, my father
insists that Chambers only meant to frighten David
into silence, or so he believed."

"What about this Anderson fellow?" Matthew
asked. "What does he know?"

"Nothing, anymore. Josiah promised me, after
David's funeral, that he would finish what he and
David had started and would bring Chambers to justice. I'd been expecting word from him regarding the
matter. Instead, I received a letter from his sister,
telling me that Josiah was killed last month in a riding
accident."

"Riding accident," Matthew repeated tonelessly.
"Well, that's just dandy. So what are our friends in
the next car following you around for? Chambers
must think you know everything. Isn't that what your
daddy dragged me into this for? Chambers put a
period to your husband's life, and now he's aimin' to
do the same to yours, and there's not a damned thing
your daddy can do to stop him."

"There's one thing he could do," she said quietly,
"but never will."

Matthew understood what she meant. "That's true
enough. He could tell the authorities what he knows
about Chambers. He figured he'd let me try to save
him the trouble, I guess, but if we come out of this
alive, Mrs. Call, you can believe I'll be payin' your
daddy a little visit to set him straight about such
things."

Her expression was solemn. "Do you think we will? Come out alive?"

Matthew let out a breath. "It all depends."

"On what?"

"On a whole lot of things. On just what kind of man Drew Quinn is. On how much of the truth I know about this whole mess. On whether you're holdin' back anything I should know. Now, I can't be sure, but Mr. Quinn looks like a fella with real steady nerves—not exactly the card you'd want to draw in a game like this. And you—" he regarded her thoughtfully, "look like a woman with a whole lot on her mind."

"Do I?"

"Uh-huh." Still contemplating her, his eyelids narrowed in a lazy, drooping manner. "Don't s'pose there's anything more you should tell me, is there?"

Her expression was blank. "No, Marshal. There's not."

"There'd better not be," he said, "'cause if there is, Mariette Call, I can promise we'll both live to regret you not tellin' me about it."

5

Marshal Matthew Kagan had fallen noticeably silent over the past several miles since they'd
pulled out of Lathrop. He sat beside the window, taking in the scenery with a thoughtful frown, tilting his
head back and forth and sometimes leaning forward
to look as far ahead as he could. He checked his
pocket watch often, as if he were expecting something, or someone, to arrive at any moment.

"Did you find a moment to eat anything at all,
Marshal?" Mariette asked, breaking their silence.

He looked at her. "What?"

"Did you eat in Lathrop, sir?" she repeated. "That
was the purpose of our stop there, I believe." A fact
she realized all too well, of course, since he'd practi-
cally carried her into the dining room, shoved her into
a chair in the middle of it, and gruffly told her to
order some food and stay put until he returned.

"Unless Drew Quinn's some kind of idiot," he'd

said, "he won't so much as look at you with all these folks around. So you just sit there and fill your belly and we won't have anything to argue about later on."

Mariette was quite sure she'd never known anyone so condescending. Even so, she'd found herself unwilling to disobey the man; she was certain that his idea of an argument and hers would prove to be vastly different.

Now he scowled and looked back out the window. "I had better things to do than eat, Mrs. Call."

"Like speaking with Mr. Quinn and his associates?"

He looked at his watch again. "Saw that, did you?"

"How could I help it? Everyone in the dining room saw." The confrontation had been interesting to watch; none of the men had so much as raised their voices, but the tension in the air had been palpable.

He made a grunting sound and looked out the window.

Another moment of silence passed before Mariette impatiently pressed him, "Well? What did you say to him?"

"Nothin' you need to worry about," he replied. "I was just settin' a few matters straight. If you're going to play a game, you got to make sure your opponent understands the rules."

"I see."

"I hope so."

"Then I don't suppose you would care to say where you disappeared to for so long, afterward?"

"Don't s'pose I would," he admitted, looking at his watch. "Reckon you'll find out pretty quick, anyhow."

"I will?"

"I'd say you'd best depend upon it, ma'am." He looked at her. "Do you know how to ride a horse?"

Mariette could feel her eyebrows rising despite her every effort to keep the surprise off her face.

"Yes," she replied slowly. "I know how to ride."

"Thank God for that, at least." He stuffed his watch back into his vest pocket. "Listen to me good now, for a minute, 'cause a minute's just 'bout all the time we've got." He leaned a little closer and Mariette, feeling like some criminal accomplice, did the same. "You know better'n just about anyone the kind of man Elliot Chambers is. He's rich and powerful, and even though he's done a lot of illegal things, there's never been any way to prove it. He's too smart to get caught, which is just why your husband ended up the way he did, and why that hired killer is tailin' you right now."

"Yes, I understand that," Mariette said.

"I'm not sure what your daddy was thinkin' by havin' me take you to Santa Ines, 'cause there ain't a whole lot of legal ways I can protect you. I'm out of my territory a ways, and even if I wasn't, there wouldn't be much I could do. If there was some evidence you had on Chambers, that might be different, but Mr. Drew Quinn is a whole other matter. Until some connection to Chambers can be made, he's a matter for local authorities, and that ain't goin' to help us out any. What I mean is, we can't just sashay into some sheriff's office and tell him you got a man tryin' to kill you when you can't exactly prove it. And you know full well Drew Quinn won't try anything until he's sure no one'll find out about it."

"Yes," she whispered. "I know. Mr. Quinn was rumored to be quite a professional at his trade, even in Washington, D.C." She thought of all the things David had told her about the man, and shuddered.

Marshal Kagan nodded curtly. "That brings our choice of roads right down to one, honey. We're going to have to make a run for it."

Mariette stared at him. "Make a run for it?"

"That's right. Now let's go."

"Go?"

"That's right."

He bent to pick up her traveling bag, and Mariette said calmly, "I'm not sure you've noticed, Marshal Kagan, but the train is presently moving."

He chuckled. "I may be gettin' old, Mrs. Call, but I ain't that far gone. Damn!" He lifted her bag and shook it. "What'd you pack in here? Bricks?"

"No, books," she said, standing involuntarily as he shoved her out of the seat. "Marshal Kagan, you cannot be serious!"

"Books," he repeated dismally. "Leave it to a schoolmarm to pack books instead of necessities. Women teachers ain't like any other kind of female." He stood and pushed his hat firmly on his head. "Bet you didn't even stick a change of underthings in there. We'll have to leave it behind. Here, take this thing." He picked up her purse.

Mariette felt thoroughly confused. "But— Marshal—you can't mean to . . . to . . ."

Ignoring her, he frowned at the purse. "Well, for Pete's sake! What've you got in here? More books? What are you, one of these gals with a fixation or somethin'?"

She snatched the purse away and held it tight.

"You are mad, sir! The train is *moving*!"

Taking her by the elbow, he pushed her into the aisle. "Better mad than dead, honey. Get a move on, now."

"My bag!" she cried.

"I said we'd have to leave it."

Mariette struggled to free herself. "I can't. I must have it! Those books are invaluable and I must have them!"

Much stronger than she, Marshal Kagan propelled her along, and Mariette's voice grew shrill with panic.

"They were David's! *They were David's!* I can't leave them behind!"

"Hellfire and damnation!" Angry, he turned and snatched up the bag. "All right! I've got it! Now come on!" He shoved her toward the back of the train.

Mariette went willingly but told him over her shoulder, "If you think, sir, that I'm going to jump off a moving train, you are quite wrong."

"I gave up thinkin' anything much about women a long while ago, Mrs. Call. Tell the truth, it'd be more profitable tryin' to read the mind of a mule."

The white-capped attendant in the back of the car stood when they reached him.

"Everything ready?" Matthew asked.

"Yes, sir, Marshal. The engineer sent back a message at that last quick stop in Morrano to tell you he'll do just what you said, and wishing you good luck, sir."

"Thank you. We'll need it."

With a slight jolt, the train began to slow, and the man said, "There he is, sir, just like he said."

"Your friend, in the next car . . ." Matthew motioned to the car in back of them.

"He said he'd do his best, sir, and would tell the other passengers there's a sick child on board who'd do better with the window blinds down. There's no way of knowing how it came out," he admitted.

"That's all right," Matthew said, rummaging with one hand in a vest pocket and pulling out money. "We'll take what we can get. This is for you," he said, pushing the paper bills at the man, "and this is for your friend."

The man's expression grew inscrutable, and he pushed the money back. "No, Marshal. You and the lady will be needing this. Please don't."

Matthew put the money back in his pocket without a pause.

"Then I'll thank you this way," he said, shaking the attendant's hand firmly. "If you ever need help, with anything, you get in touch with the federal marshal's office in Los Angeles and ask for Matthew Kagan. They'll know where to find me."

The man looked briefly bewildered, then smiled. "Thank you, sir. I'll remember."

He opened the door to the back of the car. "Station's coming up right away. It won't take but another minute to slow down sufficient. Best make yourselves ready."

Mariette stared out the open door at the land moving rapidly by and felt the harsh wind tug at her hair and clothes.

"Good luck to you, ma'am," the attendant said, just as Mariette froze and grasped either side of the door.

"This is madness!" she cried.

A big arm came about her waist, lifting her off her feet and moving her onto the car's open terrace.

"Now, don't go all hysterical on me," Matthew said, setting her on her feet. Mariette responded by turning and latching on to him with both hands, pressing her face, her whole self, into his solidness.

"That's what I like in a woman," he said with a laugh, holding her safe. "Lots of self-confidence."

The train kept slowing, so much so that Mariette thought it would stop, and yet she held on to Matthew Kagan, pressing her face into the damp, salty heat of his neck until he said, "This is it, Ettie Call. I'll carry you off if I have to."

"No," she murmured. Understanding what she was supposed to do, she turned, gripped the handrail, hugged her purse, and, when the big hand on her back pushed, walked down the car's stairs and onto the depot landing in the small town of Ripon. Just like that. Matthew Kagan walked off behind her, a few feet further, and the train they'd been aboard gently rolled away, car after car, shaking the platform upon which Mariette stood, paralyzed.

Matthew stared after the increasingly speeding train, and when he finally turned to her, his face wore an expression of satisfaction.

"The blinds were down," he said, moving toward her even as the train moved into the distance. "Quinn won't find out we're gone until the next stop, unless he was lookin' beneath his window blind when we got off." He grasped her elbow, held it for a moment as Mariette tried without success to stop her body from trembling, then said, "We've got a long ways to go. Think you can hold up?"

Mariette knew it was foolish pride that made her answer, "Of course I can," when what she really wanted to do was collapse.

A tall man approached them from out of the shadows of the ticket office, his sheriff's badge glinting in the midday sunlight.

"You Marshal Kagan?"

"'Fraid so," Matthew replied, extending a hand to shake the one offered him. "And this is Mrs. Mariette Call."

The man tipped his hat at Mariette. "Mrs. Call, I'm pleased. I'm Sanford Layton. We got your wire an hour ago, Marshal. Came just in time to stop the livestock train from going through."

"Then my horse got held back here?"

"Oh, yes, sir, he surely did," the sheriff assured him. "We took him off the train as soon as it arrived and old Sam put him in the stable. He's down at Dr. Martin's, now. Sam is, I mean."

"Oh, hell," Matthew muttered.

"Broke Sam's leg clean in two."

"Hell," he muttered again.

"Hope you don't mind me saying so, Marshal, but that's one mean-tempered horse you've got. I'd be happy to loan you my rifle if you'd like to shoot him."

Mariette felt the oddest desire to laugh but cleared her throat instead. Marshal Kagan, she saw with some amusement, answered the man with a perfectly straight expression.

"Well, that's good of you, Sheriff, but shootin' that old dog's a pleasure I believe I'll put off a while longer. Been resistin' the urge too many years now to give in so sudden-like."

Sheriff Layton nodded curtly. "Of course. I imagine you'll want to savor the moment when the time comes. I surely would, if that horse was mine. Well, the stables are this way, if you'll come along. I found a good, healthy mare for the lady, and we rounded up some supplies I imagine you'll be needing. Now, I'd appreciate it, sir," he said as they began walking, "if you'd explain just what the devil this is all about."

6

The banks of the Stanislaus River were thickly covered by oak and cottonwood trees; so thickly covered, in fact, that the horses occasionally had some difficulty moving through them. The cream-colored mare Sheriff Layton had secured for Mariette was a sweet and responsive creature, willing to try any direction Mariette put her in, regardless of how impossible it seemed, even to Mariette. Marshal Kagan's mount, on the other hand, was a fully different matter.

The horse's name was Ugly. Mariette hadn't been surprised when Matthew Kagan told her that, for it surely was the ugliest horse she'd ever seen, and the most ill-tempered, as well. The first thing the mottled piebald did upon seeing his master was bare his teeth and make a sound that made Mariette take three steps back.

Sheriff Layton, lifting a big rifle into the air, said, "I was able to pick up a new Winchester for you, Marshal. Sure you wouldn't like me to hold his head?"

Marshal Kagan declined once more, though he thanked Sheriff Layton for the rifle as well as for the other supplies, and spent the next ten minutes saddling the big steed and jumping with practiced ease around each vicious kick that came his way.

There were only three reasons why Mariette could understand Marshal Kagan letting the wretched creature live: the big stallion possessed heart, strength, and abundant energy. They had been riding for three hours now and had only been forced to stop on account of her good-natured mare. Mariette had to admit, as frightened as she was of the temperamental steed, that Ugly was a marvelous mount. The mare followed his lead willingly, just as Mariette, out of necessity, followed Matthew Kagan's.

Clearing a particularly thick stand of trees, Mariette found Marshal Kagan waiting for her.

"You all right?" he asked.

Though weary, Mariette nodded. "Yes. Thank you."

"Drink." He handed her the canteen they'd shared over the past few hours, and Mariette drank willingly. When she was done she passed it back to him, and delicately wiped her mouth with her fingertips.

"Will it be much longer, sir?"

Pulling the canteen from his mouth and capping it, he said, "We'll ride until dark, try to make Knights Ferry. That'll be a couple hours at least. We've got the lead on Quinn and we'll take what we can get."

"Will he follow us?"

"Oh, yes, ma'am. He'll follow, sure enough. I don't imagine Elliot Chambers is payin' him to sit around and twiddle his thumbs. We made the first move. Next one's his. That's how this little game goes. But we've got a few advantages on our side now, at least."

"Advantages?" Mariette repeated with some bewilderment. They were in the middle of nowhere, riding into the other side of nowhere, and being pursued by dangerous criminals. There was very little about this situation that she would call advantageous, save the fact that she might still have the opportunity to avenge David's death.

"Unless I'm far mistaken, Mr. Quinn's pretty much a city boy. Those fancy clothes . . ." The expression of disgust on Matthew Kagan's face finished the thought. "But he'll be lookin' to hire himself someone who can lead him through this territory, and I've sent some wires to make sure he gets the right man." He smiled in a way that reminded Mariette of a well-pleased cat cornering a mouse. "But that'll take him awhile, and by the time we reach those mountains over there"—he pointed into the distance where Mariette saw the ragged blue tops of the Sierra Nevadas pushing up through the golden valley—"we'll be in territory I know like the back of my own hand. When Mr. Quinn and his friends follow us there, I reckon they'll get themselves a few little surprises."

The Sierras. Mariette drew in a breath. "We're heading for the mountains?" she asked with some measure of unease, hoping Matthew Kagan wouldn't hear the worry in her voice. She'd crossed the Sierras by train before, but the thought of physically being in that rugged place was daunting.

"We surely are, Ettie Call," he replied, pushing his hat up and wiping the sweat from his forehead with one shirt sleeve. "Best set your mind to it." His black hair, she saw for the first time, was heavily peppered with silver, and his eyes, when he looked at her again, were starkly blue against his dark clothes and coloring. He was, she thought, painfully handsome. Mariette didn't realize that she was staring until he said, with an amused grin, "Find what you're lookin' for yet?"

"Oh!" She dropped her gaze and fumbled with the reins. "Forgive me, sir. That was quite rude of me."

He chuckled. "If that's what that was, honey, then you can be rude anytime you please. It won't bother me a'tall."

Mariette felt herself flushing and couldn't meet his eyes. They would be mocking her, she knew, just as he was mocking her. A man as handsome as Matthew Kagan would be well used to being stared at by women; how humorous he must find it, then, to be gaped at by a plain middle-aged widow whose chances of ever finding another husband were obviously slim. Oh, yes, he'd find such a woman's regard quite amusing, she thought bitterly.

"We'd best get on our way," he said quietly, almost gently it seemed to Mariette. "Come on, Ugly." He tried to turn his horse's head in the direction he wanted to go, and Ugly responded with an unpleasant noise. "Now, come on, you old dog," Matthew Kagan said angrily, struggling with the beast to no avail, "we're going this way. *This* way. Oh, hell," he muttered, giving up and casting a chagrined look at a laughing Mariette as he let Ugly do as he pleased. "I guess we'll go this way."

It was beyond dusk when they finally stopped for the night. Keeping to the river, moving through the trees and shrubs, Matthew had discreetly avoided the few towns and farms that were settled along the way. Now, as he led Mariette into the small clearing along the bank where they would make their camp, he felt

confident that their trail would be almost impossible
to follow. Tonight they'd be able to rest easy; tomorrow morning would be a different kettle of fish.

"Are we stopping here, Marshal?" Mariette asked
behind him, sounding just as weary as she looked.

Matthew brought Ugly to a halt and dismounted.
"Yes, ma'am. This is where we'll bed down." He held
the mare still while Mariette dismounted with an
aching groan. "How're you holdin' up there, Ettie? It's
been a hard ride today, but tomorrow will be worse."

She closed her eyes and stretched, rubbing the small
of her back. The motion pulled Matthew's gaze to her
full breasts and then down to her slender waist, which
he unintentionally envisioned spanning with his hands.

"It is Mrs. Mariette Call, sir. Not Ettie. And I am
perfectly fine, I thank you." Her gray eyes opened and
Matthew dragged his up to meet them.

"I'm sorry, ma'am. What'd you say?"

She gave him a look of impatience. "My name, sir.
It is Mrs. *Mariette* Call."

Lord! She was more worn out than he'd thought.

"Well, for Pete's sake, Ettie. I know what your
name is. You haven't heard me callin' you Annie or
Sue or anything else, have you? Now, why don't you
go sit down over there by the river while I take care of
the horses? I think you need some rest."

"I am fine," she informed him tightly, snatching
the mare's reins out of Matthew's hands, "and I'll
take care of my own horse."

"Suit yourself," he said, wondering why she should
sound so angry when he hadn't done a thing wrong.

"I assure you, sir, I will."

And she certainly did, Matthew thought an hour
later as he relaxed on his bedroll, watching Mariette

kneel beside the river and wash her hands and face. She was an interesting woman. She surely was. He knew full well that she was dog tired, yet she'd insisted on doing everything for herself and wouldn't let him lend her a hand. She'd cared for the little mare, had rolled out her own bedding; when he asked her if she was getting hungry, she went to the saddlebags Sheriff Layton had packed, pulled out a can of beans, some dry biscuits, and jerky, and dished them up a little cold supper. She hadn't asked him why they couldn't have a fire, and she hadn't asked why they couldn't wander up the hill to Knights Ferry and stay in a warm, cozy hotel. She hadn't asked anything of him at all. In fact, she'd barely spoken to him, and Matthew, for the life of him, couldn't figure out why. After all, he'd been as polite to her as he was capable of being, and if she was angry about being stuck with him in the first place, well, that sure wasn't his fault. If she was going to be mad at anyone it should be her father or, better yet, her dead husband. Now there was the culprit, right there.

Professor David Call.

He even sounded like a fool. Matthew could almost picture him. Bald, skinny, all his muscles in his head. A mathematics professor. Lord! How'd a man like that ever end up with a woman like Ettie? It wasn't a wonder she didn't have any kids. The brainy fool probably hadn't had the first idea how to go about doing anything right in bed. He'd probably bored her to death with—with mathematics, or whatever it was mathematics professors talked about. And there she knelt by the river, gazing up at the stars, looking so sad and pretty that Matthew would have knocked some sense into the man who'd left her all alone, if that man was still alive.

Those black mourning clothes she was wearing had to go, he thought. Folks would remember them if they chanced to see her, and if Drew Quinn went asking after a widow-woman, dressed in black . . .

"Ettie."

She turned to look at him, and Matthew was stricken anew at the smooth purity of her skin. Her hair, without her hat on, was a honey-blond color, braided and coiled upon her head and shining in the moonlight.

"I've got to go up to the town for a while." He nodded toward the lights on the hill above them and started to rise. "It won't be for long. Should be back in an hour or so." Brushing off his hat, he set it on his head. "Think you'll be all right by yourself?"

"I imagine so, Marshal," she replied evenly, "unless you think someone might hear the horses and come to investigate."

"Anything's likely, honey. You know how to shoot a gun?"

She shook her head, looking vaguely guilty.

Matthew reached into one of his coat pockets and pulled out a small revolver. "Come on over here, then, and I'll give you a little lesson."

Mariette did as she was told, and when she stood in front of him, he said, "This little gun should be easy enough for you to handle. Don't be scared of it. Now, turn around." With a hand on her shoulder he turned her, then pressed the gun into her right hand. "All right. Hold it with both hands, just like that." He loomed over her from behind, using his fingers to wrap hers around the gun the way he wanted them. "Now, if you find yourself in a situation where you figure you'll have to shoot or suffer, you pull this little lever down right here, just like that, until you feel that click. That means the gun's cocked, and you can't shoot the thing without it bein' cocked."

"Oh, I see," Mariette said with some surprise, thinking of how embarrassed she would have been the day before if she'd actually tried to shoot Drew Quinn without her gun being cocked. "Then what?"

"Then you point it straight as you can, firm up your grip, and pull the trigger. Now, I don't want you shootin' rabbits or shaky leaves, Ettie Call, but if you find yourself in a spot where you've got to shoot, you aim damned steady, and you aim to kill. Understand?"

"I understand, Marshal."

"Good. Now, don't leave the gun cocked, or you're like to shoot yourself in the foot. You just tug this lever down a little further and squeeze the trigger easy—easy, now—and it'll take the gun back to where it was at the start. There, see?"

"Well, my," said Mariette, much impressed. "Isn't that clever?"

He chuckled. "Clever enough, but don't go playin' with it while I'm gone. It ain't no toy. Now hold still, 'cause I've got to find somethin' out."

He was still behind her, and Mariette froze when she felt his hands circling her waist.

"Marshal Kagan! Just what do you think you're doing?"

"Fingers touch," he said. "Knew it. You ain't got no waist a'tall, Ettie."

"So sorry," she said dryly.

"Oh, honey, if you only knew."

His hands moved to her hips and she jumped. *"Marshal!"*

"Hold still," he commanded. "Don't know how you expect me to do this with you jitterin' all over the place."

"Would you mind explaining yourself, sir?"

"I don't s'pose I would, but I don't cherish the idea of the conversation we'd have afterward, so right now I think it's best if you just hold still and keep quiet."

He knelt and Mariette felt him place one hand at her waist again and another at her shoes, and then she realized he was measuring her, and what his trip into the town was for. Understanding that, she almost smiled, because it was clear he took his task quite seriously.

"I have a gun, sir," she said, "and I know how to use it."

Matthew laughed. "Why, Ettie Call. You're teasin' me. Didn't realize you had a sense of humor." He stood and met the smile she gave him over her shoulder. "But like I always said, there's nothin' better'n a good-lookin' woman with a sense of humor."

Her smile died, to be replaced by a rigidly unhappy expression, and she turned away and stuffed the gun in her skirt pocket.

"Have a nice time in town, Marshal."

She walked toward her bedroll, sat on it, and began to rummage through her bags.

With a sigh, Matthew gave up trying to figure her out. He'd known plenty of women in his day, had flirted with most of them, and bedded a few, but he'd never before come across a woman who made him feel like he was something that crawled on its belly every time he tried to be friendly.

"I'll give a whistle when I get back. Make sure you don't shoot me."

Pulling a few books into her lap, she didn't look at him. "I'll not make any promises, sir. I'll just have to see what kind of mood I'm in when I hear you whistle."

A couple of hours later, as he pushed through the brush and back into their camp, Matthew made sure to whistle loudly. It wasn't so much that he thought she'd really shoot him, but he'd learned long ago, from his mama, that it was always best to humor a woman in a bad mood.

Mariette hadn't even heard him. She lay on her bedroll, sound asleep, books strewn all around her and the little gun resting close to her head.

Quietly, Matthew knelt beside her and set near her bags the things he'd bought off a readily charmed woman's clothesline. In the moonlight, Mariette Call looked so . . . what? He didn't know the words even to think them. His younger brother, Jimmy, who liked reading books, would know the right words. Matthew only knew what he felt, and what he felt made him purely uncomfortable.

He took up the little journal she'd been reading, and in the moonlight strained to read what was written on the open page.

Lesson Plan, August 5th, 1893: McGuffey's Fourth. Page 63. Three . . . eight . . . five. First is Capitals. Second is banks.

Matthew put the journal aside and looked at the other books Mariette had been reading. One of them, strangely enough, was McGuffey's Fourth Eclectic Reader. He turned to page 63, where he found a poem entitled "Freaks of the Frost."

"'Freaks of the Frost,'" he murmured. "What kinda name is that for a poem?"

He read the first few lines.

The Frost looked forth one still, clear night,
And whispered, "Now I shall be out of sight:
So through the valley and over the height
In silence I'll take my way."

"Ettie," Matthew said aloud, "you're a strange woman."

He picked up another of the books, a volume, he saw, of the collected works of John Donne, whoever that was. It fell open, on its own, to a well-worn page.

"A val-e-dic-tion forbiddin' mournin'," he read slowly, squinting at the words before reading the first two verses silently.

As virtuous men pass mildly away,
And whisper to their souls, to go,
While some of their sad friends do say,
The breath goes now, and some say, no:

So let us melt, and make no noise,
No tear-floods, nor sigh-tempests move,
T'were profanation of our joys
To tell the laity our love.

"Well, good Lord," Matthew said with affront. "I didn't think the government allowed this sorta thing. You'd think they'd at least make 'em write it in English."

"It is English, Marshal Kagan."

Matthew looked at Mariette, who was gazing back out of sleepy eyes. She reached up and took the book away from him.

"I would appreciate it, sir, if you'd not make free with my things."

Stifling the irritation that her tone of indignant

superiority wrought in him, Matthew picked up the gun and stuffed it in his pocket. "Any trouble while I was gone?"

"None."

"Good. I brought some things for you to wear." He motioned to the pile of clothes. "They'll be short on you, likely, but at least they won't be black. Drew Quinn'll be askin' after a widow-woman, you know." He prepared himself for the argument he was certain she'd give him, being a proud woman and not wanting to cast off her mourning too soon.

But she said, quietly, "Yes, I realized that. Thank you, sir."

Something was wrong, Matthew thought, staring at her. There was a strange feeling—in his chest—like he was sickening. He was only a few days away from turning forty, but surely his heart wasn't ready to give out on him yet. It'd never given him any trouble before. Why should it be acting up all of a sudden?

"You're welcome," he said, rising, thinking that he didn't want his heart to give out right there, so that he'd die at Ettie Call's feet. "Good night."

"Good night, Marshal Kagan."

He stumbled away, toward his bedroll, still looking at her, wondering how much longer he was going to live and if she was going to wake to the unpleasantness of his stiff body in the morning. But he felt better once he lay down, and decided he wasn't going to die after all. He was only sickening, which was bad enough. Glancing at where Mariette lay, feeling again that strange ache in his chest, thinking how much he hated being sick, especially in front of women, Matthew wondered if he wouldn't rather be dead, anyway.

7

He woke her while it was still dark, and they were on their way before the sun touched the sky.

"There won't be much cover till we near the mountains," he explained as they ate a cold breakfast of biscuits and dried beef. "So we'll ride far as we can till it's light, then keep our heads low and hope for the best. Try to reach Jimtown tonight. If we can't manage that, we'll stop at Chinese Camp and find somewhere out of the way to bed down. Might be able to manage a real bed for you tonight, Ettie, if everything goes well."

"Please don't worry about that, Marshal Kagan. I slept very well last night, I assure you."

Even in the darkness she could see his look of disbelief.

"Clothes fit all right?" he asked.

Mariette ran a hand over the dark brown suit she'd pulled on that morning. "Yes, thank you. The skirt is only a little short, but the jacket fits perfectly."

"Should keep you warm, then. That's good."

They traveled in silence for several hours, until the sun was fully overhead. The trees and shrubs thinned and finally died away altogether as they rode away from the river and into golden hills dotted with oak trees and manzanita. The land was so beautiful it nearly stole Mariette's breath.

"This is like my home," Matthew said, slowing to ride beside her. "Not quite so pretty, but close enough."

The pride in his voice was unmistakable, and Mariette felt compelled to ask, "Where is your home, Marshal Kagan?"

He glanced at her. "I don't guess I told you, did I? Well, Mrs. Call, it appears we're bound to be neighbors. My family's home is in the Santa Ines valley."

"Oh," Mariette murmured, so surprised she was momentarily bereft of speech. "That's . . . lovely, sir. It will be nice to have an acquaintance there." And then, when the strange feeling she had at the thought of seeing him occasionally in the future receded, she realized something else. "And you say it looks like this? Beautiful as this is?"

"Oh, Santa Ines is prettier'n this by far," he replied confidently. "Prettiest place in California. Leastways, that I've ever seen. You'll think you've died and gone to heaven when you set eyes on it."

"I'm so relieved!" she said with a laugh. "I was rather worried about that, I'm afraid. I thought perhaps it might be a desert, like Los Angeles."

"Nah, it's nothin' like that. Santa Ines is all gold and green, hot summers and mild winters. Early springs and late falls. Evenin's are best, especially after a hot day. The winds come up, cool things off some, and it's real pleasant." He grinned at her with a kind of boyish charm that made Mariette's heart beat erratically.

"You said that you have family there?"

"My little brother and his wife and kids," he answered. "My daddy and granddaddy came out to California from back east before I was born and set up a ranch in Santa Ines. Named it Los Robles, which means 'The Oaks' in Spanish, because there's lots of oaks there. It's my brother's now, but I still call it home whenever I get a few days to visit. I was born and raised there. Guess that gives me the right to call it home for a while longer. Until I retire, anyway."

No wife, then, Mariette thought, ignoring the foolish relief that rushed over her and taking note, instead, of the sudden death of his smile. "Retire? Do lawmen do such things? It doesn't seem the sort of occupation one could set aside so easily."

"No. Don't s'pose it is."

A moment of silence passed, and then Mariette asked, "Why did you become a lawman, Marshal Kagan? Instead of a rancher, I mean?"

"Aw, well, ranching—" he gave a shake of his head, "ranching never appealed to me the way it did to Daddy and Granddaddy and my brothers. All that cattle. Lord! Daddy had his sons out workin' the damned critters before we could hardly sit a horse, and I got my fill of 'em right quick. Can't hardly think of a thing I hate doing more than herding those dumb animals around. That's prob'ly what hell is, you know. Poor lost souls herding cattle from one end of Hades to the other, then back again." He said this with a perfectly serious expression, and Mariette, coming to understand something about Matthew Kagan's sense of humor, laughed. "Surest thing in the world to make a man take up religion," he added.

"Your father must have been upset to know how you felt," she said.

"Oh, yes, ma'am, he surely was. That was the first and only time we almost came to blows over somethin'. I'll never forget it. Daddy was so worked up I thought he was going to keel over, and I sure expected him to disown me forever and kick me out. Not that I'd've blamed him. He and Granddaddy had worked their hearts out building up Los Robles, tryin' to make somethin' good for their children and grandchildren. And my older brother Johnny had died a few years before, so Daddy had it all figured out that I'd be the one to carry things on. But I just couldn't. I love Los Robles, and I sure loved my daddy, but I didn't know any way to get around the way I felt about those damned cows. I would've lost my mind tryin' to do it. God's honest truth, I would've lost my mind."

"What happened? With your father, I mean."

"Well, we fought the matter out one night. We'd been fightin' about it for years, really, on and off, makin' everybody in the family unhappy, 'specially Mama. But by the time I turned seventeen things came to a head. I still can't recall exactly how we ended up shoutin' the way we did that one night. Just kinda happened, I guess. One minute we were sitting around the dinin' room table havin' supper, and the next Daddy and I were out in the yard yellin' all kinds of crazy things at each other. And Mama . . . poor Mama, standin' there on the porch with my grandparents, crying like her heart would break." He gave a sigh. "My little brother Jimmy—thank God for Jimmy—he always loved ranching, just like Daddy.

He got between us and yelled that if I didn't want Los Robles, then he'd take it, and he wanted it. Well, that brought us to a standstill, sure enough. Good old Jimmy. He was only eleven or twelve at the time, but he knew what he was talkin' about, I reckon. Daddy settled down some, though he was still plenty mad. He stood out there in the yard and said some things that hurt pretty bad, 'bout me not bein' a real Kagan, and all, and that Jimmy was more of a man than his big brother."

"Oh, Matthew," Mariette murmured, not realizing she'd used his name. "That must have hurt."

"Well," he said gruffly, shifting in his saddle, "it ain't somethin' I'd care to go through again. Like I said, Daddy had good reason to be angry, and I don't think he meant all of it. He tried to apologize later, after Mama got through with him, but I was pretty foolish. I packed up my things and left Los Robles that night and didn't go back till I was twenty."

"Your poor father," she said, thinking of how distraught her own father had been when she last saw him. "He must have felt terrible."

"We never talked about it. I'd changed an awful lot by the time I came home, had been through an awful lot. Daddy . . . I think he knew the minute he set eyes on me the way things were. He didn't ask any questions, didn't press me. He just said I could stay if I wanted or go if I wanted, it didn't matter. Los Robles was always going to be my home. I'd always have a welcome there waitin' for me."

Gladness and relief filled Mariette, which was what any decent human being would feel, she told herself, purposefully ignoring the strength of the emotions.

"What did he think of you being a lawman?" she asked.

"I wasn't one then. I mean, I had been for a couple of years, sort of, but there wasn't nothin' official about it. I'd been deputized by an old marshal I'd come across in El Paso. Langley Tines." He smiled at the memory. "Good ol' Lang Tines. I used to tease him, call him Old Lang Times . . . like that song they always sing on New Year's eve."

"You mean, 'Auld Lang Syne'?"

"That's the one. Used to tease him somethin' fierce with that, but good ol' Lang just took it. He was a good-natured fella, old enough to be my daddy, but, my Lord, the deadliest man I ever met. Scared the hell outta me the way he could shoot. Never seen another man could match him." He gave a small sigh. "Good old Lang."

Mariette waited for him to finish the story, but when he remained silent she prodded, "You were his deputy?"

"Huh? Oh, well, yes, I was. Sort of. It wasn't anything official. We just happened on each other one night. I was drunk in a saloon in El Paso, gettin' into all kinds of trouble, and he kept some other fellas from killin' me. I don't recall what it was they wanted to kill me for, 'cept for bein' such a dumb, pesky kid, maybe. Next thing I knew I woke up in the local jail, and Lang was there ready to bail me out if I'd promise to help him catch some horse thieves he was chasin' into Mexico. Wasn't anything Lang hated as much as he did horse thieves. He used to say, 'A good horse is worth a man's life, 'specially in this country.' And he meant Texas, of course, when he said country, 'cause as far as he was concerned the United States was second-rate stuff compared to Texas."

Mariette was surprised. "But wasn't he a federal marshal?"

"Who? Lang Tines?" Matthew Kagan spoke as if she'd lost her mind. "Never. He was a Texas man, through and through. He was a Ranger before he became a territory marshal, and before that he served in the Rebellion like a true Texas Confederate."

"But, how did you become a federal marshal, then?" Mariette asked with honest confusion. "Usually a man must be highly recommended to attain that honor."

"That's true enough," he admitted, "but Lang wasn't just any territory marshal. He was the best. Anywhere. He took me under his wing, taught me everything he knew. In a lot of ways, Ettie, he was like another father to me. Those years I had with him were hard. Damned hard. Things happened that I wish I could take out of my life. But Lang, you know, he was a good man, and he believed in the law. He always said, 'The only difference between us and animals is the law,' and he was right. I've known men who've crossed that line. Men who weren't nothin' but animals, and worse.

"Well, old Lang was always after me to take up the law in a more permanent way. He said I had a good feel for it, and I guess that's true. It's always come natural enough to me, at least. He wrote some letters to a friend of his, the federal marshal in Houston, and asked him to see if he couldn't find a place for me somewhere."

"And you became a United States marshal," Mariette concluded.

"Not then. Not until after I'd gone back home and been there for a few months. I had word from Lang's friend then, askin' me to come back to Texas and take a job with him there. By then I didn't want nothin' to do with Texas, and I wrote and told him so. A month later I got a wire from the U.S. marshal's office in 'Frisco asking me to take duty in Baja California." He glanced at her. "Lang's friend had written him, see, and that's how he came to offer me the job. I talked it over with my folks." He shrugged. "They weren't all that happy about it, but I'd just been sittin' around mostly since I'd got home, not doin' much other than gettin' in the way. So—" he released a tense breath, "I took it. Packed my bags and left again."

He smiled at her in a way that said he was done talking, and Mariette smiled back, wondering how much of the story he'd left out. She longed to ask him what had happened to make him leave Texas, and what had happened to Langley Tines; but she knew somehow, perhaps instinctively, perhaps from the brittle quality of his smile, that to press him would be painful for him and unwise for her. Her own smile felt suddenly strained, and she said, "And you've been a marshal ever since."

"Ever since. It ain't much of a job, but it's a job."

"Please don't say that."

"Huh?"

"Don't," she said. "It's a very fine profession, sir. Very admirable, and you are obviously quite good at it to have survived these many years." His look of surprise made her turn her attention to the reins in her hands as she forced herself to continue. "And I'm . . . I'm most grateful to you, Marshal Kagan, for what you're doing for me. I want to apologize for what I said to you yesterday, about my father and about you working for him. It was wrong of me to make such assumptions and I deeply regret doing so."

"Oh . . . well."

His stilted tone made Mariette glance at him, to find that he was staring forward, frowning and rubbing his chest with an absent hand, as if he had an ache there.

"It's all right, Ettie. You don't need to say such things and, ah, we probably oughta, ah, get a move on, anyhow. Anybody lookin' could see us a mile away, with nothin' but this open land. Don't know what I was thinkin' to lazy around talkin' like that."

He sounded angry, and Mariette felt as if she'd done something wrong. Taking up his reins and putting his heels into Ugly's flanks, he set off at a gallop, leaving a bewildered Mariette to follow.

They made Chinese Camp by nightfall, and Matthew had no difficulty buying shelter for them for the night. The Chinese family who willingly accepted his voucher in exchange for the use of their small animal shed also lent them blankets and, laughing away his and Mariette's feeble protests, fed their ravenous hunger with as many steaming bowls of rice and chicken as they could devour. Later they lay comfortably, side by side, on a bed of fresh straw that had been placed down after the few sheep who usually occupied the shed had been pulled, protesting, out of it. Matthew yawned loudly, then said, "You'll have a bath tomorrow night, Ettie, and a proper bed. Promise."

Except for the night before, Mariette had never slept on the ground. She had never been exposed to harsh living of any kind, though she had foolishly believed that traveling in stagecoaches and railway cars was an unpleasant indignity, albeit both sufferable and necessary. Now, lying comfortable and warm and replete in an enclosure so small that it caused her shoulder to rest only inches from Matthew Kagan's, she felt so content and happy that she almost wanted to laugh aloud. Matthew Kagan was a big man, so big that she imagined he might crush her as easily as he pleased, yet he lay still, relaxed. Mariette could envision the easy smile on his face. She had never before slept with a man, not even her husband, who had only ever shared her bed for the few moments he'd required to attempt the creation of the child they had both so badly wanted. And those occasions, even, had been few. David had been a tender and considerate man, yet, at the same time, the physical act always left him embarrassed and upset. He left her bed after each short encounter murmuring pained apologies, as if he had visited some grave indignity upon her, as if he would never forgive himself. Her bed had become a lonely place for Mariette. Lying beside Matthew Kagan, knowing he would stay beside her until morning came, was an experience quite out of her knowing, and quite shamefully nice.

"Ettie? You asleep already? Did you hear me?"

"A bath would be lovely," she said, "but this is lovely, too, Marshal Kagan. Doesn't the air smell nice?" And it did, she thought. Everything smelled wonderful. The fresh straw, the clean, cold air, and most of all him, smelling like leather and wool. "David always thought the ocean air was the most refreshing, but this is so much better, I think. Everything seems better, here. David wouldn't have known that, of course. In all his life he never went farther west than Chicago, though he did travel to Europe often."

"Why did you marry that man?" Matthew asked all of a sudden, shocked at himself for doing so, shocked even more that he should care about what the answer was. He didn't even *know* this woman, he told himself. She was as good as a stranger; worse, she was an unfriendly stranger.

Her head turned toward him, but he couldn't see her face in the darkness. He could, however, hear the amusement in her voice when she said, "What?"

"Your husband. Why'd you marry him?"

He made it sound, Mariette thought, as though she'd done something criminal. Her happiness began to dim as she wondered if he asked the question out of simple curiosity, or because he found it difficult to believe that any man would marry her.

"He asked me to. That's why."

"Well, for Pete's sake," Matthew said irately. "That ain't any reason to get married, just 'cause some fella asks you to."

"It isn't?"

"'Course not. Why, any fella in the world could walk up to you out of the blue and ask you to marry him, but that don't mean you'd do it. I could ask you right this minute, right here and now, and you'd turn me down flat."

"Yes, that's true," she admitted thoughtfully. "Of course, you wouldn't ask."

"That ain't the point."

She sighed. "I suppose you're right. And there were other reasons why I married David. We'd known each other for a few years, in Washington. He was my friend."

"Your friend?" Matthew repeated, wondering what that had to do with anything.

"Yes. My good friend. I was so surprised, of course, when he asked me to wed him," she said. "He was considered quite a catch in our social circle. He came from a well-established family, and he was financially secure and highly respected in his profession. I had always enjoyed his company, but I'd never thought he would ever think me anything more than a close acquaintance. And, of course, I was an old maid."

Matthew made a snorting sound. "You ain't no old maid," he told her.

"Oh, yes, I am," she returned matter-of-factly, without offense. "And I was then, too. I was twenty-nine when David proposed and thirty when we wed. Long, long on the shelf."

"Women," he muttered. "You could put all their brains together and still not have enough sense to divide two in half." When Mariette laughed, he said, "So go on. What'd ol' Dave say to make you jump off that shelf you'd put yourself on?"

"Quite a great deal, actually. I was difficult to convince, you see, as I simply couldn't believe he actually wished to wed me. But David was persistent. He wanted a wife with whom he could be comfortable, one who would support and understand his goals toward his profession. A younger woman might have too many other expectations of him, and he honestly felt he might not be able to meet them. David was, oh, shy, I think you might say. He disliked being too involved in society, in crowds and parties and gatherings. Not that he was unfriendly. It wasn't that. He simply liked quiet evenings at home, reading in his study and working on mathematical theories. He worried that a younger woman might become bored with such a life."

"But what about you?" Matthew asked. "Didn't he worry about you bein' bored?"

"Oh, no. I was twenty-nine, with little hope of ever marrying. He thought . . . he knew I should be willing to trade my single life for any kind of marriage. Even a quiet one." Speaking more softly, she added, "No woman wants to be a spinster."

When Matthew's big hand suddenly pressed over both of hers, squeezing them, Mariette drew in a sharp, surprised breath.

"Did he say that to you?" he asked angrily. "Did he say those kinda things?"

"No!" she answered quickly, almost breathlessly. Her hands seemed paralyzed beneath his strong fingers. "Of course not. David was a gentleman. There wasn't any need to speak of matters we both understood."

"He never threw that kind of nonsense at you when you was married, did he? Because if he did, if he ever hurt you that way, then he wasn't nothin' but a—"

"My goodness, Marshal! I don't know why it should matter to you, but no, David was always very kind to me. He was generous and gentle and . . . and very romantic."

Matthew abruptly pulled his hand away and rolled onto his back. "Sure. I'll just bet he was."

"He was!"

"Spent his evenin's workin' on mathematical stuff, did he? That's so romantic it just about makes my heart go flippity-flop. No wonder you didn't have no kids."

His words stung Mariette badly. She sat up, unable to stop the hurt that flooded her, making her voice sharp and bitter. "You—you callous, insensitive brute!" Her misery and loss seemed fresh to her, suddenly, and so strong that the rest of what she wanted to say strangled and died in her throat. With a sob, she scrambled toward the shed's low gate, but Matthew moved more quickly, and she found herself lying beside him instead, hugged tight in his arms while his hands petted over her soothingly.

"Ettie. I'm sorry. I'm sorry. Don't cry."

She made a fist and hit his shoulder, which was about as effective as hitting a rock and only made her cry that much harder.

"I'm sorry," he kept murmuring. "Don't cry, honey. Please, don't."

"Let me go!"

"I will, in a minute. I'm so sorry, Ettie. I shouldn't've said what I did. It was damned stupid. You go on and hit me again, if you want. Let me have it real good."

"No," she cried against his jacket, hitting his shoulder anyway.

"Oh, come on. You can do better'n that. Here." He pulled back a little and took hold of her impotent fist, aiming it at his face. "Right here. Do it good'n'hard, Ettie, just under the eye. That'll make you feel better. Go on, now." He tilted his head back to give her better access, and closed his eyes. A moment passed, Mariette's harsh breaths the only sound between them, before she tentatively pressed her fisted knuckles against his cheekbone. Matthew opened his eyes and gazed at her. Mariette gazed back, frightened, her fingers pressed against his skin.

"Ettie," he whispered, taking her hand, pushing her and it down into the straw as he leaned over her, "we're in a whole lot of trouble here."

There was nothing tentative about their first kiss, for either of them. Mariette met Matthew's mouth as if it were the most natural thing in the world to do, as if she had every right to do so. When his hands went around her, crushing her to him, Mariette responded in kind, sliding her hands beneath his jacket to run over the hard muscles in his back, to press him as close as possible. When his tongue parted her lips she readily met it with her own. She felt, deep in herself, that this was right and good, that he was hers and had been for as far back as her memory could go. He touched her body, her breasts and hips though her clothes, and then, tugging her skirts up, he touched her legs, stroked and gripped them with a kind of desperation. Mariette touched him, too, amazed at how familiar he was to her fingertips, as if they had known him hundreds of times before.

His mouth moved over her face, her neck, and he murmured her name, "Ettie."

She wanted him. She loved him. His heavy body felt wonderful when he moved on top of her, rocking against her until she made a place for him to lie.

"Please," she whispered, her hands in his thick hair. "Please, Matthew."

But he stiffened suddenly and groaned.

"Lordy," he said, sounding utterly miserable. "What am I doing?" He tried to pull away, to lift himself off her, but she could feel how difficult it was for him. "I'm sorry," he said, not looking at her. He closed his eyes briefly and said again, "Sorry, Ettie."

She made no effort to hold him. Her hands dropped into the straw and she waited for him to lift his shuddering body away, though it seemed for a moment as if the struggle to do so was almost too great. He was like a fly caught in thick syrup, power-less to free himself. At last he pushed away from her, rolling onto his back with a thud.

For the space of a minute they were silent, breath-ing hard. Then, as Mariette smoothed her skirts down, Matthew said, "That's been comin' since just about the moment I set eyes on you, and I think maybe you knew it, too, but for all that, I'm sorry." He felt as low as a worm for attacking her that way, after he'd hurt her feelings and gotten her so upset that she wouldn't have the sense to shove him away if she wanted to. But damn him if he wasn't glad, too. Kissing Ettie Call was more potent than kicking back a shot of Granddaddy Kagan's stump liquor, and a whole lot better tasting. He could hardly wait to do it again. And she'd wanted him, too. He knew that as sure as he knew his own name, and the thought made him unbelievably happy.

In spite of her labored breathing and the pounding of her heart, Mariette's mind was strangely clear. Of course he was sorry, she thought bitterly, feeling wholly foolish and struggling with an unexpected feeling of disappointment. He wouldn't want her to misunderstand what had happened. They were alone together, and he was a healthy man with normal urges. For that, any woman would do. Even a plain woman like herself. She mustn't let herself think there was any more to it.

"Please don't apologize, Marshal Kagan," she said in the cool society tone she had mastered in Washington. "Nothing happened. It was simply a mistake. I was distressed and you meant to comfort me. I think it might be best if we both tried to forget this unpleasant episode."

"Unpleasant?" he repeated. "You want to *forget* about it?"

"Yes." Snatching up a cover, she turned on her side, away from him. "Good night, Marshal Kagan."

Unpleasant! Matthew thought furiously, rubbing at the sudden ache in his chest.

"Fine!" he said, turning on his own side. "If that's the way you want it, then that's the way it'll be."

"That's the way I want it."

"Then that's the way it'll be."

She sat up again. "And my name is not Ettie! It is Mariette. Mrs. *Mariette* Call."

"You mean Mrs. Professor David Call, don't you?" He said the words as if they were an insult. "He was such a perfect husband, no reason you should try bein' anything more." And then he sat up, too, to add, "I don't s'pose you ever found anything he did unpleasant!"

Momentarily bereft of speech, Mariette threw herself down on her side again. "Good *night,* Marshal Kagan."

The taut dismissal in her tone only enraged him that much more, so that he shot back, "Good night, *Mrs.* Call," and flopped down again, himself.

8

"We'll stop here for a spell," Matthew announced sharply.

Those were the first words either of them had spoken since they'd saddled up and started on their way that morning.

He brought Ugly to a halt and dismounted, then moved by instinct to help Mariette dismount. She accepted his help in silence, and in silence untied her heavy traveling bag from the saddle, then turned and walked to seat herself on a large rock beneath the shade of a nearby oak.

Matthew watched her settle herself, then, with an angry shake of his head, moved to take care of the horses.

The damned stuck-up woman. What had he ever seen in her? Whatever it was, he must have been out of his mind at the time. He couldn't wait to get rid of her. And once he did he didn't ever want to set eyes on her again. Mrs. Mariette Call. It would serve her right if he did call her that. It was a stuck-up name for a stuck-up woman. Fit her like as glove.

Securing the mare to the low branch of a tree that both hid and shaded them, Matthew stole a glance at Mariette. She had dug out that little red journal she was always looking at, and one of those poetry books that had been her husband's. She was glancing at each of the books in turn, her expression filled with frustration and bewilderment. Watching her, Matthew couldn't help but wonder what she was doing.

The place he'd chosen to stop was on a hill, beyond which the gold valley spread wide. Mariette sat with her back to the magnificent view, studiously bent over her books. Restless, Matthew wandered toward the edge, finding himself somehow beside the rock on which Mariette sat. Five silent minutes passed before he said, in as normal a tone as possible, "Hot today, isn't it?"

"Yes," she agreed. "It is quite warm."

He lifted a hand and rubbed the back of his neck. "You like that kinda thing, huh? Poetry?"

She didn't even lift her head. "Yes, I like it very much."

More silence passed, and Matthew realized she wasn't going to make conversation with him. Well, fine. He'd made an effort. If she didn't want to meet him halfway, then forget it. He kept rubbing the sore muscles in the back of his neck. It seemed like sleeping on the ground made him stiff and achy all the time, nowadays. Not that he'd gotten any sleep last night, of course, lying beside Miss Prim-and-Proper, but that was beside the point. The point was, he thought with sober honesty, that he was getting too old for this kind of thing anymore.

Forty years old, for heaven's sake. He was going to be forty in only a few more days.

What would he do with himself? he wondered, setting a foot on a fallen log and leaning on his knee with one hand, letting his eyes roam over the beauty of the surrounding land. He'd never thought about it before, because he'd never believed he would live to be so old, also because it had never occurred to him that the government would ask a willing, able-bodied lawman to hand in his badge.

Now that his retirement was staring him in the face, he supposed he ought to try to make some plans. Jimmy and Elizabeth would expect him to live at Los Robles, of course, but he wasn't sure that settling down in Santa Ines was such a good idea. Visiting there for a few weeks was all right, but more than that and he'd start feeling like an intruder rather than a member of the family.

Maybe he could travel. There were plenty of places he'd always wanted to see. Montana, the Dakotas—

Mariette cleared her throat loudly, all of a sudden, and asked, "Do you like poetry, Marshal Kagan?"

It seemed strange for her to call him that after what had passed between them the night before.

"Well," he said slowly, glad to talk if she was willing, "I don't know much about it, I s'pose. Not that kind you're readin', anyhow. The kind of things I know that rhyme ain't fit for female ears, if you know what I mean."

Mariette couldn't hold back the surprised laugh that escaped her lips. "Yes, I know what you mean, Marshal."

Matthew gazed out over the valley again. "Your husband sure must have liked it. He had all those books."

"It was one of the things we had in common, David

and I. We both loved poetry so much. He used to recite poems from memory, and I always enjoyed listening to him. He had such a nice voice." She sounded wistful. "We spent many a pleasant evening together that way."

Matthew almost said something about what a fun couple the Professor David Calls must have been, but restrained himself. "My little brother and his wife like readin' aloud in the evenin's after supper. Elizabeth, that's my sister by marriage, she's the one reads poetry and the like. She ain't what I'd call a romantic person, but she thinks poetry is. Romantic, I mean."

"Oh, it is!" Mariette agreed quickly. "When David would recite for me—oh, it was so romantic." Although she knew very well it had only been so for her, because what David had enjoyed about reciting poetry was the accurate detail he gave to meter and form. "One poem in particular was his favorite. 'A Valediction: Forbidding Mourning,' by Donne. Have you ever heard of it?"

Matthew groaned, thinking of the verses he'd read two nights before. "What kinda name is that for a poem? Sounds like somethin' you'd sing at a funeral."

She laughed outright again, with so much amusement that Matthew laughed, too. Mariette Call might be a prude, he thought, but at least she had a good sense of humor. She laughed at his jokes, anyway.

"It's a very good title," she said, smiling up at him in a way that made his hands start sweating. "John Donne wrote the poem for his wife, when they were about to be separated for a lengthy period of time. What he says in it, basically, is that their love for each other is so strong that a separation cannot breach it. They are two parts of a whole, like the two parts of a compass. She is the center, staying in one place, and he is the leg that moves and makes the circle. But, you see, even when he is on his journey, making the circle, so to speak, they are still joined, and she, being his anchor, will always draw him back."

"Yeah?" Matthew was honestly impressed and couldn't reconcile this interesting explanation with the vague words he'd read before. "That's pretty good. Real smart. Who is this Donne guy? Some friend of your husband's? A mathematician?"

"Goodness, no! John Donne lived in the seventeenth century, in England. He was a minister."

"Oh, well, that's even worse. No wonder he wrote poetry," Matthew said with a good-natured shrug.

"What do you mean?"

"Ministers. Preachers. Nothin' they like better'n the sound of their own voices. Makes sense they'd force folks to read all their flowery words, too."

Mariette regarded him curiously. "You're not a churchgoing man, I presume, Marshal Kagan."

He chuckled. "Not when I can help it. My sister by marriage always makes me go when I'm home, but I stay clear of it, otherwise. Not that I've got anything against God, mind you, but me and Him have some serious differences of opinion. We just leave each other alone. He goes His way, and I go mine. That's all."

"How very sad," she murmured. "I always thought a man who lived as you do would need a strong faith just to keep himself sane."

"Sane!" He made a sound of bitterness. "The only thing I need to do, Mrs. Call, is keep myself *alive.* Lots of folks have religion, but what good does it do 'em? Lang Tines was a prayin' man. Night and day he was at it, faithful as St. Peter. Made me do it, too, on my knees, no less. He always said, 'Keep God on your side, boy, and He'll get you through the fire and water.'"

"Fire and water?"

"That's outta some verse in the Bible Lang was always quotin'. Somethin' about men riding over your heads and going through fire and water, but God brings you through."

"Into a place of abundance," Mariette said.

He nodded. "That's right. A place of abundance. My God, what a lot of claptrap. Old Lang sure didn't end up in a place of abundance. All his prayers weren't nothin' but a waste of time. Mine, too, I guess. I prayed hard as I could, but either God wasn't listenin' or didn't give a damn. I learned the best lesson of my life from that." He slipped his gun from its holster in a fluid movement and held it up for her to see. "In this world, the law is God, and this nickle-plated boy right here is the judge and enforcer. If you're going to make it through the fire and the water and come out on the other side, Ettie, then you're going to have to do it on your own, or maybe with a little help from your fellow man."

"Oh, Matthew," she said sadly, "whatever happened to make you feel that way?"

He put his gun away. "Going through the fire and water, I guess. You tend to go through a lot of that when you're a lawman."

"You tend to go through a lot of it simply being alive," she returned gently, "but that doesn't mean—"

He put a hand in the air to stop her. "Hush!"

A moment passed while they both listened, then he reached down to grab her arm. "Horses, comin' right up the hill. Come on."

"But—!"

There wasn't time to explain. He pulled her off the rock and along toward the ledge, then started down the steep, dusty hill, dragging Mariette behind him. They didn't go far, only to a deep crevice sheltered by large rocks and shrubs.

"Get in." He shoved Mariette into the small space and crowded in behind her, facing outward, his gun in his hand. "Damn!" he muttered. "Wish I had my rifle."

Mariette's hands were pressed against his shoulders and Matthew felt them trembling.

"Don't worry, honey," he said. "The only thing that's going to happen to you today is gettin' a little dusty from these rocks, here. I promised you a bath and a decent bed tonight, and you're going to live long enough to have 'em!"

"What if it isn't Drew Quinn?" she whispered. "What if they steal our horses?"

He responded with a low chuckle. "I hope they try it. They'll join the rest of Ugly's victims. Quiet, now."

The sound of horses coming to a halt above them was loud, as were the voices that spoke, though Mariette couldn't make sense of any of the words. She was quite sure it was impossible, but the intruders seemed to be speaking in—Gaelic? Matthew Kagan's shoulders relaxed noticeably beneath her hands, and when he turned to face her he wore a broad, boyish grin. Setting a finger over his lips to keep her from speaking, he motioned that he was going to climb above their hiding place.

Silently, he climbed out and up, disappearing in the brush and leaving Mariette huddling into the crevice, regretting the loss of the big, heavy shield of his body.

The men above continued to speak; she heard Ugly's unmistakable angry snort. Another minute passed and someone began to climb down the hill.

"Matthew!" she whispered frantically, and the footsteps stopped. When they started up again they were slower, moving toward her, and Mariette froze with panic.

The shooting end of a rifle nosed its way into the crevice, followed by the face of a big Indian. Merciful heavens! Mariette had never seen an actual Indian before and had never realized what big people they were. This Indian, in particular, was huge.

His dark, surprised eyes took her in slowly, from top to toe, and then he frowned.

"Ma'am?" he said, and Mariette, folding her hands over her chest as if she were going to pray or start pleading, replied, "G-good afternoon."

He lowered the gun and stepped back, and at the same moment a sharp sound to one side caused both their heads to turn in that direction. A flash of color flew past Mariette, hurtling into the Indian and sending him sprawling to the ground.

"Dammit, Jus!" Matthew Kagan shouted into the face of the man he'd pinned beneath him. "How many times have I told you not to fall for that old trick?"

"For God's sake!" the Indian shouted back. "I could have shot you, you fool! What do you mean by jumping me that way?"

The angry expression on Matthew's face died away. "Well, hell, Jus. I'm only gettin' you back for that dunking you and Bertie gave me three months ago. Didn't think I'd let that pass by, did you?" He grinned.

The big Indian muttered something about crazy white men, and pushed Matthew off him. "I don't know why I didn't rip that wire you sent me from Lathrop to shreds," he said, standing and brushing himself off. "This is the thanks I get for trying to help a friend." He grabbed his rifle when a laughing Matthew held it out to him. "And where have you been, anyway?" he demanded. "We set out this morning to come looking for you."

Matthew cast a glance at Mariette, who had come out of her hiding place. "We've been doing the best we could, Jus. Don't know why you'd worry. This is Mrs. Mariette Call."

"Mrs. Call," the Indian said in a perfectly cultured tone that was at odds with the long, braided black hair that swung forward as he politely inclined his head, "I am pleased to meet you." He turned back to Matthew. "You can't understand why I'd be worried when you send me a wire like that?" He straightened and began to recite dramatically, "'Trouble. Stop. Need help. Stop. Intercept man Drew Quinn at Ripon. Stop. Quinn dangerous. Stop. Take all care. Stop. Act as guide to track me down. Stop. Will meet at Hetch Hetchy five days.'"

Matthew lifted his eyebrows. "You got a pretty good memory, there, Jus. Bet you could recite poetry, too, if you put your mind to it."

"Recite poetry!"

"Ettie," said Matthew, "this here is Justice Twelve Moons. His real last name is Drohan, but he don't use it because it's too confusin'."

"Oh," said Mariette, feeling adrift in strange waters. "I'm pleased to meet you, Mr. Moons . . . ah . . . Drohan?"

"Thank you, ma'am. Please call me Justice."

"Who'd you send after Quinn?" Matthew asked.

"Slow Bear. He was on his way ten minutes after we got your wire."

"Bertie." Matthew nodded his approval. "Good. He'll know what to do with Quinn, and he'll probably enjoy himself doin' it."

"Justice!" A loud voice boomed over the side of the hill. "Are ye needing me to come and shoot anybody, lad?"

"No, Da!" Justice shouted back. "It's Matthew I found. We wouldn't want to waste the bullet."

A large, stocky, red-haired man peered over the hill's ledge. "Why, Matty Kagan," he said in an admonishing tone. "Where have ye been, boyo? Kathleen sent us on our way this morn and said not to come back without ye."

"Hello, John," Matthew greeted warmly.

"And look! Ye've brought a lovely colleen along. 'Tis a mercy true and sure, after all these years, may God above be praised. But what do ye mean, leaving a lady to stand in such a place? Bring her up at once, lads!"

Both men moved to lend Mariette aid, but the sharp look Matthew shot at Justice made that man drop his hand.

"That gentleman is your father, Mr., ah, Justice?"

"Yes, ma'am."

"John Drohan? As in the Drohan Mining Company?"

"Yes, ma'am."

"Oh, my," Mariette said, unable to keep from staring at the half-breed son of one of the richest men in California.

"You'll be staying at my family's home tonight, Mrs. Call. It will be a great pleasure to have you. And Matty boy, of course," he added in a teasing Irish lilt.

Matthew set an arm about her waist to propel Mariette up the hill. "Told you you'd have a bath and bed tonight," he said, then added, flashing a smile at her incredulous expression, "I just didn't tell you where."

9

"I fell in love wi' her name first," John Drohan explained as he spooned another serving of potato pudding onto his plate, "long before I'd set eyes on her. I just knew, y'see, that a man couldn't help but fall in love wi' a woman named Angry Fire in the Sky. A woman wi' a name like that, says I to meself, is a woman worth having." He winked at his handsome Cherokee wife who sighed with long-suffering patience. "The trouble," he went on happily, "was that I'd always promised meself a wife named Kathleen, so when we wed I asked her to grant me that one wee favor. She's been my sweet Kathleen ever since, haven't you, my love?"

Mrs. Drohan, who had earlier admitted that she preferred being known as Angry Fire in the Sky, turned to Mariette and said, "The Kathleen part I'll admit to. For the sweet I make no promises. My father named me better than my husband has."

Mariette laughed and accepted the plate of bacon and cabbage Angry Fire in the Sky passed her.

From the age of sixteen, Mariette had acted as her father's hostess for every kind of social function imaginable, and in all the years that had passed between then and her marriage she had met and conversed with a great many unusual and interesting people, yet never before had she found herself in the midst of people like those in the Drohan family.

There were two topics the wealthy Irish immigrant enjoyed speaking about, and those were himself and his family. Mariette learned his entire history during the several hours that passed pleasantly in the Drohans' elegant home, from his childhood in Ireland to the hard mining labor he'd endured in Montana to his meeting and marrying his wife to, finally, the rich gold mine he'd struck in the hills of California. With just as many humorous details, Mariette had also been told everything about John Drohan's fine, handsome, intelligent, brave, and incomparable sons, of which there were three: the eldest, Justice Twelve Moons, the second, Liberty Slow Bear Walking, and the last, Freedom Good Path.

"I had the pleasure of meeting your husband, Mrs. Call, while I was at Harvard," Freedom Good Path said from where he sat across the table next to his bride of three months. Like his older brother, Justice, Freedom was quite dark and his Indian features were startlingly handsome. Unlike his brother, his blue-black hair was cut short and neat, and he was dressed in the manner of a wealthy eastern gentleman.

"Did you? While he was visiting there?"

"Yes. He gave a lecture at the medical college on the dependence of the medical sciences on the mathematical sciences. It was fascinating, and he was a skilled lecturer. The dean gave a dinner for him that night and I was fortunate enough to be invited. Your husband was one of the most brilliant men I've ever met. His death is a sad loss to the scientific community, as well, I know, to yourself."

"It is good of you to say so, sir. David would have liked to know that you remembered his lecture. He was so fond of visiting other universities. He was a great believer in the importance and value of a higher education."

"I hope Matthew will be able to bring his killer to justice," Freedom said sincerely. "If anyone can do it, Matty can."

"We'll get Drew Quinn, sure enough," Matthew said almost lazily, pushing his empty plate aside, "but Elliot Chambers may prove to be more slippery."

"Elliot Chambers!" John Drohan repeated with disgust. "God save us. The man has his hand in every manner of evil-making, from slavery to murder. He should have been put a stop to long ago."

"He surely should have," Matthew agreed. "There've been rumors about Elliot Chambers's doings for years, 'specially in smuggling, but there's not much the government can do without any proof, without names and dates and places. When he's got powerful men like Senator Hardesty on his payroll there's little chance of findin' out those kinds of things before they get covered up."

Mariette felt a pang of conscience, thinking of David's journal. She hadn't trusted Matthew Kagan enough to tell him about it before, but now, after all he had done and was doing for her, she wondered if she didn't at least owe him that much faith. Looking up, she found him gazing at her with an apology in his eyes, and she realized that he must have mistaken her sober reaction to his words about her father. The realization made her understand something about the man; for all his gruffness and humor, for all the bitterness he carried in himself of things long past, Matthew Kagan was a kind and considerate man. He was also a man who made friends easily. The Drohans clearly considered him an honored guest in their home. Mariette wondered if even the president of the United States would be treated with as much deference here as "Matty" Kagan was. At least three times in as many hours she'd been told of how, seventeen years earlier, the brave and fearless Marshal Kagan had captured the outlaws who'd been killing Drohan miners and stealing their gold. He'd come to help them then because much of the gold being stolen affected their federal shipments, but in the following years he'd come simply because they'd asked him to, and had lent them aid outside of his duties as a federal marshal. The family seemed to regard him, now, as their own personal guardian angel.

He looked especially handsome tonight, sitting there freshly bathed and shaved, his thick black-and-silver hair brushed smooth and his teasing blue eyes dancing with the contented pleasure of being with good friends. Mariette thought of the way he had kissed her the night before, of how his heavy body had moved against hers in need, of how bereft she had felt when he'd pulled away, and of how she wished he hadn't. Her face grew warm at the memories and she wondered if she were blushing.

They stared at each other for several moments, oblivious to the curious glances they drew from the others at the table, and Matthew's expression changed from apologetic to questioning. He opened his mouth to speak to her, but an attractive serving maid with dark hair and dark eyes leaned over him just then, her breast brushing his arm, and he was distracted.

"*Perdon, señor,*" she murmured as she filled his wineglass.

"Oh, that's all right, sugar," he assured her, smiling up at her in a charming manner that made Mariette turn her eyes away.

"Will ye be needing me to go with ye, then, boyos?" John Drohan inquired. "I'd be happy to come along and lend a hand."

"I, also," Freedom added, though his Cherokee wife, who hadn't yet spoken a word during the meal, said, vehemently, "No!"

Justice said, "No, Da. Matt and I will manage well enough, and once Slow Bear arrives there will be three of us."

"Ah, well, yes," said John Drohan thoughtfully. "Bertie's a good lad, surely. Just don't let him shoot anyone, Justice. Yer mother and I will be sadly done in if Bertie shoots somebody."

With a sound like a snicker, Justice sipped his wine, then promised, "I'll do my best, Da." He exchanged glances with Matthew, who had to cough to cover his laughter.

"Poor Da," Justice said two hours later as he relaxed in a chair in Matthew's bedroom, sipping a large glass of whiskey. "Can you imagine him thinking that anybody could keep Slow Bear from doing anything he pleased?"

Propping up his legs, Matthew relaxed in the chair opposite Justice, closed his eyes with a sigh, and cradled his own glass of whiskey in both his hands. "He's just tryin' to think positive, Jus. That's how daddies do with their children. 'Sides, Bertie hasn't actually killed anybody yet." He sipped his drink. "My Lord, your daddy's whiskey sure is smooth."

"That's because it's good Irish whiskey yer drinking there, boyo," Justice replied in an affected brogue. "The best in the world."

"Mmmmm," Matthew intoned contentedly. "My little brother swears by Scotch, you know."

"Always knew there was something wrong with Jim," Justice replied, then got to the heart of what was on both their minds. "What do you think about all this?"

Matthew opened his eyes and stared at the ceiling. "I think it's going to be a lot of trouble, Jus. Ettie— Mrs. Call—she's had a pretty rough time already. I don't want her to be hurt anymore. I surely wish I could think of another way to do this without draggin' her into it."

"She's a nice woman," Justice said. "Never saw Mama's clothes look so good before."

"Huh?"

"Mama's clothes," he repeated. "The ones Mrs. Call was wearing tonight. She has a mighty fine figure."

"Who does?"

"For the love of heaven, Matt! You can't think I'm talking about my own mother!"

Matthew sat up and gave him a furious look that made Justice's skin tingle. Then, just as abruptly, anger was replaced by confusion, and Matthew began to rub at his chest.

"Matt, what's wrong?"

"I been havin' this ache," he said. "Right here. Can't think what it is."

"Your heart?"

"Don't think so. Here, you feel." Matthew reached over and grabbed one of Justice's hands, placing it forcibly against his wool shirt.

"Dammit, Matthew, I don't want to feel your chest!" Justice tried to pull his hand away.

"No, wait a minute." Matthew insistently flattened his friend's hand against himself. "Don't you feel that?"

"It doesn't feel like anything!" Justice protested, at last pulling his hand free and rising to his feet. "Do you want me to go get Good Path before he leaves?"

Matthew rubbed at his chest and felt angry. He'd never had to ask for help from anyone before. "Well . . ."

Justice was out the door before he could say another word, and was back two minutes later with Freedom behind him.

"You're having chest pains, Matthew?" Freedom asked with concern, kneeling in front of Matthew and opening the small black bag he'd brought. "Why didn't you say something earlier?"

"Well—uh . . ." Matthew was thoroughly embarrassed. "There's nothin' wrong with me! Jus is havin' fits, is all."

"Twelve Moons doesn't have fits," Freedom said, pressing his stethoscope beneath Matthew's shirt.

"He wanted me to feel his chest," Justice said, as if that fact alone was absolute proof of Matthew's being stricken with a dire illness.

"How long have you been having these pains?" Freedom asked, listening to Matthew's heart intently.

"Since about three days ago, I guess. Or two days, maybe."

"Since you met Mrs. Call," Justice noted. "Bet she's what's wrong with you."

"What are you talkin' about?" Matthew demanded. "You've lost your mind, Jus."

"I saw the way you were looking at her during dinner," Justice told him. "And before dinner, too."

"Then you need to get yourself some spectacles, 'cause you didn't see nothin' a'tall."

"Quiet, please," Freedom requested, moving the stethoscope to another spot on Matthew's chest.

The examination proceeded in silence for a few minutes, except for Freedom's request that Matthew remove his shirt and the grumbling glares that Matthew and Justice exchanged.

"Is it a sharp pain?" Freedom spoke at last. "Has it ever traveled to another part of your body? Your shoulders, or down one of your arms to your fingers?"

"No!" Matthew replied emphatically. "And it ain't no sharp pain. It's just an ache. Kind of. I think it's just 'cause I'm gettin' old."

"Is it accompanied by any other sensations? Dizziness? Black spots floating before your eyes?"

"Black spots!" Matthew guffawed in ludicrous disbelief. "It's just an ache, Dom, I ain't smokin' opium, for Pete's sake."

Freedom looked at him patiently.

"Oh, hell! I guess it does start out with this kind of breathless feelin', and then . . . well, I s'pose I start feelin' a little light-headed, maybe."

"Mmmm. And does this happen at any particular time during the day or night? When you stand up suddenly? Or after you've done something strenuous?"

"Nah. It just sorta hits me. The first time it happened Ettie and me—Mrs. Call and I—was just talkin'. There wasn't nothin' strenuous 'bout it."

Justice shook his head. "He's in *love*. That's what it is."

"I ain't in love!"

"How would you know?"

"Well, how would *you* know? You don't know nothin' 'bout it! I only just *met* the woman."

"Sometimes that's the way it happens," Justice argued. "Haven't you ever heard of love at first sight?"

Matthew gave a snort of disdain. "Love at first sight. Sure, Jus. Sounds to me like you're the one's been smokin' opium. You been seein' any black spots, lately?"

"Gentlemen, please," Freedom said, standing and holding up a hand to silence them. "Twelve Moons, maybe you should wait outside."

"Yeah, and go find yourself a pair of eyeglasses while you're at it," Matthew suggested tartly.

"Better yet," Justice returned, "I think I'll go find Mrs. Call and see if she'd like to go for a walk in the gardens. She'd enjoy seeing the greenhouses by moonlight, I bet, and I'd surely enjoy showing them to her."

Matthew stood, thinking of what Justice had told him about what he and his brothers used those greenhouses for on moonlit nights. "You ain't takin' Ettie out to them greenhouses, Jus. I'll break your legs first, if you try it."

"See?" Justice looked at his brother and made a sweeping gesture toward Matthew. "It's love. That's what's wrong with him."

"I think you're right," Freedom agreed. "I think Matthew must be in love."

"What!"

"I'm sorry, Matt," Freedom said sincerely, "but I can't think of another explanation. You're as healthy as a man can be, more healthy than most men wish they were. I'm sorry," he repeated.

"Hell!" Matthew grabbed his shirt to pull it on. "I don't believe it! What kinda doctor are you, anyhow? Prob'ly got your degree at the college of Zulu!"

"Matthew—"

"Forget it! I ain't listenin' to a word you say, you—you witch doctor!"

Freedom laughed. "Matthew, please, don't be so upset. What's so terrible about being in love?"

"What's so terrible?" Matthew repeated, staring at him. "What's so terrible? Don't you know *anything*?"

"I know about being in love," Freedom replied, folding his stethoscope to put it in his bag. "I suffered exactly the same things you are when I met Bird Singing, and fell in love just as quickly, too. I think ten seconds passed from the moment I set eyes on her before I was ready to fall down at her feet and offer myself up as her lifelong slave." Matthew groaned loudly, and Freedom chuckled. "It's a miserable condition initially, true, but all that changes once you accept what's happened, and then it's quite pleasant. I've enjoyed myself immensely."

"Yeah? Well, you're still a newlywed. You don't know nothin', yet, far as I'm concerned. I'll come back in a few years and then we'll see what you think about it."

"Maybe we'll be able to compare notes," Freedom said, taking up his bag and closing it. "Perhaps you'll be long married to Mrs. Call by then."

Matthew gaped at him. "Married to Ettie—have

you lost your mind? I only just met the woman! I don't know a thing about her, 'cept for that she hates me. And besides that, she treats me like my brain's the size of a pea!"

The brothers exchanged amused looks.

"And even worse," Matthew went on, "she's still in love with that dead husband of hers. That Professor David Call. Ain't a man breathing on this earth can compare to a dead man's memory."

"Professor Call was a fine man," Freedom admitted, "but you're a fine man, too, Matt, and Mrs. Call doesn't seem like the kind of woman who'll grieve forever." He set a hand on Justice's shoulder. "I need to go. Bird Singing is waiting for me." He took a stunned Matthew's hand and shook it. "Good luck with Mr. Quinn and his associates, and please be careful."

He moved toward the door, but Matthew sprang in front of him. "Wait a minute, Dom." He set one hand against the wooden door. "You ain't going nowhere till you tell me how to remedy this."

Freedom's expression was bewildered. "Remedy what?"

"This! You know"—he lowered his voice and glared at a laughing Justice—"this love thing. I got to know how to get rid of it."

Freedom smiled. "I'm sorry, Matthew. There isn't any cure, I'm afraid. If someone ever comes up with one, he'll make a fortune."

"Damnation! What a thing to happen to a man. I'd rather be dead."

"You'll be fine," Freedom assured him, opening the door. "Just accept the way you feel about Mrs. Call and don't fight it. Things will go much easier for you that way, I promise."

＊   ＊   ＊

Creeping quietly along the moonlit hallway, Mariette felt like some kind of criminal. It was well past midnight, and everyone in the Drohan household, or so she hoped, was abed. She wished she were, too, but the discovery she'd made, after having spent the past several hours poring over David's journal, made sleep impossible. She was absolutely brimming with triumph and had to share her news with Marshal Kagan.

Clutching the books in her arms more securely, she counted each heavy wooden door she passed, praying that she'd not mistake his room. When she reached the one she thought was right, she nervously glanced all around and then very quietly knocked.

Silent seconds stretched with no response. Mariette tried again, a little more loudly, and whispered, "Marshal!"

Nothing.

Drawing in a breath, she reached for the doorknob. Just as her hand closed around it, it twisted beneath her fingers and the force of the door being flung open dragged her along. The next thing she knew she was slapped up against Matthew Kagan's hard, bare chest.

"What in the—?" His arms went around her to keep her from falling.

"I'm sorry!" she apologized in a small, horrified voice, trying to lift her face from his shoulder.

He helped her, taking her shoulders and holding her at arm's length. "Ettie! What in God's name do you think you're doing?"

Though the room was lit only by the moon,

Mariette could see that he was wrapped in a bed sheet and nothing else.

"Oh, my heavens!" she uttered, mortified, spinning around. "You're n-naked!"

"Be quiet!" he whispered harshly, walking past her to shut the door. "What did you think I slept in when I had a bed handy? My boots?" Turning, he moved toward her, saying, "Do you have—" and Mariette gasped and whirled away again, her face so hot it burned and her body shaking so badly that her knees knocked.

"Well, it's plain you didn't look me up for no midnight rendezvous," he said dryly, gripping the sheet around his waist more tightly.

"I—I . . ."

"Do you have any idea what John Drohan would do if he found out you was here like this?" he demanded, stepping toward her and stopping when she jumped away once more. "Dammit, Ettie, don't tell me you never seen a naked man before." She violently shook her head. "Hell!" he muttered. "What was I thinkin'? 'Course you ain't never seen a naked man. Mr. Perfect Professor prob'ly wore a nightshirt to bed every night. Bet you never saw anything more excitin' than his knees your whole married life long." He stalked across the room and picked up his pants. "Keep your head turned, then, or you'll get yourself a real eyeful."

She heard him getting dressed and asked, in a shaking whisper, "What would Mr. Drohan do to us if he knew I was here?"

Matthew gave a short, hard laugh. "He'd make certain your last name was Kagan before the sun rose in the sky, that's what. John's a strict Catholic. He don't put up with folks sneakin' into other folks' rooms at night, 'specially not in his own house, which is why his sons always meet their women out in the greenhouses, I reckon." Having explained this fact, Matthew prepared to tell Mariette a few things about the general foolishness of sneaking into strange bedrooms at night, especially into one that housed a man who had just spent several sleepless hours alternating between cursing every aspect of the affliction called love and remembering all of the alluring things he'd discovered the night before about the woman who had afflicted him in the first place.

He paused long enough to pull a shirt over his head, and then, as he opened his mouth to begin his lecture, he unexpectedly caught sight of Mariette's bare feet and ankles. The nightgown she had on was several inches too short for her, with the result that her legs were exposed from just above her ankles down. Matthew had seen a number of very attractive, well-shaped women wearing nothing but what they'd been born with in his day, and he'd always appreciated such scenery as fully as possible. But the sight of Mariette Call's bare, narrow ankles and long, bony feet jolted him with such an astounding, erotic shock that he actually heard a buzzing sound in his ears. Whatever he'd been about to say evaporated and he unwittingly moved toward her, as helplessly drawn as a dumb moth is drawn to its fiery death.

"I like that thing you got on, Ettie."

His tone surprised Mariette, for it said what his words didn't—that he thought she'd look a whole lot nicer *without* what she had on.

"Th-thank you. It's Mrs. Drohan's."

She didn't hear him come up behind her until he

was quite close. Her feet instinctively started in the opposite direction, but Matthew's big hands gently closed over her shoulders, holding her in place. "It's real nice," he whispered, so near that she felt his warm breath against her neck. "What'd you come here for, Ettie?"

"Oh . . . I . . ."

"Why, Ettie, honey, you're shakin' like a leaf. You cold?" His arms wrapped around her, enveloping her. "I'd like to warm you up," he murmured against her ear, and then his mouth pressed against her neck once, and then again, moist and soft. "You make me crazy, you know?" One of his hands moved up to cradle her chin, his fingers caressing her cheek and throat, turning her head so that he could kiss her neck more freely.

"Matthew, please." She closed her eyes as his other hand tried to coax the books from her arms.

"Mmmmm, I like it when you say that. You said it last night, 'member?"

"No," she said weakly.

"You make me crazy," he said again, giving up his quest for the books and using his hand instead to tug the soft cotton material of her gown and wrapper away from her shoulder. "Dom says there's no cure for it." He kissed her at the place where her neck and shoulder joined.

His words reached Mariette's brain a moment later, like a dim signal light struggling through a thick fog to aid drifting vessels such as Mariette, at present, was.

"What?"

"Hmmm?" Matthew's mouth traveled the curve of her nape.

Mariette straightened and lifted her head, bringing Matthew's explorations to an end. "What did you just say?"

"What?" He was so distracted and aroused he couldn't even remember his own name, let alone what he'd just said.

"Dr. Drohan said there's no cure for it?"

"For what?" he asked, mystified.

His hands had taken hold of her shoulders again, but Mariette squirmed against his strength to turn and face him.

"For what you just said!"

The accusing look on her face filled Matthew with dread and, as that familiar ache began to throb in his chest, he had the horrible feeling that he'd said something to her like, "Ettie, you make me sick and Dom says there's no cure for it."

He glanced desperately around the room, seeking some kind of escape, but when nothing inspired came to mind, he fell back upon every man's basic survival tactic in dealing with women who have the upper hand and pretended that *he* was the one who had the right to be angry.

"Well, it don't matter what I said, 'cause I didn't mean it, whatever it was, and a fella can't be held responsible for what he says when a woman comes to his room in the middle of the night dressed like you are, anyway!"

"Oh!" She stepped away from him, affronted. "So you didn't mean what you said!"

Good God, he thought, panicked. What had he said? Had he said he loved her? Or that he wanted her?

He cast out a nervous, conciliatory smile. "Well . . . I *might* have meant it."

"Might have!"

"Dammit, Ettie, keep your voice down, unless you want to find yourself shackled to me for life! What'd you come here for, anyway? Just to get me out of bed and argue? My Lord, but you're a contentious female."

"Contentious!" she repeated, stunned, then shut her gaping mouth and shoved the books at him. "Here! And this is the last time I'll ever try to be helpful to you, sir! I came to tell you that I'd finally unraveled my husband's journal, which documents in detail all of Elliot Chambers's illegal activities, and what thanks do I get? I find myself molested, sir, and insulted, and—and *pawed!* Well!" She stomped toward the door. "I regret that I ever came! I regret thinking that you'd be grateful to me or believing that you could ever be a gentleman!" She turned and glared at him. "Because you *aren't* a gentleman. I don't know what I've done to make you want to make fun of me so by kissing my neck and saying all kinds of things that you don't even mean—"

"Ettie!"

"—but I w-wish you'd stop!"

"Ettie!" he repeated, moving toward her. "I ain't makin' fun of you." He stood in front of the door to keep her from leaving. "How could you say such a thing? How could you even think such a thing?" Matthew was honestly bewildered. Surely she knew how sincere his desire for her was. It seemed impossible that she couldn't know it, because he'd never known anything like it, or her, before, and if an old, hardened man like himself could feel such wonder in such a way, how could a young, beautiful woman like Mariette not?

"I ain't makin' fun of you," he repeated earnestly. Love was a terrible thing, he told himself. *Terrible.* It turned his brains to mush and made him behave like an idiot and say things he couldn't even recall. Matthew wished with all his heart, in that moment as he stared into Mariette's tear-filled eyes, that he'd accepted that six-month assignment in Barstow.

Suddenly remembering the rest of what Mariette had said, Matthew's lawman instincts came fully to life. He straightened and said brusquely, "No more nonsense, Ettie Call. We're done actin' foolish for the night. Did you just say one of these books has some information on Elliot Chambers in it?"

The solid, even tone of his voice was strangely soothing to Mariette. She was used to being spoken to like that by both her father and husband, used to being told what she must do and that she must behave accordingly. The way Matthew Kagan sometimes spoke to her, as if he were speaking to a lover, only confused and upset her. She hadn't any past experiences of such things to guide her, but this, having a duty to do, she understood.

"Yes," she replied softly, lifting a hand to wipe the moisture out of her eyes. "My husband's journal. I don't know how he discovered so much about that man, but he did and he documented everything quite carefully. In a kind of code. Look." She pulled the red leather book from those in Matthew's arms, moved closer to him, and opened it, flipping the pages over with gentle care. "Here, this entry."

It was almost impossible to read in the darkness, but Matthew squinted at the round, exact letters on the page she held up and said, "Looks like some kinda lesson plan."

"Yes, it does. I think that's what David wanted anyone who wouldn't know better to think it was. But anyone who knew David well would at once think such entries strange, because David was a university professor. These entries look like the kind of notations an elementary teacher would make, though if you were an elementary teacher, you'd realize at once that they don't make any sense at all. To an untrained eye, however, they would look perfectly right. I'm sure David must have believed Elliot Chambers's men would pass this over, never realizing what it was."

A silence passed while the importance of that information sank in, to both of them. Mariette suddenly felt as if she'd never really known her husband of three years, and Matthew realized that he'd just stumbled upon something far more valuable than gold.

"My Lord," he said. "This is what Chambers is after. He must know your husband kept some kind of written record, and since he hasn't found it yet, he's certain you must have it." He searched her eyes intently. "Are you sure about this, Ettie?"

"Absolutely."

"And you've figured out this code?"

"Yes," she said solemnly, nodding.

Matthew took the journal from her and walked toward the small table in the middle of the room, setting all the books on it and groping for the match holder. "Come on over here and get comfortable, Ettie," he said, lighting the lamp and turning the wick so that the light it gave wasn't too bright. "We've got a long night ahead of us."

10

The night was long indeed, as well as rather unpleasant, especially for Mariette. Once she had explained her late husband's code, which mostly utilized poetry found in elementary primers, Matthew Kagan turned into a tyrant. Every bit of playfulness fled him, leaving behind only a stern, intent lawman who insisted that they would unfold every mystery David's journal held before the sun next rose in the sky.

He set up a system and inducted Mariette as his fellow laborer without even asking. First he read from the journal, then Mariette read the corresponding passages out of the different primer and poetry books, then Matthew wrote down in the journal's margins the important words and phrases David's code pointed to. When each entry was deciphered to his satisfaction Matthew would sit back, look at her, and explain what it meant whether Mariette wanted to know or not, which she generally didn't. She didn't want to know about young girls being kidnapped in China and sold to Elliot Chambers, who in turn sold them into prostitution rings in the United States and Europe and washed his profits clean with the help of men like her father, in bank accounts held under false names in respectable institutions all over the world. She didn't want to know about all of the miserable wretches who were addicted to the opium Chambers illegally imported into the country. She didn't want to know about the reign of terror he held over a number of wealthy and important men, or what it was he knew about those men, or anything about blackmail at all. She didn't want to know about the bribes he made to ensure political decisions came down in his favor. Such things were hard to know, hard to hear, in spite of the truth they imparted—that Elliot Chambers's wealth was born out of nothing more than the misery of others, and out of nothing less.

David had discovered it all, though Mariette couldn't fathom how. It was all there, names, dates, account numbers, everything the government needed to bring Chambers down.

It was nearly dawn by the time all but the last few pages of the journal were deciphered, and a grim-faced Matthew ordered an exhausted Mariette back to her own room, warning her to be quiet and careful. He kept the journal and the books and said he'd finish figuring out what little was left by himself. Mariette was glad to let him do so. She didn't cherish the thought of seeing again that last final entry, the one David had made the day he died, telling who was responsible for his death.

She lay down on her bed with relief the moment she was safely back in her room, but only minutes seemed to pass before a maid was there, waking her to greet the day.

They left for the Hetch Hetchy valley immediately after breakfast and would have left sooner if Matthew had had his way. Sitting at the table, eating with impatience, he was just as serious as he'd been the night before, perhaps even more so. He gave her no greeting when she arrived and took her place, and he paid little mind as John Drohan cheerfully spent the entire meal giving both him and Justice plenty of advice about what they needed to do to capture Drew Quinn.

He shook off his doldrums once they set out, however, and as they began the climb into the Sierra Nevadas he finally regained the easygoing smile Mariette had come to expect from him. The beauty of nature seemed to affect Matthew Kagan powerfully, or perhaps it was simply the freedom of being in such a place, the freedom of *going*. It affected her, too, and in much the same way. Being away from towns and cities, from people, and moving through untamed lands was nothing short of exhilarating.

It took three days of riding to reach the Hetch Hetchy valley, and during that time Mariette saw natural beauty surpassing anything she ever had or could have imagined. The mountains provided challenging terrain to travel, indeed, but the rocky hills never failed to give way to welcome meadows, so breathtaking they stole one's senses.

There was an abundance of multicolored wildflowers in these mountains. Larkspur, lilies, columbine, goldenrod. And wild irises that Matthew plucked when they stopped to rest on their second day. When Justice wasn't looking, he pressed the beautiful flowers into her hands, reddening and grumbling something about her maybe liking to have some.

Matthew and Justice Twelve Moons took turns riding off alone, sometimes for hours at a time, and took turns, as well, guarding their small camp in the evenings, so that Mariette rarely saw the two men together. This didn't particularly bother her. Though she liked Justice very well and found him to be good company, Mariette preferred being alone with Matthew. He made her happy, even as her dear David had never been able to do, and he did it in the simplest ways. He made her laugh and he let her know that she was safe. And his eyes told her plainly that he truly desired her, in spite of all her faults and plainness. By the end of the third day Mariette had come to believe, absolutely, that sitting under the stars with Matthew Kagan, enjoying the warmth of the campfire and listening to his humorous stories, was the most pleasant thing a person could do on earth.

"We'll reach Hetch Hetchy tomorrow mornin'," he said after they'd already spent an hour talking by the fire, and Mariette heard at once the change in his tone, the seriousness of his words.

"Do you think Drew Quinn is following us?" she asked quietly, refilling his coffee cup.

Matthew nodded. "Bertie's bringin' Quinn and his boys right along, staying a few miles back."

"You've seen them?"

"It'd be hard not to. Bertie's keepin' 'em out in the open, puttin' up as much dust as he can and lettin' the damned fools shoot their guns whenever they please. He's havin' himself a real good time with 'em. Says he hasn't had so much fun in a dog's age."

Mariette gave him a bewildered look. "You've spoken with him recently?"

"Uh-huh. Met up with him last night, late. He told Quinn he'd seen some bear tracks earlier and was going to make sure there weren't any nearby." Matthew laughed. "Bertie said that was some sight, the look on those boys' faces when he said that. Had to bite his tongue real hard to keep from laughin' himself silly. He was tempted to hide in the bushes and make noises and scare 'em, but he didn't want to take a chance with Quinn bein' the kind of shot he is."

"Oh," said Mariette, the smile that had started on her face at his story dying. "He's very good at shooting guns, or so I've heard."

"Bertie says he's never seen better or faster. Quinn's the kind of man who uses his ears as well as his eyes to find his target, and that's a deadly talent. Which is why, Ettie Call, you're going to do exactly what I tell you to do tomorrow when we make ready to draw Quinn out. The only thing I need outta Quinn is proof that he threatened you with intent to harm. When I've got that, I can put him and his friends away for good."

Mariette lowered her eyes, unable to tell Matthew that if all went well tomorrow, Drew Quinn wouldn't be alive to put away. "And Elliot Chambers?"

"If even half of what's in your husband's journal proves true, Chambers won't have a prayer of escapin' justice."

"Then David and Josiah won't have died in vain," she murmured.

"Death is death, Ettie," he said curtly. "Don't try to make it anything more by givin' it some kind of value. Your husband didn't have to die and neither did

Josiah Anderson." His voice grew angry. "Why didn't he tell the law about what he was doing in the first place if he was so all-fired smart? Why didn't he have some people who know what they're doin' to back him up and keep him from gettin' killed like he did?"

The sharp words hurt, and Mariette felt the sting of tears. "I—"

"Hell!" Matthew muttered, tossing the remains of his coffee into the fire with a violent swing of one arm. "I don't know what it is makes me say things like that lately. If Mama was alive to hear me, she'd box my ears good, I swear." Then he added, more gently, "I'm sorry, Ettie. I shouldn't've said that about your· . . . about Professor Call."

"It's all right," Mariette whispered. "I've asked myself the same question a hundred times or more since he died. David wasn't the kind of man you'd ever expect to do such a thing. He was so quiet and reserved in every way. I don't think I'll ever be able to understand why he made the downfall of Elliot Chambers his own personal crusade. I wish he hadn't."

"I'm sure you do," Matthew said quietly. "I imagine you miss him pretty bad."

"Yes."

"Well," he said, then let out a sigh.

They sat in silence for almost a full minute, listening to the popping and crackling of the fire, until Mariette asked, "Why haven't you ever married, Matthew?"

He lowered his head so that she wouldn't see the pleasure the sound of his first name on her lips gave him. She'd said it a few times over the past few days, and the way it made him feel sometimes made him nervous.

"I promised myself a long time ago I never would, 'cause it'd mean havin' to give up my badge and that ain't somethin' I'd ever do on my own if I could help it."

"You'd have to give up your badge?" she said. "I don't understand."

"'Cause it ain't any kind of life to offer a woman," he explained. "Bein' the wife of a lawman. She wouldn't've seen much of me, not hardly enough to have a regular marriage, and it's a fairly dangerous way to make a livin'. I didn't want to marry some little gal and end up leavin' her a widow all of a sudden, maybe with some kids to have to take care of all alone. So I promised myself I wouldn't get married."

"It sounds very lonely," she said, thinking of what she knew of being alone.

He shrugged. "It ain't so bad. There's a lot to be said for bein' a free man. I can do what I like when I like, and go wherever it strikes my fancy. And I don't have no bossy female always tellin' me what to do. Except for Elizabeth," he amended with a smile. "My sister-in-law. She bosses me around plenty, but I don't have to live with her for more'n a few weeks at a time, so that's not too bad."

"All you say is true," she admitted, "but on the other hand, you don't have anyone to share your life with. Your troubles or joys."

"Or my laundry," he put in. "That's what I really miss about not havin' somebody to share things with."

Mariette laughed with that sudden, childlike delight that charmed Matthew right down to the soles of his feet. Humor seemed to surprise her, as if she had never experienced it before, as if the laughter sprang out on her so suddenly she wasn't prepared for it. He didn't think he'd ever heard anything nicer in his whole life than Mariette's laughter, and he wished there was some way he could hold on to it, bottle it up somehow and always have it to hear.

"So what'd you think of it?" he asked, suddenly becoming serious. "Bein' married."

"Oh, it was fine."

"It was *fine*?" he repeated.

"Yes, I liked it very well."

"Good Lord, Ettie. You make it sound like a trip to the mausoleum."

Her smile was almost mischievous. "Not quite so bad as that," she said, "but David and I did live a quiet, respectable life. We were not in the habit of getting drunk and shooting up the house, in any case."

Matthew made a face at her. "That's not what I meant and you know it. For a woman who just went on about sharin' joys and troubles, you don't exactly sound like an advertisement for marriage."

"Oh, well," she said, sounding more wistful, "I don't think you could consider mine and David's marriage an example of what a real marriage would be like. What I mean is, David and I didn't wed because of love or a grand passion. We were friends. We respected each other. We were comfortable together."

"Sounds great," he commented dryly, thinking to himself that if Mariette had been *his* wife, she never would have spoken about marriage that way. And she certainly never would have used the word "fine" to describe the kinds of things they would have shared.

"I know it doesn't sound very exciting," she admitted, "but I was so happy with David. I'd had to live with Papa all of my life, after Mother died." She seemed to think better of her words and stopped speaking.

"Go on, Ettie," Matthew persuaded. "Tell me."

Mariette curled her fingers into the material of her skirt, trying to keep them warm. "It's just that . . . I've always wondered why she married him. My mother, I mean. She was such a nice woman. I was only eight when she died, but I remember her well. She was from Massachusetts, and had the most wonderful way of speaking. She was so gracious and gentle and loving, and my father is so—" she searched for the right word, "difficult."

Matthew heard the pain in her voice. "Aw, Ettie," he murmured, his hand crossing the small distance between them, coming to rest on one of hers. He squeezed it and rubbed his thumb across her fingers.

"He wasn't cruel to her, or anything like that," Mariette went on, "but his heart was given to his career. Politics was his mistress." She paused for a moment, looking thoughtful. "I was born in Sacramento. Papa was already an assemblyman by then. I grew up knowing politics the way some children know songs and stories." She gave a miserable little laugh and Matthew squeezed her hand even harder.

"After Mother died there were only the two of us, and he suddenly had to pay attention to me because she wasn't there to look after me any longer. He felt guilty, I think, for having neglected her for all those years, so he made a conscious effort to keep me involved in his life."

"And 'cause he loved you, honey," Matthew said softly.

"Yes, I think he did," she allowed. "Once, when I was little, I fell from my horse and I woke and found him sitting beside my bed, crying."

"'Course you did," Matthew said soothingly. "He's

your daddy. I bet he was scared to pieces over the thought of you bein' hurt."

"I used to remember that all the time. The way he looked when I opened my eyes that day, the way he kissed me then and spoke to me. I used to live off that memory later on when we were in Washington, when I saw so little of him, when I was no more important to him than my mother had been. I was a suitable hostess for his political gatherings. Nothing more. Nothing less."

"Ettie . . ."

"No, it's the truth. He often told me how glad he was that I hadn't the beauty to attract a husband, for he needed me so much to take care of him."

Matthew muttered a few words beneath his breath that Mariette pretended not to hear.

"So you see," she said when he'd fallen silent, "David rescued me. He knew how unhappy I was and he offered me a means of escape. He made a sacrifice of his own happiness. I tried to refuse him but he did press me so, and I was thankful afterward. I did try to be a good wife, just exactly as he wanted, and I don't think he ever regretted—at least, he never seemed to regret—marrying me," she finished, staring into the flames of the fire.

"Any man who ever regretted havin' a woman like you, Ettie Call, is what I'd call a complete fool."

She squeezed his hand without realizing what the action did to him, how it made his heart turn over in his chest. "You are gallant, sir. Just like a knight of old."

"I wish I was, Ettie. I surely do. I wish I was a whole lot more'n what I am." He pulled her up as he himself stood. "Here, come on with me a minute."

He took her out of the camp, away from the fire, until they stood in darkness, then he put his arms around her and held her close. Mariette readily accepted the embrace, because she wanted him so very much, and because she'd never before felt the kinds of things that Matthew Kagan made her feel. She wanted to remember the way this felt forever, his big arms wrapped around her, holding her warmly, his big hands on either side of her waist, tucked against her intimately. She set her own arms about him and lifted her head, praying that he would kiss her. But his head, too, was lifted. Toward the stars above.

"Look at that," he said, the words filled with amazement.

Mariette looked, and felt anew the wonder that only a million and more stars could inspire.

"It's beautiful."

"Yes," he agreed, almost breathlessly. "So beautiful. I don't know God very well, but when I see this . . ."

"Yes," she whispered.

"There's some things a man can't understand about himself," he said. "Some things he can't change, or control. That's the way this is for me." He crushed her tight, suddenly, and buried his face against her hair. "Ettie," he murmured, as if he were making a sorrowful apology.

She stroked a hand gently on the back of his neck. "Oh, Matthew. It's all right. I understand."

He let out a breath and held her even tighter.

"There's not so many places like this anymore," he said more calmly after a moment. By degrees his hold on her loosened, until they were able to look at each other in the moonlight. "Twenty years ago there wasn't so many towns here, or railroads or anything. Now just seems like everything's closin' in on a man. It just seems"—his voice grew hushed—"like a man don't have nowhere to be himself, anymore. There's nowhere a man can be free."

"I understand."

"Do you?" He searched her eyes. "Do you, Ettie?"

"Yes."

He moved his hands up to either side of her face and caressed her cheeks with his thumbs.

"Tomorrow, when we get ready to draw Quinn out, I want you to do everything I tell you to. Everything to the letter, Mrs. Call."

Mariette stared at him.

One of his thumbs touched her lips. "I want you to promise me that, Ettie. I want to hear you say you'll do what I tell you to and nothin' more. No tryin' anything foolish just because you hate Drew Quinn."

She swallowed heavily. "Wh-whyever would I?"

"I dunno. Women can't help themselves sometimes, they're such contrary critters."

"Really, Marshal!"

"Yes, really."

"I am not a contrary woman."

He smiled and bent to kiss the set line of her mouth. His fingers slid up into her hair. "Ain't you, though, Ettie? Then why didn't you tell me 'bout your husband's journal before you did? Don't you remember that first day on the train, when I asked if you was holdin' anything back from me?"

Her expression filled with guilt. "I didn't *know*. I mean, at that time I didn't *really* know that—that . . ." She fell silent, unable to lie to him.

Matthew chuckled and kissed her once more, a

little longer, wanting to erase the worried expression from her face.

"Didn't you, Ettie? But it don't matter. No, don't look at me that way, 'cause I'm tellin' you the truth. It don't matter a'tall. The only thing that matters to me is hearin' you give me that promise."

"Oh."

He wanted to kiss her again so he did, teasing her with his tongue before lifting his head and saying, somewhat out of breath, "I'm waitin', honey."

In her life, especially during her marriage, Mariette had always behaved just as a proper woman should. She had never reached for a man, including her husband, and had never been the one to initiate any kind of physical embrace or kiss. But Matthew seemed to want her kisses; indeed, he actually seemed to enjoy them, and as Mariette couldn't think of any other way to avoid giving him false promises, she discarded the proper behavior she'd formerly cherished, threw her arms about him, and pressed her lips to his.

He froze, which only made Mariette kiss him more frantically, and then, uttering a deep groan, Matthew gave way and returned the kiss with an enthusiasm that filled Mariette with hope.

"Well, you said he was in love, Twelve Moons, but I sure wouldn't have believed it until I saw it with my own eyes."

Neither Mariette nor Matthew was able to react to the intrusion with any kind of speed, but when Matthew finally did manage to lift his mouth from hers, he did so giving out a low, threatening, involuntary growl.

Justice, standing with his brother by the fire, said, "It's incredible, isn't it?"

"Sure is," his brother agreed. "Looks like a whole lot of fun, too."

"I'm going to kill them," Matthew said.

Mariette was blinking, trying to make her brain function.

"Matthew?" she murmured confusedly as he straightened and loosened his hold on her.

"We've got company," he said.

Mariette turned her head and saw a grinning Justice standing beside another, also grinning, man by the fire, a tall stranger whose half-braided, waist-length hair was the most amazing red-gold she'd ever seen. It shone in the firelight like bright, new copper pennies.

"Oh, my goodness," she said without thinking. What strange people lived in these mountains. This man, dressed in leather from the moccasins on his feet to the heavily fringed shirt on his back, looked like more of a wild Indian than Justice Twelve Moons Drohan did.

Matthew took her hand and led her toward the men, both of whom had started laughing.

"Come and meet Liberty Slow Bear Walking, honey. Just as soon as I've introduced you," he said, still growling a little, "I'm going to strangle these damned hyenas."

11

Before they arrived, Matthew explained to Mariette why he loved the Hetch Hetchy valley. It was as beautiful as the more famous Yosemite valley, with waterfalls just as spectacular and glacier-made mountains just as incredible, but few people knew about it, much less ever went there. That was why it was so special to Matthew. This was where he came when he needed to think things through, when he'd had enough of human faces and wanted to be alone.

When Mariette saw the valley, she understood.

"Oh, Matthew, it is so lovely."

Mounted beside her on Ugly and sharing the same panoramic view that she did, Matthew replied, "Sure is. You know, I love Santa Ines like I loved my parents, but this place always does somethin' to me. I've seen the Grand Canyon and all that, but this beats everything else as far as I'm concerned."

"The waterfalls!" she said. "It's just amazing."

"That first one there is called Tueeulala. The bigger one is Wapama."

"Indian names."

"That's right," Justice said as he rode up on her other side. "The Yosemite Indians were here long before the white man came. Almost everything in the valley is named out of the Miwok or Yosemite tribe languages."

"Hetch Hetchy is Miwok," Matthew said knowledgeably. "It means 'a grass with edible seeds.'" When Justice laughed he added, reddening, "Well, that's what John Muir told me, anyhow."

Mariette stared at him. "You've met John Muir?"

"Oh, I've run into him a few times. Here and there."

"How fortunate you are," Mariette told him. "There isn't a senator's or assemblyman's wife in Washington who wouldn't give her right arm to have John Muir as a guest at her table. He caused quite a stir when he visited there last year, and was feted by all the best families."

Matthew chuckled. "That's a hoot. I can't imagine John sittin' at some fancy table. Bet he wished he was out campin' the whole time." Ignoring her shocked expression, he looked past her to Justice. "I got that funny feelin' up my spine, Jus. I'd 'preciate it if you'd stay close, just in case Quinn tries somethin' foolish."

His expression suddenly sober, Justice nodded.

As Matthew led them on the descent into the valley, Mariette leaned toward Justice and whispered, "Does he really know John Muir?"

"Better than he knows how to speak Miwok," Justice replied.

Mariette laughed and Matthew turned in his saddle to glare at them.

"Stop flirtin' with Ettie, Twelve Moons, and keep an eye out for your brother."

"I'd rather flirt with Mrs. Call," Justice replied smoothly. "It's much more pleasant."

"Yeah? So is keepin' all your teeth in your mouth."

Justice said something in Cherokee that made Matthew flush and turn forward again and mutter, "Just wait till it happens to you, friend. We'll see how touchy you get."

Their descent to the valley floor was slow and cautious. Matthew repeatedly set his hand in the air, bringing all of them to a halt as he stopped to look about and listen. More than once he exchanged silent, meaningful glances with Justice.

As they neared the flat, open meadow, he stopped once again.

"What's wrong?" Mariette whispered, only just then realizing how silent it was. There weren't any natural sounds—no chirping, no twittering, no buzzing; it was as if every living creature had fled.

Matthew made no reply, only nodded at Justice and nudged a strangely docile Ugly forward in a different angle than they'd gone before. She saw his hand move forward to check the rifle on his saddle; a clicking sound behind her made Mariette glance at Justice. His rifle was now resting across his lap, ready to fire.

Swallowing, Mariette reached for her purse—where her own gun still resided—unhooked it from the saddle's horn, and tied it to her skirt belt.

Staying just inside the trees, they moved along the edge of the meadow until they reached a place where the distance between the mountains they'd just left and the mountains up ahead was most narrow.

Mariette knew little of what Matthew's plan regarding Drew Quinn was, but he had told her that the mountains on the other side of the meadow provided their best chance for keeping safe.

"Where was Bertie leadin' Quinn?" Matthew's words, though spoken in a low voice, sounded loud in the strange silence.

"Lower valley," Justice replied just as quietly. "Behind us."

"It's gone wrong," Matthew said so softly that Mariette almost didn't hear the words. "Quinn's ahead of us." He scanned the mountains.

"Yes," Justice whispered. "Where?"

Matthew didn't answer. All he said was, "I hope to God Bertie keeps his wits."

He backed Ugly toward the mare, reaching out a hand and sliding it around Mariette's waist without taking his eyes from the opposite mountains.

"You're going to ride with me, Et—"

Gunfire filled the air, and the mare stumbled, just as if someone had punched it in the side. The animal reared violently onto its hind legs, whinnying fiercely. Stunned, Mariette saw the sky and trees whirling past as she flew into the air, her arms and legs powerless. More gunshots rang. The mare kept shrieking, Mariette kept flying.

Suddenly Mariette found herself crushed against Matthew's chest, his arm so tight around her waist that pain lanced through her ribs. Her face was twisted against his shoulder and Mariette watched in horror as the docile mare that had carried her so far and so well thrashed wildly. Above the mare's madness, gunfire continued sputtering, and then Matthew was shouting, "The falls!"

Justice Twelve Moons lifted his rifle, aiming at the mare. A scream shook Mariette's body but when Matthew's leather-gloved hand came down on her mouth it stopped. She closed her eyes against the sight of Justice's rifle. Beneath her, Ugly's hot body felt taut and strong, full of ready energy. He moved restlessly, as if he were dancing. Justice's gun was louder than the others and then the mare was silent.

"The falls!" Matthew repeated, his knees jerking as he dug his heels into Ugly's flanks.

Ugly eagerly shot forward, and Mariette was flying again. She gripped the cloth of Matthew's shirt beneath his jacket and held on for dear life. His arm like steel around her, his big body bending her backward, Matthew leaned low and shouted encouragement at the demon on which they rode.

Ugly moved across the flat meadow in swift, long-stretching strides, so smoothly that Mariette believed the exertion actually appealed to the beast. When they reached the mountains on the meadow's far side, Ugly clawed his way upward like a cat climbing a tree, snorting as if he were a hungry wild animal tearing apart its prey. When the time came to stop, the horse actually seemed angry, and Matthew had to wrestle down Ugly's defiant head to slow him.

The gunfire had died away; now all Mariette could hear was the splattering of the airy waterfall Matthew had pointed out to her earlier. Tueeulala.

"Matthew," she said, frightened.

"Not now," Matthew returned curtly, guiding his sweating, hard-breathing horse through the rocks.

They moved directly toward the sound of the water, until Matthew stopped Ugly completely. "This is it. Come on."

He dismounted, then pulled Mariette down. She was shaking so badly that her legs gave way the moment she touched earth, and Matthew had to pick her up and carry her.

"Quinn's right behind us," he said, striding through the thick bushes until they came to a small cavern, just outside of which he stopped and put her down. "Now you listen to me, Ettie Call." His turned her to face him and his fingers bit into her shoulders as he dragged her close. "You stay right here where I put you and you don't come out till I tell you to come out. Understand?"

Mariette found that she couldn't speak. Her lips moved, but no words came past her chattering teeth.

"I won't let any harm come to you. I swear it," he promised fiercely, then kissed her. "Now you get in there and stay put." He pushed her through the cavern's small entrance into a damp darkness. "Get back as far as you can and don't come out until I tell you to. No matter what happens, Ettie, don't come out until you hear me tellin' you to."

"M-M-Matth . . ." she tried, but he had already walked away. Peeking around the opening, she saw him swing up on Ugly, turn the lathering horse in the direction from which they'd come, and ride away. She stood there, hugging her arms to comfort herself. Long minutes passed, and she heard nothing but the falls and saw no one. Her trembling began to calm. She thought suddenly of her gun and realized that she must get it ready.

Unlacing the drawstrings still tied to her belt, she freed her purse, then knelt on the damp ground to pull the big gun out. It was so much heavier than the little gun Matthew had given her on their first night together, when he'd left her alone to find new clothes for her. She was glad, after having carried it for so long, that she would finally have some use of it.

"Pull back the little lever," she murmured, using both thumbs for the task. It clicked and she let out a breath. "There." She wiped the back of one shaking hand across her heated forehead and tried to slow her breathing.

David had hated guns. He'd thought hunting a detestable sport, not worthy of civilized men, and he'd never allowed a gun inside their home, even for protection.

Staring at the weapon where it lay in the dirt, she tried to imagine David in the moment when he had known he was going to die. Had he wished, then, that he'd had a gun in his hand? Would he have aimed it at another being and been able to pull the trigger? Try as she might, she couldn't envision such a thing. She could only see David as he had been the night before his death, sitting in their drawing room beside the fire, reading his beloved poetry. And she could see him at one of his lectures, standing before a captive audience, enslaving them with his subtle humor and wondrous intelligence. She could see him dancing, as he'd enjoyed doing at the few parties they'd attended, whirling her around and around in a waltz. And she could see him dead, his body lying askew on his bedroom floor, white and still, so much of him broken and bloodied. That was what she could see most clearly of all.

The sound of horses approaching made Mariette lift her head. She wiped her wet cheeks and stood, taking the gun with her. The horses stopped too far away for her to see the riders, but when they dismounted and began walking through the shrubs she called out, "Matthew?"

Drew Quinn pushed into the open. "I'm sorry, Mrs. Call, but Marshal Kagan isn't here. I hope you won't mind having my company, instead." He glanced at the big man who followed behind him, one of his apes. "Or should I say, our company?"

Mariette stared at him and said nothing. She felt, suddenly, very tired, as if she might lie down upon the ground and fall asleep. Except for the waterfall, everything was quiet again. Her fingers tightened around the stock of the gun, and she lifted it.

She had never really looked closely at Drew Quinn before, she thought. She'd always believed him a boy, but she realized now, gazing at his haggard face, that he wasn't young at all. His skin was drawn, worn, full weary. He seemed as old as the earth. When he saw the gun in her hands, pointed in his direction, he laughed.

"I've never liked killing women, but you make it easy, Mrs. Call."

"Where's Matthew?" she asked.

"Gone," Quinn replied. "Gone, gone, long away, Mrs. Call. He can't save you now. Put the gun down and I'll give you a chance to pray before you die."

Mariette's lips were dry. She licked them and lifted the gun higher. She could hear Matthew's voice in her mind.

If you find yourself in a spot where you've got to shoot, you aim damned steady, and you aim to kill. Understand?

"Yes." She closed one eye and with the other found Drew Quinn's chest in the gun's sight.

"Put the gun down, Ettie. I've got him."

Mariette blinked in disbelief, clearly hearing

Matthew's voice coming from somewhere above her, but it took no longer than a blink before Drew Quinn's gun was in his hand, pointed straight at her. His smile never wavered.

"You must possess some kind of magic, Marshal," Quinn commented calmly, his eyes on Mariette. "I just saw you ride back across the meadow not more than five minutes ago."

"What I possess ain't magic, it's a damned good horse. Put your gun down easy, Quinn, or I'll aim mighty low when I shoot."

"You've got it wrong, Marshal. I'll give you three seconds to lower your rifle before I send Mrs. Call to join her husband."

"That isn't going to do you any good, now, boy. If you hurt Mrs. Call you'll surely die. If you want to live, then you put down your gun and deal with me."

"Then we'll meet in hell," Quinn said. "Lewis may not be too smart"—he nodded toward the man behind him—"but he can shoot that rifle he's holding well enough to kill a big target like you."

"It looks like there'll be nothing but dead bodies lying around," said Justice as he stepped out of the bushes, his rifle pointed at Quinn's henchman. "Put it down slowly, friend."

Lewis did as he was told. Quinn's eyes remained on Mariette, but his smile began to waver.

"Deal with me, Quinn," Matthew said. "It's your only chance."

"Chance for what?" Quinn asked. "Chambers will have me killed anyway. I might as well take Mariette Call with me."

"Don't be a fool. You know how valuable you are to the United States government. Nothin's going to happen to you if you agree to give evidence against Chambers. I give you my word you'll be kept safe."

Quinn began to look uncertain. "Bradley!" he shouted. "Drohan!"

Liberty's head appeared from behind a rock. "No need to shout, Mr. Quinn. I'm right here."

"What the hell are you doing? Where's Bradley?"

"He's just where you left him, down the road a way. Except now he's tied to a tree." Liberty lifted his rifle and aimed it at Quinn. "This is the damnedest party I've ever been to. Everybody but Lewis has a gun pointed at somebody else. We should have a photograph done."

"Put the gun down, Quinn," Matthew repeated. "Deal with me. I'll keep you safe."

"I don't want to spend the rest of my life in prison!"

"It's better'n bein' dead, boy. You'll go to prison, sure enough, but that don't mean you can't make a few bargains about where and how in exchange for your cooperation. Think about it, Quinn. You stay alive, you've got some power. You harm Mrs. Call and you'll be facin' Old Nick with your balls shot off."

A tremor ran through Quinn's body. The gun shook slightly in his hand. Still looking at Mariette, he said, "You'll keep Chambers away from me? He's got ways. . . ."

"On my word of honor," Matthew promised, "you will be kept safe."

"All right." Quinn carefully released the hammer on his gun. "All right, Kagan." Bending, he set the gun in the dirt, then straightened and lifted both hands in the air. "We'll deal."

"No," Mariette whispered, taking a step toward him. Her arms ached from holding the heavy gun and she forced her shaking hands to grip the weapon more firmly.

Ignoring her, Justice moved forward to pick up Quinn's gun, and Liberty moved to tie Lewis's hands. Matthew started descending the hill.

Mariette saw none of this. She saw only Quinn, standing there in front of her. He was looking back strangely now, as if he couldn't believe she was still pointing a gun at him. "Uh, Kagan?"

"Put it down, Ettie," Matthew said quietly, moving toward her. "It's all over."

"No!" Her voice was taut, angry. She took another step toward Quinn. "Please move away, Mr. Twelve Moons."

Justice and Liberty finally looked at her. "Mrs. Call?" Justice said, moving away.

It seemed impossible to draw in enough air; every breath was a victory against the terror that possessed her.

"Don't do it, Ettie," Matthew said more sternly. "David wouldn't have wanted this."

Quinn's eyes widened and Mariette knew that he understood. She was going to kill him. He was going to die, and he knew it.

Her labored breathing made it difficult to speak. "Now you know how David felt."

He let out a scream when she pulled the trigger, a scream so sharp that Mariette didn't hear the gun's report.

And he kept screaming.

Mariette opened her eyes and looked. Quinn had fallen to his knees, but he was still alive. And screaming.

Clenching her teeth, she aimed and shot the gun at him again.

"What a woman," Justice said in amazed admiration.

"I'm in *love*," Liberty declared.

Mariette shot the gun again. And again. Quinn had started crying, his hands folded across his chest. Mariette shot over and over, but nothing changed. Quinn simply stayed where he was, kneeling before her, weeping like a frightened child.

She shook the gun. "No. No, no, *no*!"

"Ettie," Matthew said from beside her now. "That's enough."

His hand closed over the gun, but she jerked it free and glared at him. "Why won't it work!" she demanded furiously. "I did what you said!"

"Honey," he whispered, his eyes filled with sorrow. "He wouldn't have wanted it."

Gazing at him, Mariette suddenly understood. The gun dropped to the ground with a thud.

"You *bastard*!"

Her hand shot out, slapping Matthew hard enough to swivel his head.

"Ettie . . ."

She turned and walked away, blindly, not caring where she went. Liberty threw himself down on his knees as she passed him.

"I realize you don't know me very well, Mrs. Call," he said, "but would you marry me?"

She kept walking. Liberty's disappointed voice drifted after her. "Does that mean no?"

Matthew gave her an hour to herself and then he went looking for her.

Sitting on a large rock, looking out over the beautiful valley, Mariette heard him as he came up behind her.

Neither of them spoke for a few minutes, and then Mariette asked, "How did you know?"

He moved closer, sitting beside her.

"About the gun? Or about you wantin' to shoot Quinn?"

"About the gun."

"That first day, when we were on the train, I picked up your purse to hand it to you. Remember? I'm not much of an expert on women's purses, but yours seemed mighty heavy. There wasn't time to think about it at the moment, but it stayed in the back of my mind the rest of that day."

"When did you take the bullets out?" she asked stonily.

"That night, after you'd gone back to sleep. I was almost to sleep myself before it struck me why your purse might be so heavy. When I saw that Colt"—he shook his head—"honey, I could hardly believe it. There was only one reason I could think of why you'd have a gun like that, and I knew you were serious about what you intended to do."

"Yes, I was," she assured him bitterly. "I made a vow at David's grave that I would kill the man who'd killed him. It was a sacred vow, the only thing I could do to repay him for all he'd given me while he was alive." She lowered her head. "You ruined it."

"Honey," he said gently, "you can't believe he would have wanted you to do that. For you to take another person's life? Your husband never would've wanted that."

Her hands curled into fists on her lap. "No, he wouldn't. But *I* wanted it. Every time I remember the way I found him . . ."

Matthew tried to put his arms around her, but she pushed him away.

"Listen to me," he said softly, touching her chin

with his fingertips, trying to turn her toward him. "Listen, Ettie. You don't have any idea what it's like to kill another human being. Plannin' on it, thinkin' about it, isn't the same as actually doing it. It's not somethin' you can make right once it's done. It's not somethin' that can be fixed. Aw, honey, I know you're hurtin'." His fingers touched the tears on her cheek. "I know you miss your husband, but killin' Quinn wouldn't make anything better. It would only make things worse. There's nothin' in this world that's as heavy as that burden, knowin' you took another's life."

She sniffled, and Matthew slid his arm around her waist to draw her close. This time she didn't resist but with an almost relieved sigh nestled against him.

"I've killed sixteen people in my life, outright," he said, smoothing his free hand over her hair, "and I've helped to hang dozens more. I can't even count the number I've sent up for judgment who've ended up being shot or hanged for their crimes. They're with me every day, every night. I see their faces in my dreams. And the ones I killed by my own hand, I know all their names, the names of their folks, their children. When I close my eyes I can see exactly how it happened with each of them, how I killed them, the way their faces looked when they knew they were going to die, the words they said, if they were able to speak. I can remember it all, perfectly."

"Oh, Matthew."

"I couldn't let you know somethin' like that, Ettie. Killing Quinn wouldn't've erased the memories you have of the way your husband died. It only would have added to them. I couldn't let that happen."

She pressed her face against his chest and said

nothing, and Matthew held her and respected her silence.

"What will happen now?" she asked at last. "To Quinn?"

"We'll take him and his boys over to Mariposa—that's a three-day ride from here—to the county courthouse, and have him formally charged. I'll send some wires and get the investigation on Chambers going. It shouldn't take but a week or so for the federal government to send enough men to take care of Quinn. I'll turn everything over to them." He lifted his head to look at her. "And then, Mrs. Call, we'll finish getting you to Santa Ines."

12

Mariette sat on the balcony outside her room at the Mariposa Hotel, enjoying the beauty of the early evening sun. The day had been warm, so pleasant; now the breeze was coming up, promising a perfect night.

They had been in Mariposa for a week now, and this was her last day to relax. Tomorrow she and Matthew would board the early morning stage and resume their journey to Santa Ines.

On the afternoon they'd arrived Matthew had sent her directly to the hotel with Justice, while he and Liberty had taken Quinn and his two men to the county jailhouse. Mariette, once Justice had secured a room for her, had fallen into bed fully dressed and slept for the rest of the day and through the night.

She'd been wakened the next morning by one of the hotel maids, who had come at Marshal Kagan's request and had brought with her, also at Marshal Kagan's request, a tub and several pails of hot water.

"He sent this up as well, ma'am," the girl said as Mariette undressed to bathe, and placed a large box on top of the bed. "And he said I was to take your other things away and have them laundered proper, if you please, ma'am."

"Thank you," Mariette murmured, going to the box and lifting its lid. An elegant white-and-lavender striped silk waist blouse met her eyes, beneath which lay a simple, brown wool Newport suit. Beneath these were new cotton undergarments. On top lay a note.

> *I knew you didn't have any clean things. Hope these fit. Sorry they're ready-made. M. K.*

Two hours later, Marshal Matthew Kagan, just waking from his own much-needed slumber, received a note of his own.

> *To a verray, parfit, gentile knight. Thank you very much. The clothes fit beautifully. M. C.*

Matthew read the elegantly written script over and over. He didn't have a notion as to what a verray, parfit, gentile knight was, and he didn't care. The words made him feel hot all over, and light-headed. He carefully folded the note and tucked it away in one of his saddlebags. In his own wide scrawl he wrote another missive to Mariette, asking if she would have supper with him that evening when he finished his duties at the courthouse. When he had bathed and shaved and dressed and was on his way out, he slipped the note under her door.

Mariette spent the rest of the day anticipating the shared meal. She hadn't set eyes on Matthew since he'd sent her to the hotel with Justice, and she missed him. This worried her a little, for she didn't want to have such feelings for a man who would shortly be out of her life almost completely. Yet she couldn't make herself stop, and so resigned herself to the fact that she was in love with Matthew Kagan.

She'd admitted it to herself before. Several times, in fact, during the three days they had journeyed from Hetch Hetchy through the Yosemite Valley to Mariposa. Every time she caught him staring at her, every time he showed her some favorite sight of his, some mountain or meadow, every time he took her walking in the evenings, after they'd eaten with the others by the campfire, and had taken hold of her hand and led her through the darkness until they could look up at the stars, Mariette had silently said that she loved him. She loved him. It wasn't like anything she'd ever known before and it frightened her, the way he made her feel, the way just looking at him made her heart come alive in her body, the way the sound of his voice could bring tears to her eyes. His tenderness frightened her even more, so much that sometimes she prayed he would leave her in Santa Ines and never come back, because then she might return to being herself, her old, plain, reliable self, and not this foolish woman who dreamed impossible things and wanted a man she couldn't have.

When she had opened the door to his knock that first evening, it was to find that Matthew wasn't alone. He stood before her, handsome and apologetic, while behind him Justice Twelve Moons and Liberty Slow Bear beamed beatifically.

It was a sight that recurred continually throughout the following days and evenings, no matter how desperately either Matthew or Mariette wished things otherwise. The two Drohan brothers seemed determined to be with them every possible moment, and if they weren't dominating the conversation at mealtime they were teasing Matthew or flirting with Mariette and generally making pests of themselves. They took turns entertaining Mariette during the daylight hours, and in assisting Matthew with his tedious legal chores; but at night the brothers made a united effort to keep Mariette and Matthew from doing anything more than speaking about the case at hand or simple generalities. They clearly found this quite amusing, although Mariette, for the life of her, couldn't understand why.

She longed to spend some time alone with Matthew, even if just an hour. She wanted one last opportunity to think only of him, to speak only with him, one last opportunity to commit everything about him to memory before their journey ended. Once they arrived in Santa Ines, Matthew would efficiently finish his assignment and would get her safely settled, and then he would leave. After that, Mariette knew that she'd see very little of him again. She'd understood only too well what he had tried to tell her that night when they'd stood under the stars, when he struggled to explain how such sights affected him, and how dearly he held his freedom. He desired her physically, but there would never be anything more between them than that, at least not for him. He needed to be free, and Mariette, loving him, would never try to take something that precious away from him.

She would be content to have only a few more hours alone with him, she thought as she stood and pulled on her jacket. Only a few more hours, and then she would begin to distance herself from him to make their eventual parting easier for them both. With the Drohan brothers making such constant nuisances of themselves, however, she doubted she'd even have Matthew to herself for more than a few minutes here and there until they reached Santa Ines.

A loud knocking signaled the timely arrival of her dinner companions, and, stopping only long enough to collect her small purse, Mariette made her way to the door.

She hoped, as she set her hand on the doorknob, that Liberty Slow Bear would leave her in peace tonight. If he asked her once more to marry him, she truly believed she might commit an act of violence.

Opening the door, she found Matthew standing in the hallway.

Alone.

"Evenin'," he said almost hesitantly, turning his hat in his hands.

Mariette bent forward to look around him.

"Good evening," she returned.

"You, ah, ready to go?"

She glanced down either side of the hallway.

"I am. Are Mr. Drohan and his brother joining us later?"

Matthew's lopsided smile looked a little guilty. "Not tonight. You know how the marshals who're takin' Quinn back east arrived today?"

"Of course."

"Well, there was only four of 'em, and I figured that was about two shy of what's needed." His smiled broadened. "So I deputized Jus and Bertie and assigned them tonight's watch."

Mariette stared at him. "Oh, Matthew, that's *wonderful.*"

"I thought so, too," he said, pleased by her response. He straightened and formally extended his arm. "Would you allow me the honor, ma'am?"

Mariette, in turn, made a grand curtsy and set her hand on his arm. "I shall, kind sir. Thank you very much."

"Not a'tall. My pleasure." He pulled her into the hallway and shut her door. "And now, Mrs. Call, wha'd'you say to paintin' this here town red?"

"That would be fine, Marshal," she said as they walked toward the stairs, "though I've always been partial to blue."

Matthew's laughter could be heard all the way out to the street. "Tonight, Ettie, we can paint it any color you please."

He had known before that Mariette did everything perfectly. But tonight, in Mariposa's fanciest dining establishment, watching her from across the small, candlelit table they shared, all of her movements, her words, seemed more than perfect to him.

He'd known before that her hands moved with an easy, fluid grace, yet tonight he felt as if he'd never seen them, they were so stunningly feminine and beautiful, just as she was.

The way she talked, the way her words came out so round and full, made him think he'd never heard the like. Whenever she laughed he had to draw in a sharp breath just to keep his heart pumping. When she smiled he felt his skin grow hot. The fact of the matter was, Matthew didn't know how he got through the meal without making a complete fool of himself. Somehow he did it; Mariette never laughed at *him*, anyway, though she did laugh at all his jokes.

Greedy for as many memories of her as he could

take away with him, he made the night last as long as he could. He ordered champagne before their meal, the best available wine with their meal, and a thick, sweet apricot liqueur afterward. As to the meal itself, he simply handed Mariette the menu and told her to order whatever she thought they'd like, and she did. Cheese soup, wilted lettuce salad, stuffed Tennessee ham; it was all very good. Matthew enjoyed every bite, in spite of the fact that he didn't pay any attention to what he was eating.

He walked her back to the hotel slowly, toying with the slender fingers that were curled about his arm. It was late, the night was dark. Stars blinked gloriously in the sky, blind to every unhappiness on earth. Their conversation had changed in the past hour, from boisterous to happy to contented. Now it had grown solemn. By the time they entered the hotel they'd stopped saying anything at all, and walked up the stairs in silence.

Matthew stopped at her door and pulled his hat off his head.

He felt like a schoolboy. "That was . . . a real good meal," he offered lamely, silently kicking himself.

"Yes, it was wonderful. Thank you, Matthew."

He stared at the floor. "You're welcome."

Silence passed, then she said, "I suppose I should turn in. We have an early start in the morning."

Matthew nodded. "That's right. An early start. Have to be up early."

More silence, until Mariette said, "Well. Good night, Matthew. Thank you."

"Sure. You're welcome. Enjoyed it." He bent and kissed her cheek. "'Night, Ettie. Sweet dreams."

"Good night."

She turned and opened her door and Matthew walked away toward his own room.

A half hour later, dressed in her nightgown, Mariette sat on her bed, brushing out her hair and struggling to make some sense of her feeling of loss. A very soft knock fell on her door and she lifted her head in surprise.

She pulled her wrapper on and went to open it; Matthew, standing in the hallway, stared back at her, his blue eyes intent.

"I want to stay with you tonight," he said quietly.

Her heart began to pound in her ears. She pulled in a breath, let it out unevenly. She had never felt more sure of anything in her life, or more frightened of anything, either.

"Yes," she whispered, stretching one hand toward him. "That's what I want, too."

He moved forward, grasping her hand and pulling it to his mouth. His other hand wrapped around her waist, taking her into the room with him. Releasing her hand, he kissed her mouth, and as Mariette's arms went about his neck, Matthew closed the door.

13

She lay against him, warm and drowsy, smiling contentedly, trying to keep her fluttering eyes open.

Stroking his hands over her back, Matthew kissed her and whispered, "Sleep. I'm not going anywhere. Unless you want me to."

Yawning, snuggling into him, Mariette said, "No, please stay with me."

He kissed her again.

"I don't want to sleep," she murmured. "I'm too happy for it."

"Me, too." His hand drifted down to smooth over the curve of one hip. Nibbling at her ear, he said. "I'm sorry 'bout your bed, honey."

"It's all right." She gave another yawn. "It's really very comfortable this way."

"I've never enjoyed breaking a bed more." He tickled the shell of her ear with his tongue, felt her press against him. "But I shouldn't've done that to your pretty nightgown."

"Oh." The word came out rather breathlessly. "It's . . . it's perfectly all right, Matthew."

"I couldn't help myself," he murmured, kissing his way down her neck, pushing her onto her back. "I never wanted a woman more than I do you. Ettie, you make me plumb crazy."

"Oh, Matthew. I've never—"

His mouth had just closed over the peak of one breast, but he pushed up all of a sudden and kissed her to silence.

"I know, darlin'." He smiled at her tenderly. "Bein' with you is the sweetest thing I've ever known. You're all new and untouched. Why should that make you pink up?" he asked, amused at her embarrassment. "Don't you know how that makes me feel? To know I'm the first man to touch you this way, to see you this way? I wish I knew all the pretty words to tell you what that does to me." He grew suddenly serious. "I hope I ain't gettin' you pregnant, Ettie. I should've been more careful."

She gazed at him with utter incomprehension, then blinked and said, "I don't think I can get pregnant. With David . . . well, he was always so disappointed when I didn't conceive."

He kissed her again, thoroughly, making a needy, growling sound, and when he lifted his head and spoke, it was with conviction.

"Bein' disappointed with you, Ettie Call, is a little like bein' disappointed to be alive. I've never known a more beautiful woman in my life. I've never known anything more beautiful than Ettie Call."

"Oh!" She sounded as if she might cry.

"Shhh," he whispered, running his hands over her, molding her body to his as his mouth traveled downward once more. "Go to sleep. I'm going to have my wicked way with your helpless body."

"Please do," she murmured, her voice filled with emotion, her hands tangling in his soft, thick hair. "Then it's my turn."

The light was just coming through the curtains when a soft sound woke him. Matthew opened his eyes, reaching for Mariette. Confused when he didn't find her beside him, his muscles tensed, but then he saw her sitting at the small table only a few feet away, and he let out a breath and relaxed.

She had pulled on her night wrapper, which was the only garment she had on the night before that was still nearly intact, and she was gazing at a small photograph in the dim morning light.

She gazed at it for a long while, sometimes stroking it with reverent fingertips. At last she murmured something too soft for Matthew to hear, then lifted the picture to her lips and kissed it. Opening a book on the table, she put the photograph inside, then carefully closed the cover.

Matthew shut his eyes when she rose and pretended that he was asleep when she slipped into the bed and pressed her body against his. She stroked his bare arm beneath the sheets, murmured his name twice, then fell quiet and still. When he was certain she was fully asleep, Matthew opened his eyes again.

Moving slowly, careful not to wake her, he crept out of the broken bed and moved to the table. He recognized the book at once—*The Collected Works of John Donne*—and picked it up. He opened it at the place where Mariette had set the photograph, some-how knowing that "A Valediction: Forbidding Mourning" would greet his eyes.

It was a wedding picture. Mariette was in it, stand-ing, dressed in a fancy white dress, not smiling, not looking at all like she should, with her head, her whole body, draped in a long netlike veil and clutch-ing a big bunch of white flowers in one hand while her other hand rested on the shoulder of the man sit-ting in front of her.

Professor David Call hadn't looked anything like what Matthew imagined. He wasn't bald and skinny. He wasn't even old. He'd been a regular-looking fel-low, middle-aged, blond, with light-colored eyes. What Matthew figured most women would call handsome. His features reminded Matthew a little of his own brother, except that Jimmy didn't have a mustache and Jimmy was a big, muscular man. Professor Call looked as if he'd been tall, not skinny, but certainly slender. He was elegantly dressed in the picture, in his fine wedding clothes, as proud as a king, his face filled with intelligence and self-assurance. And Mariette, Ettie, standing there in back of him, looked as beautiful and distant as a queen. Professor David Call's queen.

An almost unbearable thrust of pain speared Matthew, so unexpectedly that he had to blink back the sudden, unwanted tears that welled up before he could stop them. Hot rage made him grit his teeth, and he forced his fury down with a shuddering breath.

You damned fool, he thought, hating David Call with every cell in his body. *Look at you. Pompous, stupid fool. You knew what you'd just gotten, didn't you? Sure you did. Just look at you. Sittin' there as pleased as can be, as if you'd just struck gold. Why didn't you take better care of her? How could you be so stupid to leave her here with nothin' but men like me to take advantage of her loneliness? To sit around and kiss your damned photograph?*

Matthew couldn't bear to think of that, of her sitting in the early morning light, after she'd made love with him, and kissing David Call's picture.

He put the photograph back in the book and started looking for his clothes. He dressed quickly, not letting himself think. He left her room without looking at her, without leaving a note, without saying good-bye.

Mariette paced her room restlessly, dressed and packed and ready to go the moment Matthew came to fetch her. There was only half an hour left before they needed to board the stagecoach; he would come for her soon, she knew. It had been disconcerting, and a little disappointing, too, to wake and find him gone, but she understood why he'd left so early. After all, it would have been quite embarrassing if anyone at the hotel had discovered them together. Explaining away the broken bed was going to be difficult enough.

When he knocked on the door she just about turned over a chair in her rush to get there.

She flung the door wide. "Matthew Kagan, you wretched . . ."

The mock tirade died away.

"Good morning, Mrs. Call," Justice Twelve Moons greeted politely.

Liberty Slow Bear, standing beside him, repeated the words.

"Good morning," she echoed, looking from man to man. "Where is Marshal Kagan? I thought—he told me last night—"

"He relieved us of our duty this morning," Justice said quietly.

"Oh. Has he gone to the stagecoach office, then? To make arrangements?" But she knew that couldn't be right. He'd made the arrangements for their travel a few days earlier.

"Matt left town a couple of hours ago, ma'am. There was some kind of emergency. He didn't explain it. He asked us to escort you to Santa Ines and make certain that you got there safely."

Mariette stared at them, stunned.

"I'm sorry, ma'am. I hope you won't mind."

She felt breathless, almost as if she might faint. "Of course not," she murmured.

"We'd better get your things and hurry if we don't want to miss the stage." He sounded as if he were still apologizing, as if every word was "sorry, sorry, sorry."

Mariette moved aside to let them enter the room. "Yes. Of course. Thank you."

Liberty picked up her jacket off the table. "Will you allow me, ma'am?"

Numb, Mariette let him help her into the garment.

"Here's your hat, ma'am." She had never heard Liberty Slow Bear speak in such a gentlemanly tone. Mariette lifted her eyes to gaze at him, wanting to understand what had happened, wanting to understand why they looked so sad. He held out the dark brown bonnet that Matthew had sent her three days before. It had arrived with a note, just as the clothes had, apologizing for its simplicity and explaining that it was all the town had to offer. Mariette took it and put it on, tying the ribbons beneath her chin.

Justice lifted her traveling bag and her purse. "This is everything, isn't it, Mrs. Call?"

"Yes."

He nodded and started out the door. Mariette cast a glance at the broken bed.

Liberty came up beside her. "Don't worry about that, Mrs. Call." He placed her tense, gloved hand on his arm. "Matthew took care of it with the hotel, already. We'd better go." He patted her hand and led her to the door. "Don't worry about anything, ma'am. We'll take good care of you. Everything will be fine."

14

During the three days that it took to arrive in Santa Ines, the Drohan brothers completely cast off their formerly flirtatious behavior and were transformed into perfect gentlemen. They treated Mariette exactly as she was used to being treated, as the wife of a renowned professor and the daughter of a United States senator. If it hadn't been for the way they looked and dressed, they might easily have passed for "civilized" men. Their appearance, however, as well as their large size, proved to be quite helpful on the stagecoaches and trains that took them to their destination; the other passengers gave them a wide berth and Mariette was left in peace. The only trouble Justice and Liberty gave her, in fact, was when they finally arrived in Santa Ines and stepped off the stage in front of the College Hotel.

"Please be reasonable, Mrs. Call," Justice said. "Matt told us to take you out to Los Robles, and that's what we're going to do."

*I*f you
have a passion
for great
historical
romance,
here's an offer
you'll love...

4 FREE NOVELS

Introducing
The Timeless Romance

Passion rising from the ashes of the Civil War...

Love blossoming against the harsh landscape of the primitive Australian outback...

Romance melting the cold walls of an 18th-century English castle —— and the heart of the handsome Earl who lives there...

Since the beginning of time, great love has held the power to change the course of history. And in Harper Monogram historical novels, you can experience that power again and again.

Free introductory offer. To introduce you to this exclusive new service, we'd like to send you the four newest Harper Monogram titles absolutely free. They're yours to keep without obligation, no matter what you decide.

Free 10-day previews. Enjoy automatic free delivery of four new titles each month —— up to four weeks before they appear in bookstores. You're never obligated to keep a book you don't want, and you can return any book, for a full credit.

Save up to 32% off the publisher's price on any shipment you choose to keep.

Don't pass up this opportunity to enjoy great romance as you have never experienced before.

Reader Service.

Yes! I want to join the Timeless Romance Reader Service. Please send me my 4 FREE HarperMonogram historical romances. Then each month send me 4 new historical romances to preview without obligation for 10 days. I'll pay the low subscription price of $4.00 for every book I choose to keep--a total savings of at least $2.00 each month--and home delivery is free! I understand that I may return any title within 10 days and receive a full credit. I may cancel this subscription at any time without obligation by simply writing "Canceled" on any invoice and mailing it to Timeless Romance. There is no minimum number of books to purchase.

NAME

ADDRESS

CITY   STATE   ZIP

TELEPHONE

SIGNATURE

The look Mariette gave him could have frozen hell's fires. "I am grateful to you both for escorting me to Santa Ines, but there is no need for you to worry over me any longer. I am perfectly capable of obtaining a room for myself at this hotel and of taking care of myself in the future. Thank you very much for all you've done." Clutching her purse with one hand, she held out the other for her bag.

Liberty grinned at her. "That's all right, ma'am. I don't mind carrying your bag."

Mariette's hand remained extended. "If you please, Mr. Drohan."

Liberty ignored her. "You'd better go hire a buggy, Twelve Moons. It's a long drive out to Los Robles."

"I shall count to three," said Mariette, "and then I shall scream."

"All right," Justice answered his brother. "You two wait for me over there in the shade. I'll be back in a few minutes."

"One."

"Better hurry. If she starts screaming you may have to pick us up at the jail."

"Two."

"Hell, Slow Bear, don't you know how to keep a woman quiet?"

Liberty's expression brightened visibly. He looked at Mariette with renewed interest.

"In that case, you take this." He shoved the bag at Justice and put his arms out for Mariette.

Mariette's eyes widened in disbelief.

"Three!" she cried, stepping back and opening her mouth to fill her lungs with plenty of air.

"'S'cuse me, are you Mrs. Mariette Call?"

All three of them turned. A tall, dark-haired man

stood before them, his hat in his hands. He was looking politely at Mariette, but when he saw Justice, his
blue eyes lit with recognition.

"Why, Justice Twelve Moons," he said with surprise, lifting a hand to grasp the one Justice extended.
"What are you doin' in Santa Ines?"

"Nate," Justice said with pleasure, "it's good to see
you after so long. How have you been?"

"Fine," the man replied. "Wonderful." He glanced
at Mariette, then looked back at Justice.

"Oh," Justice said. "Forgive me. This is Mrs.
Mariette Call. Mrs. Call, this is Nathan Kirkland. He's
a rancher in this area. He's also good friends with the
Kagan family."

Mariette was trying to manage the shock she experienced at setting eyes upon Nathan Kirkland. He
was quite the handsomest man she'd ever seen.
Incredibly so. His eyes were the most amazing color
of blue, as clear as fine crystal, and only made more
outstanding by the tanned darkness of his skin and
the crow black of his rather long hair.

"How do you do, ma'am?" His hand moved up to
shake hers.

"Very well, thank you, sir." Suddenly, Justice's
words about Nathan Kirkland being good friends
with Matthew's family made their way into her brain,
and she dropped his hand as if it burned.

He didn't seem to notice her disdain. "My brother
asked me to meet you here, ma'am," he said. "He was
sorry that he wasn't able to come himself."

"Your brother?"

"Yes. Virgil Kirkland?"

"Oh, of course," Mariette said with relief. "Mr.
Kirkland of the school board. He's the one who wrote

to offer me the position in Santa Ines. He's your brother?"

"Yes, ma'am. He had to go to Santa Barbara today to defend a client in court, but he asked me to come and fetch you in his place and get you settled. He's found a real nice house for you, ma'am, close to the school. I'm sure you'll be pleased."

"I'm sure I will," she assured him. "How very kind of you, sir." She took his hand and shook it again, overwhelmed at being saved from the Drohan brothers. "I *am* glad to meet you, Mr. Kirkland."

"You came with Mrs. Call?" he asked Justice when Mariette released him. "I thought Matt was bringin' her." He glanced in Liberty's direction.

"He was, but there were a few difficulties. This is my brother, Liberty Slow Bear. I don't think you two have ever met."

"No," he said, shaking Liberty's hand. "But I think I would have known a brother of yours anywhere. How do you do?"

"Fine," Liberty replied coolly, gazing past him to Mariette. He withdrew his hand and said, "You'd better go hire that buggy, Twelve Moons. The day isn't getting any younger."

"I am not going to Los Robles," Mariette stated, "and that is final."

"Los Robles?" Nathan Kirkland repeated. "I don't know why you'd want to take Mrs. Call all the way out to Los Robles when she has a house ready and waitin' for her close by. And Jim didn't say anything to me about expectin' her out at the ranch when I saw him yesterday."

"I do wish to go to my new home, Mr. Kirkland,"

Mariette told him. "I should be so grateful if you'd take me there now."

Justice put a hand on Nathan's arm and drew him aside, speaking in a low voice so that all Mariette heard was the other man's reply.

"I understand, Jus, but I can't believe she'd be more comfortable out there with Jim and Elizabeth. If there's somethin' you aren't tellin' me, then do it."

Frowning, Justice spoke again, in the same low voice, a little longer this time.

Nathan smiled and nodded. "All right. If you feel that strong about it, go ahead. Just don't get thrown in jail. Maybe you'll want to go out to Los Robles and talk to Jim first. It may be that he's had word from Matt by now. Could be he'll join you." Turning, he took Mariette's bag from Liberty and touched Mariette's elbow with his fingers. "If you'll come with me, Mrs. Call, I have a buggy over this way. I didn't say it yet, but welcome to Santa Ines."

Fifteen minutes later, he was opening the door to a white clapboard house.

"I hope you like it, ma'am. Some of the ladies from church came in yesterday to freshen things up."

Standing on the wide, covered porch, Mariette gazed inside her new home with some wonder. The house was much larger than she'd expected, yet it was as charming and pretty as a garden cottage. She stepped over the threshold and through the short hallway that led to the living room.

Nathan Kirkland looked at her anxiously. "If you don't like the furniture, we can have some different things brought in. Virgil thought you might like it the way it is because . . . ah . . . because the ladies who lived here before, Miss Ada and Miss Alice, they were

ladies and these were all their things and because . . .
bein' a woman yourself . . ." He waved a hand around
to finish the sentence.

Smiling, she said, "It's perfect, Mr. Kirkland.
Everything is perfect." She looked about at the gleam-
ing cherry wood furniture, at the polished floors and
spotlessly clean Japanese rugs, at the walls papered in
elegant, scrolling flowers. "I have never lived in such
a comfortable place before."

He seemed amazed. "Really?"

"Yes." She set her purse on a small table and
began to untie her bonnet. "My other homes were like
museums. Oh, my. What lovely lace curtains. And
everything is so clean! How kind of the church ladies
to make everything ready for me. And how good of
your brother to find such a perfect dwelling for me."

"Well, that wasn't so hard," Nathan Kirkland said.
"The Hanlan sisters, that was Miss Ada and Miss
Alice, died last month within a week of each other.
None of their kin back east wanted anything, so the
school board made arrangements to buy the house
and furniture. Virg said you could buy the place for
yourself if you like it, or just rent it out of your
salary."

"I do like it. Very much." Mariette walked around
the room, taking everything in. "Look at these beautiful flowers!" she exclaimed over a large, colorful bou-
quet set upon the dining room table in a crystal vase.

"Elizabeth brought those this morning," he
explained, following as she moved about the room.
"Elizabeth is Jim's wife, and Jim is—"

"Marshal Kagan's brother," Mariette finished for
him, her smile fading as she came back to the flowers
and touched a soft rose petal.

"That's right. She brought food, too, and got your icebox all ready so you wouldn't have to worry 'bout that for a few days. Though I'm supposed to bring you over to my brother's house for dinner tonight. My sister-in-law, Anne, she's been cookin' all day and lookin' forward to havin' you. Virg should be back tonight, too."

"That's very kind," Mariette murmured, gazing steadily at the flowers. "I should be grateful to share supper with your family, Mr. Kirkland." Her voice seemed strange to her, yet familiar, as well. In the past weeks she had moved beyond the life she'd known; she'd been as free and unfettered with Matthew, and even the Drohans, as a fancy bird uncaged. Now, as each moment passed in this new place, in this house, in the presence of this man, she felt her old self creeping back, like a thick fog taking possession, dampening her. Her voice sounded very proper, her words were exactly what should be said. She could have been in Washington, D.C.; she might have been speaking to the president. "I should like to rest for a little while, however, if you don't mind."

"Oh," he said, embarrassed, as if he should have realized that before. "Of course, Mrs. Call. Your things arrived some time ago." He waved his hat at the stairs. "All your trunks and . . . things. Virg had them put upstairs in one of the bedrooms." He blushed just saying the word and started edging in the direction of the door. "I'm sure everything's there, but if it's not, we can always track down what's missin'. Well, I'll go on and leave and come back to fetch you in a few hours. Seven o'clock. Will that be okay?"

"That will be fine, sir. I'll be ready at seven. Thank

you for all you've done for me today, Mr. Kirkland. I'm very grateful."

"You're welcome, ma'am. My pleasure. Good-bye." He opened the door and backed out. "Welcome to Santa Ines," he added as an afterthought.

"Good-bye, Mr. Kirkland," said Mariette. He gently closed the door, leaving her alone. Mariette stood beside the flowers for another minute, gazing at the lovely living room of her lovely new home, liking the way the sun dappled through the lace curtains and breathing in the heavy scent of furniture polish and the lighter scent of flowers.

She was here, now. Everything else was gone. Her father, David, Quinn.

Matthew.

All her past was gone, except for the way she spoke and acted, but perhaps she would never be free of that. Her new life was all ahead of her. A fresh, new life, all ahead of her.

She pulled a chair away from the table where the flowers were, sat in it, folded her hands together in her lap, bowed her head away from the sunlight, and, feeling the emptiness all the way to her soul, began to weep.

15

She called her new home Hanlan House, because the essence of the two women who had lived in it for most of their seventy-odd years permeated the place. Wandering through the quiet rooms Mariette found the bits and pieces left of two fully lived lives.

In the room Mariette chose for herself she found, hidden in a low drawer in the wardrobe, Miss Ada's fancy woven sewing basket, which that lady, or someone else, had made beautiful by fixing its top with fabric intricately embroidered with red and pink roses. The contents of the box were a revelation. Mariette spent the better part of two hours going through them, button by button and bit of lace by swatch of silk, becoming acquainted with the very practical Miss Ada, who had not only kept every piece of material she'd ever had left over, but who also sorted those scraps, along with buttons, threads, and needles, in little wrapped packages with detailed descriptions written on the outside: *Good Quality Black Buttons of Various Sizes, Twelve Large Safety Pins,* and *Three and One Quarter Inches No. 1 Silver Tinsel Cord.* There were emery bags with white-beaded pins stuck in neat rows, and fine, sharp scissors kept in velvet wrappers, and, on the very bottom, in the faded envelopes in which they had been sent, tied in a bundle with red silk ribbon, were the loveliest valentines Mariette had ever seen. For whatever reason she had kept her single state, it was clear that Miss Ada had been well loved by at least one gentleman, Mr. Marlon Bishop of Cicero, Illinois, who, five decades earlier, had faithfully declared his love twelve years in a row. Was he still alive? Mariette wondered, gazing at the beautiful, handcrafted cards. If so, did he know that Miss Ada had died? Had he at last given up hope all those years ago and turned his affections toward another and met with any kind of success?

Miss Alice Hanlan was of a much more gregarious nature, Mariette discovered when she found, stuffed messily in a drawer in the parlor desk, a treasure trove of cards and letters that that lady had received in her life, from acquaintances as far away as Bath, England, and Madrid, Spain. Noting the cheery, confiding nature of the correspondences, Mariette could almost envision the likable and trustworthy lady to whom they had been sent.

She felt right living in Miss Ada and Miss Alice's house, among their things. It was a house meant for women like them, like herself. She put her own belongings out among theirs—pictures of her mother and of David, and her books, set in the glass-enclosed bookcases in the parlor.

And she settled down to her new life.

She was too busy, in her first three weeks in Santa Ines, to think much of Matthew. There were a great many people to meet: the Kirklands, who took her under their wing and "brought her out," so to speak; the members of the school board and the church ladies, who showed up at her front door en masse on the day following her arrival; and the Reverend Talbot and his family, who showed up the day after that to invite her to tea in their home.

She was something of a celebrity, she discovered. Wherever she went in the small town, she was already known—Mrs. Mariette Call, daughter of the famed Senator Hardesty and wife of the renowned Professor David Call. It was also known, rather widely, that she had come to Santa Ines to be in charge of the school, a fact that astonished Mariette. It was true she'd been desperate to return to California after David's death, and equally true that she'd accepted the first position that had been offered her in this far western state. But she was certain, in spite of her haste, that none of the correspondence she had received from the school board in Santa Ines mentioned anything other than her working as a schoolteacher. What the people of Santa Ines wanted was not only a teacher, but also someone to act as a principal, to organize the educational offerings of their rapidly growing town, and to oversee the building of the new combined grammar and high school building. Most importantly, they needed someone who would be able to raise funds for the construction of the greatly anticipated new school, someone possessed of all the social graces, someone whose name would draw the wealthier residents of the area to any gathering she attended, someone who might be able to persuade those wealthier residents to dig more deeply into their pockets for a good cause.

When Mariette at last realized just why she'd been asked to come to Santa Ines, she actually laughed. She'd wondered why the school board had been so ready to hire someone without any previous teaching experience, and she'd begun to feel something of a fraud in the month before her arrival, in spite of the fact that she possessed a degree in education from a well-known east coast ladies' college. She was relieved to be given a task that she actually knew how to do, and she began to look forward to her life in Santa Ines. Every day it seemed less and less as if she had run away, and more as if she'd finally come home.

Matthew had been right when he told her that the Santa Ines valley was like heaven. The rolling hills were peaceful, beautiful, as golden as ripe wheat fields, and dotted with magnificent oak trees. There was a sweetness to the place, a beckoning. She sat in her garden in the early evenings, hearing Matthew's voice and envisioning his face, his sparkling blue eyes.

Evenin's are best, especially after a hot day. The winds come up, cool things off some, and it's real pleasant.

It was the only time of day that she actively let herself think of him and feel the pain and the wonder that he'd given her. The pain was so sharp, so fresh every time it came to her, but the wonder was strong, too, and equally fresh. She would close her eyes and relive their last night together, the way he had touched her, gently, almost reverently, the way she had shivered beneath his caresses. It had been the most perfect, the most wonderful experience of her life. What, she often wondered, had it been for him?

Fortunately, Mariette was never able to get far enough in her ruminations to find an answer to the question. Not that she needed one. He had left without saying good-bye; one didn't have to think too hard to understand what that meant. But she wasn't able to get very far with the question simply because she was never given more than ten or fifteen minutes alone to herself. Justice Twelve Moons and Liberty Slow Bear made certain of that.

They were like ghosts, appearing and disappearing at any given moment. Mariette didn't know where they stayed, where they slept, or how they managed always to be where she was. What she did know was that they were protecting her from whatever threat Elliot Chambers still posed, and for that, in the wake of Matthew's abandonment, she was grateful.

They established an odd sort of pattern from the very first day. The two men were on her porch each morning, like stray dogs, and she let them in and fed them. At least, she fed them on that first morning out of the bounty of breads and biscuits and other already prepared foods that Elizabeth Kagan had so kindly left her, because Mariette herself didn't know how to cook. They appeared on her porch again in the afternoons and evenings, ready for their supper and dinner. In the evenings, when she sat in her garden, thinking of Matthew, either one or both of them would eventually wander in, and Mariette would stop thinking of Matthew and would instead spend a pleasant hour conversing with her guardians.

In spite of the way they looked, the Drohan brothers were well educated and quite intelligent. Justice, in fact, had graduated from Notre Dame six years earlier, though more than that Mariette couldn't get him to tell. Each night she invited them to sleep in her parlor, and each night they politely declined, insisting that they preferred sleeping out-of-doors. Mariette was secretly grateful for this, because she could only imagine what the townspeople would think if she suddenly had two long-haired, wild-looking gentlemen staying in her house at night. She wondered what they thought about their presence on her porch in the first place.

As for Matthew Kagan, Mariette simply wanted to forget him. She wanted him to leave her heart in peace, to become nothing more than a fond memory. She wanted to grow old and pull him out for a happy reflection like Miss Ada must have pulled Marlon Bishop out of her sewing basket. No matter if she ever saw him again in Santa Ines. She wanted to root him out like a weed, to look in his face and feel nothing but the knowledge of his name. To better this purpose, she declared privately that she would never become well acquainted with his family, but that resolve, as she soon discovered, was an impossibility. She might have withstood Matthew's affable younger brother, James; there was nothing she could do to withstand his sister-in-law. Elizabeth Kagan was like a storm. One could see the signs of its coming, and one could prepare, but there was nothing one could do to stop it.

The food Elizabeth Kagan had brought ran out after two days. On the morning of the third, while the Drohan brothers impatiently waited on her porch for their breakfast, Mariette struggled in her kitchen, trying desperately to figure out how her stove worked. She had just set a pan of eggs and some slices of bread on top of it and had tossed a match at the wood inside when a loud knock sounded on her front door.

Angry and frustrated, she marched to the door.

"If you want your breakfast," she said loudly, flinging the door wide, "I'm afraid you'll just have to wait a little . . ."

The young woman standing on the porch stared at her and Mariette's words died away.

"Oh, I'm terribly sorry," she said, peeking out the door to find Justice and Liberty sitting in the porch chairs, hungrily eating biscuits out of a wicker basket that was smaller than the one the girl herself was holding. Two blond children, one just a baby, stood beside the men, demanding attention.

"I believe I'm the one who should apologize, Mrs. Call," said the dark-haired, dark-eyed young woman. She spoke with a pleasant but distinctive southern accent. "I meant to come later, but I thought you might be needing some breakfast. I'm familiar with the appetites of Mr. Twelve Moons and Mr. Slow Bear, and was sure they'd eaten your shelves bare by now." She lifted a hand. "I am Elizabeth Kagan, Matthew's sister by marriage."

"Oh," Mariette said, taking the girl's sturdy hand and shaking it. She hadn't expected Elizabeth Kagan to be so young. "I'm pleased to meet you, Mrs. Kagan. Matthew—Marshal Kagan told me so much about you. Won't you please come in?"

"Thank you." The girl glanced at her children. "Will you please keep an eye on George Robert and Joseph for me, gentlemen? I shall return in a few minutes."

His mouth full, Justice nodded.

Turning back to Mariette, Elizabeth Kagan lifted her skirt to cross the threshold. "Thank you, Mrs. Call. I shall come in."

Walking into the room, she looked about assessingly.

"It's lovely," she said. "I've never been in Miss Ada and Miss Alice's house before, but I have always admired it. Such a nice garden."

"Yes," Mariette replied, looking curiously at the young woman who had married Matthew's brother. She was dressed very plainly for the wife of a wealthy rancher. Everything about her, from her dark clothing to her tightly arranged and covered hair to her stoical expression, was Spartan. She reminded Mariette of some Amish women she'd once seen in New York. "I like it very well, also."

"How are you coming along?" Moving about the room, Elizabeth Kagan touched her gloved finger to a piece of furniture and frowned. "Dust," she said disapprovingly. "It's a constant battle in this dry climate. In Tennessee it was bugs and mud, in California it's dust." She continued her circumference of the room. "Do you have everything you need?"

"Well, yes, I think so," Mariette replied, wondering why she should feel so defensive. She didn't know anything about dust or how to remedy it. She had always had maids to take care of such things. "I'm still just settling in, of course."

"Of course," said Elizabeth Kagan, as if that weren't any excuse for dust. She looked at Mariette directly out of her large, black eyes. "I wish to be perfectly honest with you, Mrs. Call, for I myself will tolerate no interference in the way in which I run my home, but I did promise Matthew that I would—"

"Matthew!"

"Yes. I promised him that I would look after you as best I could, and would make certain you had everything you needed."

Striving to maintain her composure at the mention of Matthew's name, Mariette pressed her hands together, palm to palm, and replied, as calmly as she could, "That's very kind, Mrs. Kagan, but I assure you Marshal Kagan is in no way responsible for my well-being."

"I'm sorry," Elizabeth contradicted just as calmly, "but he seems to believe that he is. He made quite a scene when he arrived home two nights ago."

"Marshal Kagan was in Santa Ines? Two nights ago?"

Elizabeth set down the heavy basket she'd been holding and began to pull off her gloves. "You seem surprised," she said, untying her bonnet. "I must say, I really do not approve of Matthew's behavior. Perhaps you should sit down, Mrs. Call. You look rather unwell."

"I am fine, Mrs. Kagan," Mariette assured her curtly. "I would appreciate it if you would tell me what Marshal Kagan said to you."

"You dislike that he asked my husband and me to help you," the other woman stated matter-of-factly. "That is understandable. Matthew has always been a rather forceful man. Kagans tend to be that way. You will find, in future, that it is best to manage him with a very firm hand, just as you might manage an unruly child. Will you please excuse me for a moment?" She walked back to the door, opened it, and said, "Mr. Slow Bear, would you come here, please?"

Liberty obediently appeared at the door, a half-eaten muffin in one hand.

"Yes, ma'am?"

"Unless I am greatly mistaken," Elizabeth said calmly, "there is something afire in the kitchen."

"Oh, no!" Mariette cried. "The eggs and toast!"

"If you would be so good as to put the fire out, sir, before any damage is done, I am sure Mrs. Call would be very grateful."

Dropping the muffin, Liberty ran toward the kitchen. "Be careful of your hair!" Elizabeth called after him. With a shake of her head, she moved back to Mariette. "That hair!" she said with audible distaste. "Every time I set eyes on Mr. Twelve Moons and Mr. Slow Bear, I am possessed with an almost overwhelming urge to fetch my scissors."

With her hands pressed against either side of her head, Mariette stared at the smoke drifting out from behind the swinging kitchen door. "That wretched stove! And after I spent all morning simply trying to make it work!"

"Matthew said that you might require a cook and housekeeper, and I believe he is right. Mrs. Call," Elizabeth said firmly, "I wish you will sit down. You do look quite ill."

Mariette sank into the nearest chair without further argument. Her guest took a seat opposite her.

"Please don't be distressed, ma'am. I'm sure Mr. Slow Bear will put the fire out quickly. He does seem a capable gentleman, in spite of the hair." She folded her hands on her lap. "Now, where were we? Oh, yes, we were discussing Matthew. As I was saying, he behaved very badly when he arrived home two nights ago and found Mr. Twelve Moons and Mr. Slow Bear at Los Robles without you. To be honest, there were a few unpleasant moments when I truly believed they were going to start fighting over the matter, though James, my husband, managed to keep that from happening."

"Why?"

The young woman looked at her blankly. "Why what?"

"Why," Mariette asked patiently, "did they nearly start fighting?"

"I believe I've just said why," was the stiff reply. "It was because Mr. Twelve Moons and Mr. Slow Bear hadn't brought you to Los Robles, as Matthew had asked them to. He arrived expecting you would be there, and when you weren't he began making all kinds of wild accusations. Why, he even went so far as to suggest that *I* had something to do with your absence, as if I had scared you away, which is quite the most foolish thing I have ever heard. I nearly took my parlor broom to him."

Mariette set the fingers of one hand over her mouth and tried to keep from laughing at the vision Elizabeth Kagan's affronted words brought to mind.

"If I understand the matter correctly," Elizabeth continued, "he was concerned about a gentleman named Chambers doing you some harm. It was Matthew's intention that you stay at Los Robles until Mr. Chambers can be apprehended, and he was very angry when he learned that you had come here, instead. In fact, he was nearly on his way to fetch you and bring you to Los Robles by force when Mr. Twelve Moons and Mr. Slow Bear promised that they would guard you very carefully and sleep in your yard and never let you out of their sight. That did calm him a little, though he began to behave badly again when he discovered that it was Nathan Kirkland who'd met you at the stage and taken you home." Her expression grew foreboding. "The things that man will say! Why, I had to send the children to bed. And it was quite bad of Matthew, because Nathan is James's oldest and dearest friend, and I know he was only being kind and doing what Virgil asked him to do."

"Of course," Mariette murmured, torn between amusement and anger. "He was a perfect gentleman. I was very grateful to him."

"Certainly he was. Nathan would never do anything improper. I'm sure I don't know how Matthew could have thought otherwise."

The kitchen door swung open and Liberty strolled in.

"Fire's out," he announced. "Pretty good mess in there, though."

"Well," said Elizabeth, standing, "we'll take care of that easily enough. Thank you kindly, sir. You may return to the porch." She picked her basket up. "We'll have a proper breakfast ready for you shortly."

"We will?" Mariette asked.

"Yes. Oh, and before I forget, my husband and I would be pleased if you would come and have dinner with us Sunday after church, Mrs. Call. And yourself and Mr. Twelve Moons, of course, Mr. Slow Bear."

Liberty smiled. "I doubt there's anything that could keep us away from your good cooking, ma'am. Thank you very much."

Mariette wasn't quite so grateful. In spite of Elizabeth Kagan's kindness in bringing her food, and in spite of Matthew's lingering concern for her safety, Mariette held to her determination to keep as far away as she possibly could from the Kagan family.

"Thank you for your kind invitation, Mrs. Kagan," she said politely, "but I'm afraid I won't be able to have dinner with you this Sunday."

"Nonsense," Elizabeth replied at once. "Of course you will."

"No, thank you," Mariette said firmly, "I will not."

"Don't be foolish," her guest returned dismissively. "I promised Matthew that you would spend every Sunday afternoon at Los Robles, and you shall. We'll not discuss the matter any further." Basket in tow, she started for the kitchen door. "Come along now, Mrs. Call, and I'll show you the proper way to light your stove."

16

"*The code holds pretty much* to pattern throughout the whole journal. The only thing 'bout Professor Call's method that's confusin' is the way the entry dates jump around out of order, but since the dates themselves are part of the proof against Chambers we can understand the need for it."

Standing at the head of a table at which eight high-ranking federal officials were seated, Matthew stopped his address long enough to pull David Call's red journal out of a leather case and hand it to the man nearest him.

"If you'd turn to the entries marked August 5, 1893, sir, and if the rest of you will look up to where Marshal Brown copied those entries on that blackboard there, I'll go ahead and explain. . . ."

*   *   *

"You've done a fine job, as always, Matthew," Marshal Brown said an hour later as he and Matthew left the meeting room. "With that journal and the help of our informer, Drew Quinn, we've got Chambers on everything from banking fraud to prostitution trade. And that was some speech about David Call and Josiah Anderson you gave in there. I don't think there was a dry eye in the room." He chuckled. "I almost started crying myself."

"Ah, well," Matthew said wearily, walking beside the portly, older gentleman, "I just wanted to make sure they get the recognition they deserve. It'll mean a lot to Et—to Professor Call's widow and to Josiah Anderson's family to know their men didn't die in vain."

"When word gets back to President Cleveland, and it *will* get back to him, I'm sure he'll find a suitable way to commemorate what Call and Anderson did."

"I hope so." Matthew shook his head. "Kind of a strange thing. My last official duty is gettin' medals for two dead men."

"Matthew, I do wish you'd reconsider this," Marshal Brown said, opening the door to his office. "I've already admitted that I made a mistake in threatening to retire you because of your age, though you must admit you goaded me into it with that Shaeffer business."

Nodding a greeting to the clerk in the small waiting room, Matthew followed Marshal Brown into his formally decorated office. "Millie Shaeffer has as much right to be protected from extortion as anybody else, I reckon," he said.

"Certainly she does," Marshal Brown agreed, "but not from a federal agency. It was clearly a matter for the local authorities."

"Local authorities, my foot. The only reason you got upset about me helpin' Miss Millie is 'cause I caught your brother-in-law sneaking into her place behind his wife's back."

Reddening, Marshal Brown went to stand behind his desk. "Now, Matthew, I know we haven't always agreed about every case in the past, but the truth is, you're the best man I have. In fact, you'd be impossible to replace. I wish you'd reconsider. Things will be better, I promise. I'll make every effort to see matters from your point of view."

"Well, that's good of you, Harry, but—"

"And, of course, there would be a substantial raise in pay."

"Aw, Harry, that don't make any—"

"And additional time off each year. Paid time off. As much as you like."

"It's mighty tempting, but I don't think—"

"You can choose all your own assignments from now on and I won't say a word. I won't care if you find my own son in a whorehouse."

"I'm sorry, Harry, but the thing is—"

"Well, what *do* you want?" Marshal Brown asked, exasperated. "Just tell me. Anything, and it's yours."

"What I want, Harry, I don't think you can give."

"I don't understand, Matthew. I never knew a man who loved what he did as much as you do. How can you walk away from it so easily?"

"It ain't easy," Matthew told him softly. "I never wanted to be anything else but a lawman, and bein' a United States marshal is the proudest thing a man can know. I sure never thought I'd walk away from it on my own, but there's somethin' else now, and nothin' seems very good without . . . it." He drew in a shaky breath. "Can't even sleep nights, thinkin' 'bout it. All I can do is go and try my damnedest to have it."

"I see," Marshal Brown murmured. "I must say, Matthew, I never thought you'd fall in love, but I'm glad for you. Truly glad. I wish you the best of luck."

Gazing at Marshal Brown's desktop, Matthew nodded.

"Well, I guess that's all there is to say, then," Marshal Brown said more briskly. "All of the paperwork was taken care of yesterday, and you already know that you'll be called to testify when Chambers is tried."

"Yes."

"I'll be certain to wire you when he's apprehended. The warrant for his arrest should be issued as soon as those gentlemen we just left finish going over Professor Call's journal."

"I'd appreciate it if you would, Harry. You know where to get in touch with me."

"Oh, yes. Your brother and his wife have been faithful message givers these past many years. I'm sure I'll be sending them plenty of wires for you in the future when all your acquaintances address their pleas for help to this office."

"Thanks, Harry."

"Not at all. It's the least the government can do after all your years of service. You'll be taking up ranching, then, when you get back home?"

For the first time in days, Matthew laughed with honest amusement. "I'd rather be shot dead first. Nah, I'm going to try my hand at sheriffin'. The fella in Santa Ines, Broadman, he's been wantin' to retire for a few years now. So . . ." He shrugged.

"Matthew," said Marshal Brown in a stunned voice, "you can't be serious."

"I know, I know how all of us have made fun of the local fellas over the years," Matthew admitted, "but they're not so bad. Some of 'em are real fine lawmen. 'Sides, Harry, you ain't exactly one to be makin' fun of anybody. You can't even load a gun proper."

Marshal Brown made a *tsk*ing sound. "I know how to fill out paperwork properly, sir, and God alone knows how much of it I've had to fill out because of you. Most of it trying to explain away your wild escapades and to keep you from going to prison for the abuse of your authority."

Matthew had the grace to look ashamed, though only just a little. "I have had some times, I reckon."

"You certainly have," Marshal Brown returned dryly. "You've given me more gray hairs than my own children. If you hadn't been my most effective deputy, I probably would have gotten rid of you years ago."

"Effective, huh?" Matthew liked the sound of that. "Make sure you put that down in my final report."

Marshal Brown chuckled. "I will. And you'll remember to give Mrs. Call the message about her father?"

"I'll give it to her, don't worry."

"Thank you. Well," said Marshal Brown, "if you're ready, then?"

It struck Matthew as odd that in all the years he'd spent as a lawman he had never before thought about this moment, about what it would be like. He set it down to one of the same reasons he'd never thought about retirement, because he hadn't figured he'd ever live that long.

He remembered the day he'd been sworn in, up in San Francisco. He'd been a cocky young kid, then, with more confidence than brains, or maybe more desperation than brains. The words he'd repeated didn't stay in his head for more than three minutes after he said them. He'd been handed a gun, federal vouchers, and his badge. In the past twenty years he'd gone through plenty of guns and more vouchers than he could count, but he'd only ever had the one badge. It was the first thing he'd always made sure to have on him each day. That and his gun, though in a lot of ways the badge was more powerful.

United States Deputy Marshal.

Not everyone had believed him when he told them what he was, but they'd always believed his badge.

"It don't look like so much, anymore," he said, his voice strangely thick, his fingers lifting to the clasp. "The day I got it, it was so shiny you could see your face in it."

"It looks just fine, Matthew."

"I'll get it in just a minute, here," Matthew said, fumbling with the tiny mechanism that was as familiar to him as his own name. "My fingers are cold this mornin', for some reason."

Marshal Brown was silent. Matthew closed his eyes as the pin gave way. His badge slid free of his shirt. He held it in one hand, squeezed it.

It was hard, God, so hard. His throat felt suddenly swollen, his eyes filled with shameful tears. For the space of several seconds he was afraid he was going to break down and make a fool of himself. All of the muscles in his hand were rigid and he had to clench his teeth to unfold his fingers.

His badge fell with a dull clatter onto the wood top of Marshal Brown's desk, and the deed was done.

From this moment forward, he would never again be Marshal Matthew Kagan.

*   *   *

"James had a letter from Matthew yesterday."

It had been nearly five weeks since Mariette had first met Elizabeth Kagan, and although she'd come to like her a great deal, she never ceased to be amazed at the younger woman's talent for saying the wrong thing at the wrong time. Just now, for instance, that one simple sentence made Mariette lose count in her knitting, and this was the third time she'd tried to count that particular row.

"I give up," she muttered, gazing woefully at the knotted mess in her hands.

Elizabeth looked up from her own knitting, which was an example of easy perfection. "What do you mean? You can't give up. You've only just begun."

"I would prefer to do embroidery," Mariette said, lifting her work for Elizabeth's examination. "I'm much better at that."

Elizabeth inspected the knitting with a frown. "Hmmm."

"That's it," Mariette repeated emphatically. "I'm giving up."

"All I said was 'hmmm.' You can't stop just because of that."

"Yes, I can. That 'hmmm' said it all."

"Don't be ridiculous. I won't allow you to stop."

"Elizabeth," said Mariette calmly, "in the past weeks I've let you bully me into coming to your house for dinner every Sunday night. I've let you bully me into hiring a housekeeper, whom I'm more than happy with," she added quickly at Elizabeth's affronted look and thinking that Mrs. Keeler was, in truth, an answer to prayer. "I've let you bully me into accepting more food than I, Mrs. Keeler, or even the Drohan brothers can consume. I've even let you drag me into meeting with the church ladies every Tuesday morning in spite of the fact that all they do is drink tea and gossip. But I will not, I tell you, I will *not* let you bully me into learning how to knit."

Elizabeth set her knitting in her lap. "Well, my goodness, Mariette, just because I happened to mention Matthew doesn't mean—"

"Matthew Kagan doesn't have a thing to do with it!"

"Yes, he does," Elizabeth said patiently, "and please don't speak such falsehoods to me, for I'll not have it. I know very well that you're in love with him, and aside from that it is rude to interrupt. Now, what I meant to say is, just because I mentioned Matthew doesn't mean you should feel despaired toward knitting. It's common to be easily distracted when you first begin, but after a while it will be—"

"Elizabeth!"

"Really, Mariette. That is quite the worst habit. If George Robert or Joseph ever dared to—"

"I'm not in love with him! How could you even think such a thing!"

"That is enough! You will either behave yourself or—" Elizabeth brought herself up short. "Oh, dear, what am I saying? I'm speaking to you as if you were one of the Drohans. How dreadful. I'm very sorry, Mariette. Please forgive me."

Mariette set her knitting aside and rose from her chair. "I'm afraid you'll have to leave now, Mrs. Kagan. I am suddenly not feeling well."

Elizabeth accordingly began to put her things away. "I realize you haven't been feeling well these past several days," she admitted, "but I think at the moment you're only upset because I mentioned Matthew, which, under the circumstances, is certainly understandable, but . . ."

"Mrs. Kagan," Mariette said curtly, her head truly beginning to throb, "your audacity is beyond anything I have ever before known or ever expect to know. You could teach my father a thing or two about manipulating people, and he's a master of the art."

"Please calm yourself, Mariette," Elizabeth said more gently. "It isn't healthy to be so upset when—when one isn't feeling well. I don't know much of what passed between you and Matthew, I don't know anything, really, but I do think we need to speak of him."

Mariette felt threatened by sudden tears. She'd never been one to be so quickly overcome by strong emotions, but lately . . . She pressed her fingers to either temple. "No. I do not wish to discuss Marshal Kagan with you. I only want you to go."

Elizabeth studied her hands for a few thoughtful seconds.

"I don't entirely know what he wrote in his letter, either. James only read parts of it aloud, and the children were rather distracting last night, I'm afraid. There was one part that pleased James in particular, though, that I did hear." She lifted her gaze to Mariette's. "Matthew isn't being made to retire after all, as he thought he was. Marshal Brown told him that all of that was a mistake and apologized for it. He's asked Matthew to continue on as a deputy marshal for as long as it pleases him. So I don't imagine he'll be coming back to Santa Ines anytime soon, as we'd hoped."

The two women gazed at each other. Mariette's throat tightened and her lips trembled.

"I'm sorry, Mariette."

"Don't be ridiculous," Mariette managed as Elizabeth's sad face blurred. "Why, that's wonderful news. I'm so glad for Marshal K-K . . ." She drew in a sharp breath. "And you and Mr. Kagan m-must be so . . ."

Pressing her fingers against her mouth, she turned away.

"Please." Elizabeth stood and put an arm about her, guiding her toward the sofa. "You mustn't become too upset. I know how difficult it is, especially now, but it isn't at all good for the baby. Sit down, now, and I'll fetch a glass of water."

"I don't know why I'm crying!" Mariette said angrily when Elizabeth returned with the water and a clean handkerchief. "I wasn't even going to tell him!"

"Of course you weren't," Elizabeth said soothingly, patting Mariette's back. "He has behaved quite badly. You have every reason to be upset."

Mariette felt as if everything was falling away—the self-control she'd been so proud of these last two weeks since she found out, the bravery with which she'd held her overwhelming fears at bay. "Oh, gracious Lord, whatever will I do, Elizabeth? What will I tell people? I've been so frightened."

"I'll have none of that kind of foolishness." Elizabeth efficiently scrubbed Mariette's wet face with the handkerchief. "Everything is going to be perfectly all right, I promise you. I admit there are some difficulties, but we shall face them and we shall overcome them and that is that. Now, drink this water and calm yourself, and we will discuss the matter rationally."

Obediently, Mariette drank and, with the help of several deep breaths, calmed herself.

"That's better," Elizabeth said.

"Better!" Mariette repeated. "Just look at me!" She tugged at her skirt. "Dressed in black, mourning my husband!" she said with complete dismay. "David hasn't even been gone a year. He was so good to me. So dear to me. I've betrayed his memory, everything he did for me, everything he was. And for what? For what?" Every wretched, self-punishing thought she'd suffered during the nights struck her anew. "I've behaved little better than a whore!"

"Heavens!" Elizabeth said, quite shocked. "That's perfectly ridiculous. I do admit that it is very wrong for people who are not married to be quite so friendly with each other, and of course, I don't absolve either Matthew or you of such behavior, but even so, I do believe that you truly love each other, and you won't be the first man and woman on God's earth who have anticipated their vows. It is unfortunate that the child was created before you could be wed, but if you're going to dance you must pay the piper, and it's a small price to pay when you consider the alternatives. Besides, five years from now the townspeople won't even remember. And you may be certain the child won't suffer. The Kagan name commands that much respect in this town, at least."

"It doesn't matter how much respect it commands," Mariette said. "It will not be my name and it will not be my child's name. Matthew doesn't love me. He would certainly never want to marry me, and I should never force him to by telling him of the child."

"Mariette!"

"I meant what I said before," she said firmly. "I had already decided I wouldn't tell him. Matthew made me no promises and I asked for none. You mustn't think he didn't have a care for the consequences, because he did. He said he hoped he wasn't getting me pregnant and I told him that I didn't believe I was able to conceive, because with David . . ." She sounded suddenly embarrassed.

"I understand," Elizabeth said quickly.

Mariette looked at her shoes. "David wanted children so badly. I spent our marriage berating myself and being so angry." She set a hand over her stomach, pressing there as if she still couldn't believe she carried a life. "So you see, I'm glad, really. I want this child more than I've ever wanted anything. I will love it and will give him or her the best life I possibly can."

"But Matthew has a right to love this child, too," Elizabeth told her.

Mariette stood. "No. Matthew has a right to do what he wants to do, which is being a federal deputy marshal. I will not saddle him with a wife he doesn't want because of a child he never meant to create."

"I see," Elizabeth said. She added with practicality, "That *will* complicate matters somewhat."

"Somewhat," Mariette agreed.

"You won't tell Matthew anything?"

"No, and I want your promise that you'll not say anything to him, either."

Elizabeth was ominously silent. Mariette turned and looked at her. "Promise me, Elizabeth."

Elizabeth's expression was stubborn. "It isn't right! He should know!"

"You know how much he loves what he does! Would you take all of that away from him?"

"I don't see why he can't marry you and keep on being a federal marshal. Plenty of other men do it."

"Matthew wouldn't," Mariette assured her. "It's why he never wed in the first place. He never wanted to wed a woman and leave her alone for so long, perhaps forever. He didn't think it right."

"Oh," said Elizabeth, her stubbornness deflated with the surprise that Mariette knew more about her brother-in-law than she did. "I never realized. My goodness."

Mariette sat beside Elizabeth again. "I think I must leave Santa Ines," she said.

"No!"

"I can't think of any other way. If I go away, somewhere where they won't know me, I can say the child is David's." She restlessly folded and unfolded her hands. "I have plenty of funds. That won't be a problem. I've just bought this house out of my own money. I'll keep it for a time. For another month, at least, until I can make arrangements, although I'll be very sorry to leave when the school board won't have anyone to take my place. And I did so want to help them build the new school, but there isn't anything I can do about that, because I must think of my child first."

"Oh, Mariette!" Elizabeth sounded as if she might cry.

"I can go to Europe," Mariette went on, desperate to have things settled. "My father isn't so well known there. Perhaps to England—oh, no, I don't suppose that would do. All of my mother's relatives are there, all over the place. Perhaps France, then. Or Italy."

"Tennessee is nice," Elizabeth suggested sadly. "Please, Mariette, won't you reconsider telling Matthew?"

"No! Absolutely not. He would only insist on doing the right thing, and I won't live through another marriage like that."

"But I'm certain he loves you," Elizabeth insisted. "He must love you to have been so . . . intimate . . . with you."

Mariette sent Elizabeth a look of disbelief. "There are times, Elizabeth, when I think you live in a cave."

Elizabeth stiffened and flushed. "I understand that Matthew suffers from the same unfortunate tendencies that all men do, but I know him, and I'm sure that he cares for you very deeply. If you could have seen him that night when he came home and didn't find you there."

"He was simply concerned about my safety," Mariette told her. "Perhaps he felt badly about abandoning his assignment to the Drohan brothers and wanted to make certain it was successfully completed."

"He knew very well it was successfully completed. He followed you every step of the way from Mariposa. It's the truth!" she said at Mariette's shocked expression. "He told me himself that he never had you out of his sight, not for a moment until you reached Santa Ines and he had to go check in with Sheriff Broadman. And he was sorry that he took his eyes off you even for that, because you weren't taken out to Los Robles, as he'd meant you to be."

Mariette didn't know what to make of this revelation. He hadn't abandoned her. No, that wasn't quite right. He hadn't abandoned his assignment. She should have realized he wouldn't do such a thing, no matter what his feelings for her had become, if he'd ever had any feelings for her in the first place, other than desire.

"Marshal Kagan is a dedicated lawman," she said somewhat bitterly. "I'm not surprised that his superior wished to keep him."

"Mariette." Elizabeth's tone was earnest. "I said before that I don't know what passed between you and Matthew. Well, I mean, I do know some of what passed between you, because you are pregnant with his child, but in spite of whatever did happen, can't you at least give him a chance to tell you what his feelings are? Write him. Tell him that you love him and that you're thinking of going away. You don't have to mention the baby, but at least give him the chance to respond."

Mariette felt like crying again. She felt so foolish and plain. Why didn't Elizabeth understand? David hadn't even been gone a year, yet she'd allowed herself to fall in love with a man who didn't want anything to do with her past the one night she'd so foolishly shared a bed with him. She loved Matthew Kagan. She didn't want to think about him. It hurt too much to remember the way he spoke, the way he looked at her with those beautiful blue eyes, the way he touched her with his hands, with his mouth.

"No," she said. "That would only make Matthew uncomfortable. And that," she added with finality as Elizabeth opened her mouth, "is something I don't want to do to him. Now I don't want to speak of this anymore."

"Very well. If you are truly decided, then it would be a waste of time to argue."

"It would," Mariette agreed. A thought came to her, and she looked at Elizabeth suspiciously. "How did you know I was pregnant?"

"You may not have noticed it," Elizabeth replied,

"but I have been pregnant myself. I am not unaware of the signs of the condition."

Mariette's eyes widened. "Oh, no, I didn't think anyone else would realize until I began to show. Do you think . . . ?"

"Oh, no, I don't," Elizabeth assured her quickly. "I wouldn't have, either, except that Mr. Twelve Moons and Mr. Slow Bear said you hadn't been getting up as early as you used to. They were afraid if you came down with something Matthew would somehow blame them for it. I promised them I would keep an eye on you, and I did notice that you seemed rather pale, though at the time I thought it was simply because you were missing Matthew."

Mariette made a dismissive sound, in spite of the fact that she'd initially set her illness down to the same reason.

"But this last Tuesday I realized it must be something more, when you excused yourself from the ladies' meeting and went out to get sick in the bushes."

Mariette flushed. "I didn't think anyone saw that. I'd hoped not, anyway."

"I was the only one," Elizabeth promised. "But it was then that I realized you were expecting, and only because of the coincidence."

Mariette gazed at her uncomprehendingly.

"I did exactly the same thing in the exact same bushes when I was pregnant with Joseph. I declare, it's a wonder the poor plants haven't died yet."

A silent moment passed, and then both women burst out laughing. And they kept laughing, unable to stop themselves, until tears were rolling down their faces and until Justice and Liberty walked in to make

sure they were all right, which only made them laugh
that much harder. The men left, shaking their heads,
and Mariette and Elizabeth at last calmed.

Wiping her face with the fully wet handkerchief,
Elizabeth sighed and met Mariette's tired, relieved
smile. "That was silly of us," she said kindly, smiling
just as tiredly. "Since you're determined to be so stubborn about this matter, we should be spending our
time trying to make some plans, not in being amused."

Mariette reached out and took her hand. She'd
never had a friend like Elizabeth before. She was so
glad to have her now. "You'll help me?"

The younger woman squeezed her hand with reas-
suring confidence. "Of course I will."

17

Matthew moved silently, marking his prey. Slipping into the shadows of the stable, pressing deep in them, he inched his way toward the stall where the man stood unsaddling his horse.

Smelling Matthew's scent, some of the horses lifted their heads and whinnied, but the man didn't notice. He was humming, talking a little nonsense to his horse the way a man sometimes did after a long day's work. He was utterly preoccupied, not expecting a thing.

Slowly, slowly, Matthew moved, from stall to stall, stopping and ducking whenever his quarry turned his way and starting forward again when he turned back.

The man's stallion caught the strange scent at last, and snorted.

"What're you complainin' about?" his owner asked, patting him. "We'll get you brushed down here and you'll be all right. I know, I know. If this wasn't

Stan's night off, you wouldn't have to put up with me, but it *is* Stan's night off and . . ."

Crouching low on the other side of the dividing wall, Matthew tossed a pebble onto the wooden floor just outside the horse's stall.

His prey fell quiet. Matthew threw another pebble and heard him setting the brush down.

"What in the—?"

"Yaaaa!" Leaping out of the shadows, Matthew caught him around the waist and hurled him to the ground.

The shocked look on his little brother's face was worth all the anger that followed.

"You damned dog!" James Kagan shouted, shoving his huge brother off him. "What're you doing! Don't you think I already got enough gray hairs?"

Laughing, pleased with himself, Matthew tousled the hair in question. "You ain't got no gray hairs in there, Jimmy. You look like a kid, still." He offered him a hand and pulled him up. "You want gray hairs, have a look at the mess I got on my noggin."

"You dog," James repeated, rubbing his head where it had hit the floor. "Aren't you ever going to grow up? My Lord, I just about jumped outta my skin." He set a hand over his chest and breathed deeply. "What are you doin' home? When'd you get here?"

"Oh, I rode in this afternoon," he replied with a shrug. "I thought everybody'd be expectin' me, but I guess I forgot to mention a few things in that letter I sent last week, which ain't surprisin' considering the way my mind's been workin' lately."

"You sure didn't say you were comin' home," James agreed, "but you know we're always glad to see you." With a laugh, he added, "'Cept for when you scare the heck out of any of us. Hey, big brother"—he gave Matthew a short, hard hug—"welcome home."

"Thanks, Jimmy." Matthew patted his shoulder. "It's good to be back."

"You going to stick around a little longer this time? All you did last month when you dropped by was get everybody angry and ride off again."

Matthew looked a little sheepish. "Guess I did, didn't I? Well, I'm sorry 'bout all that. I wasn't in my right mind at the time, but all that's going to straighten out pretty quick here, I hope."

James looked at him with interest. "Yeah? That mean you're stayin' or going?"

"Well, look, Jimmy . . . ah, hell, I guess I left more outta that letter than I should have." Matthew didn't know where to start. This was harder than he'd thought, trying to explain things to his little brother, who stood there grinning at him.

"That bad?" James said. "What is it, Matt? Are you stayin' or aren't you? Or don't you know yet?"

"I'm stayin'. Jimmy—" he drew in a breath and forced the words out, "I resigned. I'm not a federal marshal anymore."

"What!"

"So I'll be stayin' at Los Robles for a spell. Not forever," he added quickly, "just for a while until I can get things settled and find a place of my own."

"You resigned! I don't believe it!"

"Believe it," Matthew said, "'cause it's the truth. I ain't givin' up the law completely, though. I'll be takin' over Hank Broadman's sheriffin' duties until the next election comes. You know how he's been wantin' to retire."

"Well, sure I do, but . . . Matt! You said Marshal Brown wanted to keep you. How'd this happen?"

Matthew glanced at the stable doors. "I'll tell you, Jim, but you got to swear to me, swear to me on Mama's grave, that you won't tell nobody else. Not sister Elizabeth, not Nate Kirkland, not even God in your prayers at night."

"All right. You know you can trust me."

"I know," Matthew conceded, lowering his voice, "but, the thing is, Jimmy, it's so damned foolish you're going to laugh your head right off. I know you are, so don't try to deny it. I wouldn't even tell you, 'cept I'll be needin' your help and I don't have no choice. Go on and promise me, on Mama's grave."

James lifted a hand in the air. "On Mama's grave, I swear I won't tell another living soul what you're about to tell me."

Matthew nodded, satisfied. "Good. Well, all right, then." He lowered his voice even more, so that James had to move closer. "Do you remember how I always said I was never going to get married?"

"Of course. That's why I married Beth."

"Right. 'Cause you knew it was up to you to carry on the Kagan name. I s'pose you could give me a punch in the nose for that now, 'cept that you and sister Elizabeth is pretty happy together, but, the thing is, Jimmy, I've changed my mind."

James straightened minutely. "Changed your mind?"

"Right. I've changed my mind and now I want to get married. Not to just anybody, of course. It's got to be to Ettie, 'cause she's the one I fell for."

"Ettie," James repeated, looking at his brother as if he were demented. "Because you fell for her."

"In love with her," Matthew corrected. "Happened just like fallin' off a cliff. One minute I was fine and the next thing you know—" he slapped his hands together sharply, "I was a goner. Never knew what hit me. Is that the way it happened with you and sister Elizabeth?"

"Uh . . . not quite."

"I never thought it happened like that to anyone," Matthew said thoughtfully, rubbing the side of his neck, "but I reckon it does, 'cause that's the way it happened to me. I've been a wreck ever since, 'specially since I left her. I can't think of anything but Ettie, don't want to eat, can't hardly sleep. Terrible. My Lord, if I was a horse you could shoot me and put me out of my misery, but I ain't, so I finally decided I had to face the way things are." He met his brother's amazed stare. "Just can't live without her, Jimmy. Can't do it, don't want to do it. I figured all I could do was try to get her to marry me. Now, I know what you're thinkin'." He put his hands up in the air as if warding off his brother's thoughts. "What would she ever want an old fool like me for, bein' the way she is, so smart and refined, and 'specially after who she used to be married to, right?"

"Well . . ."

"I know it's a long shot, but I tell you, Jimmy, I just don't have any other choice. I got to give it a try or I'll never be able to look at myself in the face again."

"In the mirror again."

"Huh?"

"You'll never be able to look at yourself in the mirror again."

"Dammit, Jimmy, aren't you listenin' to me? I just said that already."

"Sorry."

"It's all right." Matthew made a dismissive gesture. "I reckon you're too surprised by all this to think straight."

"That's one way of sayin' it," James agreed.

"Anyhow, it wasn't easy, but I went ahead and retired, 'cause I didn't want Ettie to think I'd just marry her and leave her alone all the time. I wanted her to know I was serious." He looked at James for concurrence.

James was still trying to get over the shock of the situation, but the worried look on Matthew's face brought him around. "Uh, sure. Of course! That was just what I would've done."

Matthew ran a hand through his hair. "I figured it was the thing to do, but now I'm here and I can't figure out what to do next. I mean, it's got to be done right. I can't just walk up to Ettie's door and tell her to marry me." He looked at James again. "Can I?"

James felt a little lost. He couldn't believe he was actually discussing what he was discussing. With *Matthew*. "No, I don't—no," he said with more conviction. "You shouldn't. I don't think so, anyhow."

Matthew was clearly disappointed. "I didn't think so, either, but you're the expert in these matters." He let out a tired sigh, then lifted his face toward heaven and closed his eyes and tried to envision Mariette. "With Ettie," he said, "it's got to be just right. Flowers and poems and music. All the right words. Perfect. She's so perfect. The way she talks. Things she writes. Way she smells. That's just what a woman ought to smell like, so good like that, so—"

"Good Lord," James murmured, "you *are* in love. Never thought I'd live to see this day."

Matthew opened his eyes and blinked. "Me, either."

James extended a hand, took Matthew's, and shook it solemnly.

"Congratulations, Matt. I'm glad for you."

"You'll give me some help courtin' Ettie?" Matthew squeezed his brother's hand hard.

"You bet. Any way I can, I will. You count on it."

"Thanks, Jimmy. And I won't get in the way while I'm at Los Robles. Promise."

James waved the words away. "Los Robles is your home, Matt. You're never in the way. I imagine Beth must be happy as anything to know you're here to stay. Bet she's up at the house runnin' herself ragged trying to make everything nice for you."

"Well, you know, Jimmy, that's kind of a funny thing. I figured sister Elizabeth'd be real happy to see me. She always has been before. But I walked into that house today and she looked at me like she wanted to shoot me. No, I'm serious," he insisted at his brother's look of disbelief. "Gave me a look that could've froze a polar bear, like I was some kind of skunk that'd walked into her clean house. I was awful glad the kids was there to give me a welcome."

"If Beth looked at you with anything but welcome," James retorted, "then it was prob'ly 'cause you said somethin' a little raw when you walked in without thinkin'. I know better'n anyone how she cries her heart out every time you leave Los Robles after a visit, and how she's always wishin' you'd quit your job and settle down."

"She did seem happier after I told her I was home to stay," Matthew admitted. "And she's makin' Tennessee jam cake for after supper."

"Well, there you go. You know how Beth is. It's hard for her to say the things she feels. She tries to show it, instead. That's what the jam cake's for."

"I reckon."

"You can more than reckon. That's the way it is. Now let me get finished with Andrew J. here and we'll get up to the house before Beth comes down here and reads us a sermon about bein' late for supper."

"All right, I'll give you a hand."

"I'll take care of him. Why don't you tell me some more about this gal you've fallen for."

"Like what?"

James started brushing his horse's shiny coat. "Like who she is, for a start."

"Wha'd'you mean, who she is? I thought you and Beth were keepin' an eye on Ettie for me since she got to town. Beth said she'd have her over for dinner every Sunday."

The brushing stopped. "Oh, my Lord." James gaped at Matthew. "You can't be talkin' about Mrs. Call. You fell in love with *Mariette Call*?"

The back door of the Kagan household was open, inviting the evening breeze into the stove-hot kitchen. Elizabeth pulled two cake pans out of the oven, surveyed their contents with satisfaction, and with her sons trailing her, went to set the hot pans on the back porch to cool. Laughter, coming from the direction of the stable, greeted their ears as they stepped out the door.

Her oldest son, two-year-old George Robert, tugged on his mother's skirt, pointed at the stables, and said, "Daddy!"

"Yes," Elizabeth replied slowly, wondering at the unbridled quality of her husband's laughter. She knew Matthew had gone out to greet him, but she couldn't imagine what it was that James found so very funny, or why Matthew wasn't laughing, too. "Yes, dear," she said, smiling down at her son. "It's Daddy. He sounds very glad to be home, doesn't he?"

She drew her sons back inside the house, but James's loud laughter followed, all the way into the kitchen.

18

Justice let out a low whistle when Matthew passed through the gate and started up the path that led to Mariette's house.

"My, my," he crooned, "what have we here? Why, Matty Kagan, me boyo. Yer lookin' fine as new polished silver, so ye are. May God and all the saints preserve us."

"Careful, there, Jus," Matthew warned as he mounted the porch steps. "I ain't in the mood for any of that today." He extended a hand to where Justice sat comfortably reclining, his long legs propped up on the porch railing. "How's things been?" He nodded at the front door. "Everything okay? Any trouble?"

Grimacing, Justice pulled his hand free of Matthew's and wiped it on his pants. "Your hand," he said with distaste, "is sweating like a dog's tongue. If you came here to sweeten up Mrs. Call after what you did to her in Mariposa, I'd advise you not to touch her. Damp palms aren't real romantic, if you know what I mean."

"I didn't come here to sweeten up Ettie," Matthew lied, scowling and wiping his hands on the new wool jacket he'd put on that morning. He glanced at the door again. "Is she home?"

"She's in there," Justice assured him, his eyes wandering over Matthew's fancy suit of clothes, "but I can't say whether she's receiving or not. You know, I don't think I've ever seen you dressed this way before. You look like you're about to attend a funeral. Which is just as well," he added when Matthew glared at him, "because Mrs. Call will probably kill you when she sets eyes on you. Standing her up in Mariposa isn't one of the smarter things you've ever done, that's for sure."

"Keep your opinions to yourself," Matthew suggested. "You don't know what all happened there."

Justice chuckled. "I know a broken bed when I see one."

Matthew reddened. "Oh, yeah. Forgot about that. Well, there's more to that story'n just a broken bed."

"I'll just bet there is."

"You got a dirty mind," Matthew chided. "So . . . she's all right? All settled in?"

"Pretty much. We haven't had any trouble, anyway. Slow Bear brought me up to date on Chambers and Quinn after he talked to you last night. Guess you'll be wanting us to stick around for a while?"

"For a little while longer, if you would, Jus. I'm sorry to ask you to do it, but I'll feel better having you and Bertie around until Chambers can be tracked down."

"Sure we'll stay. No trouble. It's the least we can

do after all you've done for Ma and Da, and besides, I wouldn't miss watching you court Mrs. Call for the world."

"I ain't courtin' Ettie!"

"And Slow Bear will want to stick around long enough to kiss the bride."

"I *ain't* courtin' Ettie!"

"Oh, go knock on the door already." Justice waved him away. "You're starting to remind me of Good Path when he was courting Bird Singing."

"I ain't courtin' Ettie!" Matthew repeated as he stalked to the door. "And Bertie can keep his damned lips to himself!" He pounded on the door with a hard fist. "He ain't nothin' but a randy goat, and I won't have him pesterin' Ettie with his nonsense." He kept pounding. "If he wants a woman so bad he can just go on down to Miss Beverly's and buy a good whore!"

The door swung open as he spoke his last four words, and a stout, middle-aged woman stood in its place.

Matthew pulled the fancy black fur hat off his head and cleared his throat. He'd never worn such a foolish-looking hat in his life and had sworn that morning, as he stood before his mirror staring at himself dressed up like a fool, that as soon as he got that gold ring he'd bought in Los Angeles on Ettie's finger he'd never humiliate himself like this again.

"Hello, there, Mrs. Keeler. It's good to see you."

"Marshal Kagan," she returned stiffly.

"You're workin' for Ettie—uh, Mrs. Call, now?" he asked politely. "I don't s'pose she's home so I could talk with her, is she?"

"I'm sorry, Marshal Kagan, but Mrs. Call isn't feeling well. She's not receiving visitors."

"She ain't well? Wha'd'you mean she ain't well?"

"Just that, Marshal. She's not up to having visitors."

"Well, what's wrong with her? Is it somethin' serious? Has she been sick a long time? Has she been to see Doc Hedlow?" He straightened and called to Justice, "Has Ettie been sick?"

Justice shrugged. "She sleeps in sometimes, but Mrs. Kagan said she's only adjusting."

"Adjustin'? Adjustin' to what?"

"I don't know. It's probably one of those woman things."

"Oh." Matthew nodded thoughtfully. "Sure. All right." He returned his attention to Mrs. Keeler. "Would you tell her that I came by, please, ma'am, and that I'll come back later? There's some things we need to talk about and . . . oh, here." He dug around in one of the coat's inner pockets, pulling out a small envelope. "This is for Mrs. Call from my sister-in-law. She said it's real important that Ettie—that Mrs. Call gets it soon as possible."

"I'll give it to her, Marshal," Mrs. Keeler promised, taking the envelope, "and I'll be sure to give her your message."

"I 'preciate it, ma'am." He set the hat back on his head and started for the stairs. "You keep an eye out for trouble, Jus, and don't let Ettie go nowhere, 'cause I'll be back in a couple hours."

Two hours later Liberty was in Justice's place, doing the front porch duty, and Mrs. Call, so Mrs. Keeler informed Matthew, still wasn't receiving visitors. The hour after that she was napping, and the hour after that she was taking a bath. Matthew put up with the Drohan brothers' teasing throughout the day and tried to keep himself busy by visiting with Sheriff

Broadman and playing poker in one of the town's saloons, but as the day wore on and as he repeatedly got turned away from Mariette's door, his generally good-natured disposition began to sour. All he wanted to do, he thought as he made his way once more in the direction of her house, was talk to the woman. She didn't need to get all dolled up to see him. Heck, she didn't have to get dressed at all, as far as he was concerned. It wasn't like he didn't already know what she looked like under her clothes, but he'd better not think about that now, at least not until he had that ring on her finger. Once she was wearing his ring it wouldn't matter, because they'd be just as good as married, and married people could do whatever they pleased without having to worry, which was just what he was going to stop doing the very minute she accepted his proposal.

She was probably angry with him. Well, heck, she was probably more than angry. It was a fact he had to face. Not that he could blame her, of course, because he shouldn't have gone off like that in Mariposa without even saying good-bye. But that still didn't give her the right to flat-out ignore him, especially not after he'd spent the past month and a half suffering for her so bad. So, all right. She'd left him standing on her porch and wandering around the town dressed up like a fool all day. She'd gotten even. Fine. He was able to take his licks just like any other fella, but this was the end of it. He didn't care if Mrs. Keeler opened the door and said Ettie was standing on her head in the hallway, he was going to see her and talk things out and that was that.

Five minutes later he was standing on Mariette's front porch, shouting at Justice.

"She's not here? Where'd she go? I told you not to let her go *anywhere*!"

"Now, Matthew," said Justice, putting both hands in the air in a placating gesture, "I want you to stay calm."

Matthew swung his gaze all around, as if he expected Mariette to appear at any moment.

"And I told Mrs. Keeler I'd be back," he insisted. "I said I'd be back in an hour."

"Mrs. Keeler went home soon after you told her that, so I can't be sure Mrs. Call got the message. But even if she did, I don't think it would have mattered, because when Nate got here she was so ready to leave that he barely had time to knock on the door before she was out of it and pushing him toward his buggy. I tried to tell her you wouldn't like it, but she's not under arrest, after all, and what was I supposed to do? Pick her up and toss her back in the house?"

Matthew fell ominously still. When he spoke, his voice was low. "I hope you ain't talkin' 'bout Nate Kirkland, Jus. God help me, I surely hope you ain't talkin' about Nate."

"Well, it *was* Nate Kirkland," Justice replied. "And what I'm trying to tell you, Matt, is that they already had plans to go out. You know full well that neither you nor I can legally keep Mrs. Call in her house if she doesn't want to stay. All I could do was send Slow Bear after her to keep an eye out, and nothing more. Are you listening to me? Matt? Dammit, Matthew, give me a minute to explain." He followed Matthew down the porch steps. "Where are you going?"

Matthew didn't answer, and he didn't stop walking.

He tore one of the hinges off the garden gate when he yanked it open.

"Don't be a fool!" Justice strode after him. "Matthew, wait just a minute . . . will you just . . . at least slow down a little!"

"Well, if you ask me, Matt's a fool. I've known him since I was a kid, but I never knew him to walk out on a woman, or anyone for that matter. I sure can't figure him walkin' out on someone like you."

Mariette ran the tip of one finger over the rim of her icy champagne glass.

"I shouldn't have told you. You've been so good to me, and I'm sorry to take advantage of your kindness by telling you such things. I think it must be the shock of finding him on my doorstep all day."

"Oh, well, you listened to my troubles last week. It's only right you should feel free to talk to me about yours. To tell you the truth, it's nice to sit across a table from a pretty lady again and talk. I haven't done this since . . . well, since . . ."

"Since you were courting Elizabeth," Mariette said with gentle understanding. "That must have hurt terribly when she decided not to marry you."

"I've gotten over it," he said. "It hurt pretty bad at the time, but it would've hurt a lot more if Jim and I hadn't been able to keep on being friends. And I had my ranch to keep me from thinkin' about things too much." Seeing her frown at the tablecloth, he reached out and took her hand, squeezing it in a comforting gesture. "What're you going to do to keep from thinkin' about your troubles, Mariette?"

"I don't know." She shook her head slightly. "I

don't know what I'm going to do at all. I don't want to see him, but I hardly know how I can avoid doing so if he persists in calling on me. And I can't hold him off forever. It really isn't right, and only makes matters worse. I wish I'd been brave enough to face him today and get it over with. At least I might be able to sleep tonight." She gripped Nathan's hand more tightly. "If only I knew what he wanted!"

"Could it have been about your case, maybe? Somethin' about this Chambers fellow?"

"I can't think so. He was dressed in a suit. He wouldn't have to dress so finely to tell me anything about that."

"Well, maybe he came to his senses then. That's prob'ly what it is. Elizabeth says he's in love with you, and she's generally right about these things."

Mariette thought of the note Mrs. Keeler had given her, while Mariette had stood still trembling in the hallway after listening to Matthew at her front door.

I didn't tell him anything, Elizabeth had written in her difficult, child-like scrawl. *He doesn't know anything. See him,* with the *See* twice underlined.

"I imagine so," Mariette allowed softly, "but not this time. Elizabeth doesn't seem to understand that Matthew never gave me any promises. It was just . . . wanting. I never expected anything more." She looked up at him. "I'm sure you'll think me a terrible woman, Nathan, but I did love him."

He lifted his other hand, sandwiching hers between both of his, and said to her, earnestly, "I know that, Mariette. I never thought anything else. You're a good, wonderful woman and I want you to believe that I'll stand beside you no matter what."

"Oh, Nathan, you really are the kindest—"

"You go right ahead and fetch the sheriff," a familiar, belligerent voice suddenly filled the room, causing all of the diners to turn their heads toward it. "Get the whole damned militia if you want, but keep outta my way while you're doin' it!"

"Oh, dear," Mariette murmured as Matthew pushed the headwaiter aside and stormed into the restaurant with Justice Twelve Moons behind him.

"Don't worry," Nathan said, patting her hand. "I won't let him hurt you."

Justice stopped to pick the headwaiter up off the floor, but Matthew stalked farther into the room, his furious gaze sweeping the tables. When his eyes fell on Mariette, the steely look in them made her gasp. Slowly, he moved toward her, stopping when he saw her hand still clasped in both of Nathan's. The growl he emitted before taking another step could be heard clearly through the silence.

"Oh, my heavens!" Mariette tried to tug her hand free but Nathan, with a smile on his face, held it fast. Only when Matthew reached the table did he release her.

Standing, he said pleasantly, "Hey there, Matt. It's good to see you." He held out a hand. "Jim said you were home."

Matthew's breathing was harsh. He stared at Mariette and when he spoke, the hardness in his voice made her tremble.

"Get your things."

Nathan dropped his hand. "Mrs. Call and I were just havin' somethin' before dinner. Would you like to join us for a drink before we eat?"

Matthew started breathing through his mouth, as if he couldn't get enough air in his body. The muscles of his shoulders and arms and hands seemed so rigid that Mariette wondered how his clothes contained him without bursting at the seams.

"Get . . . your . . . things," he repeated, this time through his teeth.

Mariette started groping for her shawl.

"Mrs. Call isn't going anywhere with you, Matt," Nathan told him. "She came to have dinner with me and she'll be leavin' with me."

Justice clamped a strong hand on Matthew's right arm, the hand of which had clenched into a fist.

"Matt," he warned in a low voice, "think. *Think.* He's Jim's best friend. Don't do something you know you'll regret."

Matthew held Mariette's eyes. "You either get your things right now and walk out of here on your own two feet," he told her slowly, clearly, "or I'll take you out."

"Mrs. Call isn't going anywhere," Nathan repeated.

Mariette gathered up her purse and gloves. "It's all right, Mr. Kirkland," she said quickly. "I don't wish to cause a scene."

Liberty's husky laughter came from the doorway, where he stood with Sheriff Broadman. "It's too late for that," he said, taking in the dining room's avid audience. "Bet this'll make the front page of next week's paper. We could have us a good, proper fight in here. You back up Nate, Twelve Moons," he told his brother. "I'll side with Matthew, and we'll let Hank referee."

"You don't have to go with him, Mariette," Nathan said as she pushed her chair aside. "I can take care of this."

"I know that," she said loudly and clearly, pulling

her gloves on and ignoring Matthew, who stood inches away from her, still breathing like a hard-ridden stallion and staring at her as if he'd like nothing better than to toss her over his shoulder and carry her off. "I'm sure you could handle Marshal Kagan with ease, being not only younger but also possessed of a superior intelligence and quite obviously of better manners." She arranged the shawl about her shoulders with great care. "But I'd rather not make the situation any worse than he has already done with his rude, boorish behavior and lack of common civility. I'm very sorry to leave your kind and enjoyable company, sir"—she extended a hand to politely shake his—"and I thank you for a lovely, though short, evening. I hope you will forgive me for departing so suddenly, but perhaps Mr. Twelve Moons would be so kind as to stay and lend you company. Good evening."

Having finished this dignified speech, Mariette lifted her chin and walked away from the table, ignoring Matthew and all of the staring diners. Her refined, elegant exit was worthy of her upbringing. If she hadn't exactly managed to salvage the situation, she'd at least managed to keep from making a complete fool of herself, she thought, nodding at Liberty, who gave a low whistle of praise as she passed him.

Matthew shrugged off Justice's restraining hand and leaned toward Nathan. "The only reason you're still in one piece is on account of you bein' such good friends with Jimmy all these years. But I'm tellin' you straight out—you keep your hands off my woman or I swear to God I'll knock your face so far back in your head you'll have to walk backwards to see where you're going."

He followed Mariette, leaving Justice and Nathan staring at each other.

"Well, that was plain enough," Nathan said.

Justice let out a breath. "Sure was. My Lord, I hope I never fall in love that way."

"Me, too. Think she'll be safe with him?"

"Oh, sure," Justice said, sitting in the chair Mariette had vacated. "You saw how she handled him. Though I wouldn't want to be around when he remembers what she said about you being younger. Matt's a little sensitive about his age. But he's in love. He wouldn't ever hurt her. Mmmm. This is good champagne. What's for dinner?"

"Nobody wants me," Liberty said sadly, pulling up a chair and joining them. "I asked Matt on his way out the door if he wanted me to come along and help him with Mrs. Call, and he said something very, very naughty. Ma would have washed his mouth out with borax."

"Where'd Sheriff Broadman go?"

"Home," Liberty replied, drinking out of Justice's glass. "Said he needed his wife to make him a bromo and that he hoped Matthew didn't kill him off from aggravation before he got the chance to retire first. Can't we get some whiskey to drink?"

"Sure," Nathan said, gazing around the room, meeting the stares of the other diners. "But we may have to wait until the shock wears off. Where'd all the waiters disappear to?"

"I think they carried the headwaiter into the hotel lobby. He was shaking pretty bad."

"We'll have to wait, then," Justice said. "Which is just as well. We'll want to give Matthew a little while alone with Mrs. Call before we go back." He filled the two glasses on the table with champagne and handed the half-empty bottle to Liberty. Lifting his own glass in the air, he said, "Here's good luck to Matthew."

"And to Mariette," Nathan added.

Liberty drank liberally from the bottle. "Hey, I have an idea," he said, wiping his mouth with the back of his hand. "Let's go back to Mrs. Call's after we're done here and stand on the porch and sing old Irish love songs. That'll be sure to liven things up."

"Slow Bear," Justice said wearily, "you're a walking death trap. We'll give them one hour alone. One hour, and then we'll head back." He looked at his brother severely. "And no Irish love songs out of you, me boyo, or the only thing I'll do when Matthew tries to kill you is offer to hold his hat."

19

Neither of them said a word as they walked back to Hanlan House, Mariette striding ahead and Matthew storming along behind her.

She took her key out of her purse to open the door but Matthew snatched it away, then freed the lock and tossed the door wide. With an ominous expression on his face, he stood aside to let her go in first. Setting her purse on the entry table, Mariette marched directly into the parlor and started pulling off her gloves. The fire that had been lit in the room earlier still glowed; she turned up the wick on the large table lamp. Matthew shut the front door loudly, and in another moment he appeared at the parlor door.

"That," she said coldly, dropping her gloves onto the brocatelle-covered divan, "was unforgivable."

In response he removed his hat and threw it on the floor.

Mariette stared at it, and said, "You had no right to cause such a scene, to humiliate me so publicly."

He struggled out of his coat and flung it down beside his hat.

Mariette swallowed, and took a step backward. "I'll not put up with such treatment. Not from you, not from anyone."

Matthew started unbuttoning his vest.

"What are you doing?" she demanded.

"I put this damned thing on this mornin'—I did it for *you*. Jimmy told me not to do it. He told me it was too much, too soon, but I wouldn't listen to him." He tossed the vest to the carpet and started walking toward her with slow, measured steps. "Oh, no, I wouldn't listen. Everything had to be just right. I had to get all dolled up for you, I had to be perfect, I had to be—" He fell silent, his gaze drawn to something on the mantel. He moved toward it, away from her, and grabbed the photograph. "Because of him!" He shoved the framed picture at her, the one of her and David on their wedding day. "Because *he's* what I'm up against." Matthew kept pushing it at her, until Mariette snatched away the photograph.

"Don't!"

"Don't," he repeated, seething, stalking her as she backed away. "Don't do what? Don't talk? Don't look?" His voice rose furiously. "Or don't touch your precious husband there?" He pointed at the photograph she clutched.

"You aren't making any sense," she cried. "What does David have to do with you? With anything? You never even knew him!"

Matthew fell still and let out a harsh breath. "I wish to God I had. I wish to God I knew what to do to compete with a dead man. I'll tell you one thing, Ettie. I ain't gettin' dressed up for you again. I ain't wearin' this damned suit again until our weddin' day, and after that I'm going to burn it!"

"What!"

"And I'll tell you somethin' else," he went on angrily, moving toward her once more. "I won't have you going around with Nate Kirkland. Not nowhere. I don't even want you speakin' to him."

"How dare you!" Mariette returned angrily, hugging David's photograph as Matthew backed her against a wall. "You have no right to say such things to me, to demand anything of me. Our association ended in Mariposa, Marshal Kagan, and I am no longer under your protection. I want you to leave. *Now.*"

He pulled the photograph out of her hands and tossed it onto a nearby chair.

"Have you missed me at all?" he asked just before grabbing her around the waist, jerking her forward, and sealing her mouth with his own.

She tried to push him away, to free herself, but he was hungry and insistent and too big and strong to budge. Flattening her body against the wall with his own, he lifted his head.

"Did you miss me?" he demanded.

"No!"

He kissed her again, longer, deeper, more thoroughly.

Breathing harshly, he asked again, "Did you miss me?"

Mariette was panting, too. "N-no," she managed unconvincingly.

Encouraged, Matthew's mouth traveled over her

face, kissing her eyes and cheeks and chin. "I missed you," he murmured in a voice filled with desperation. "I missed you, honey . . . you got no idea. I dreamed about you, wanted you so bad. Ettie"—he kissed her mouth—"didn't you miss me just a little?"

Mariette's eyes were closed, her hands were pressed against the muslin of his shirt, feeling the strength and heat of him beneath the thin material, the powerful beating of his heart. She wanted to lie to him again, to say something that would make him go away. He'd left her in Mariposa; if he had missed her, it was only in the physical sense. He wanted her, and he'd come back only because of that, and because she'd let him into her bed so easily once before. She ought to lie to him. He deserved it. She ought to do it.

"Yes," she whispered. "I missed you, Matthew. Very much."

With a deep groan he swooped down on her, kissing her as if he would devour her. His hands moved to caress her body, her breasts and back and hips, even as his own body pressed needily against her, and Mariette was glad. She loved him and she was thankful to be in his arms again. He would make love to her and then he would go away again. She knew that, but she didn't care. Tonight he would be with her and she would be glad for it. She would cherish every single moment.

"Ettie," he murmured against her mouth, "I love you. I love you, honey."

She was stunned, but only for a moment. Of course he would say he loved her. After what happened in Mariposa, he would probably think she expected it. Strangely, the words hurt. Even more strangely, she couldn't speak them back to him, couldn't tell him that she loved him, too, because her love would make him feel trapped and uncomfortable. He wouldn't want to have it.

With difficulty, Matthew lifted his mouth from where he'd begun nuzzling her neck and slid his hands away from her breasts to the safer curves of her waist. Gazing at her, he chuckled huskily and said, "That's better. Next time I'll know right off how to handle you and won't waste no time talkin'."

"Matthew—"

"Don't worry, honey," he said, "we'll get back to it in a minute. You'd better believe we will." He kissed her quickly. "You sure make me forget myself, Ettie. But we got somethin' else to do first, and we're going to do it right."

He drew her over to the divan and motioned for her to sit, then he picked up his coat and dug through the pockets while Mariette watched in bewilderment.

"There it is," he said at last, pulling something small out of one pocket in particular and tossing the coat on the floor again. Sitting, he took hold of her left hand. "We'll get this out of the way," he said, grinning lecherously at her, "and then we'll get back to what we was doing. You've got a lot of sleepless nights to pay me back for, honey. I sure hope you got a good, strong bed upstairs."

"Matthew, what on earth are you doing?"

"This old thing comes off first," he replied. "I ain't takin' you to bed while you're wearin' another man's ring." He started wiggling her wedding ring off her finger.

"Matthew!"

"Now, don't get all hysterical on me. I didn't say you couldn't keep the thing in a drawer somewhere.

You can give it to our daughter someday. If we have a daughter, that is."

Mariette felt as if he'd just punched all the breath out of her.

"What did you say?" she whispered.

He was too busy with her hand to answer. "Now, we'll stick this on and everything will be right as a trivet."

It was another ring he was trying to slide onto her finger, she saw through the haze of her shock. A ring with a diamond in a Tiffany setting.

"I ain't rich like Jimmy is," he was saying happily, "but I got enough to afford a decent ring, at least. Wait till you see the weddin' band I picked out in Los Angeles. It's got flowers and vines carved on it and—"

She snatched her hand away and stood, staring in horror at the ring that looked so tiny in his big fingers.

Matthew looked up at her. "What's wrong, honey?"

He *knew!* That was the only answer. In spite of what Elizabeth had written in her note, he knew about the baby and had come because of it.

"You don't like it?" Matthew was turning the ring around, inspecting it with a frown. "I thought it was real pretty, but I can send it back if you want somethin' different."

"Matthew—no."

Another loveless marriage. She couldn't do it. She couldn't, no matter that she loved Matthew so deeply. It would be unbearable. At least she and David had been matched in their feelings for each other, but with Matthew, loving him so much and knowing he could never feel the same for her, she couldn't do it.

"It's a real diamond," he said hopefully, lifting it to show her. "Half a karat."

Tears burned in her eyes. She couldn't say anything.

A look of embarrassment crossed his features. "I know it ain't what you're used to, Ettie. Prob'ly ain't nothin' like what David Call gave you, but the jeweler seemed to think it was as fashionable as anything you could find back east."

"It's the most beautiful ring I've ever seen, Matthew." She lifted a hand to wipe her tears away. "In my entire life. I promise you. But I can't accept it." When she drew in a breath she made a sob instead. "I'm very flattered, and I'm so sorry." She turned and moved toward the fire.

Matthew stared at her for a moment, then pushed the ring into his pants pocket and stood. "I didn't say everything I meant to when I came in," he said. "Guess I was too upset to remember." He gave a half laugh, sounding so uncertain that it made Mariette's heart ache. "I know you're upset about what happened in Mariposa and I sure don't blame you, but I can explain why I left."

"Oh, no, Matthew, please." Her voice was filled with distress. "I can't bear to speak of that tonight. Please, not tonight. Not after all this."

"Well," he said slowly, "all right. If that's what you want. We don't have to talk about it tonight."

Sniffling, she nodded.

Matthew cleared his throat uncomfortably. "Well, then . . . look, Ettie, I realize I ain't the kind of man you'd ever hope for . . ."

"Matthew, you are," she whispered to the fire.

". . . but I mean to do right by you. I resigned from bein' a federal marshal . . ."

"No," she murmured, setting both hands over her face.

". . . and I accepted the position of sheriff in Santa Ines, leastways, until the next election comes 'round, and when it does, well, you know, I ain't so old that I can't do a little sheriffin' for a few years. You won't have to be a teacher, if you don't want."

He'd given up what he loved most because she was pregnant with their child. Unable to stop herself, Mariette began to cry for what he'd lost.

Feeling helpless, Matthew took a couple of steps toward her. "I know I'm not rich, not nowhere like what you're used to, anyway, but I've got plenty set aside, Ettie. Plenty, I swear it." He took another step. "We'll be able to live real well, as comfortable as can be."

Mariette couldn't make her tears stop, couldn't stop the flood of emotions that his words wrought. She put a hand over her mouth, but it didn't silence her sobs. Behind her, she heard Matthew's sharp intake of breath.

"I . . ." he began, then fell silent. She heard him picking up his things, and a moment later she heard him leave, slamming the front door behind him.

" 'We'll stick this on and everything will be right as a trivet'?" James repeated. "*That's* how you proposed to Mrs. Call? What happened to everything havin' to be just right? What happened to the flowers and poems and music and all the right words?"

Groaning, Matthew pushed into a sitting position. He was stiff from sleeping in the straw all night and sore from all the whiskey he'd drunk while he'd sat in the barn, talking to Ugly and feeling sorry for himself.

"Well, I was kinda in a rush to get the thing done

with," he explained weakly, rubbing the heels of his hands over his tired, reddened eyes. "We started out mad and went downhill from there. I sure wasn't thinkin' with my head, if you know what I mean."

James chuckled and sat beside his miserable brother. He picked up the empty whiskey bottle half-hidden in the straw and set it on the ground. "Yeah, I know what you mean," he said. "My brain don't work too good, either, when other parts of my body take over. But, 'Stick this on and everything'll be right as a trivet'—that just about beats anything I ever heard far as a proposal goes. No wonder she turned you down."

"That didn't have nothin' to do with it," Matthew said roughly. "She don't want me. I was a damned fool to think she ever would. She's a fine, educated lady and I ain't nothin' but a hard, stupid old man."

James set a comforting hand on Matthew's neck. "Come on, now, don't start talkin' that way. You have to give Mrs. Call a little ground, here. She just lost her husband. He hasn't even been gone a year and somethin' like that takes some gettin' over. Why, if I lost Beth, I sure wouldn't be receptive to any kind of courtin' for a long spell. You know what Mrs. Call needs?" he asked, patting Matthew on the back.

"What?" Matthew asked dully.

"Some tender lovin' care, that's what. You've got to be extra gentle with her, real careful, like she was made of china. You've got to do what you set out to do in the first place, and that's court her proper."

"Aw, Jimmy, I just don't know."

"That's what you've got to do," James insisted. "But you need to keep a firm hand on that temper of yours and you need to give Mrs. Call plenty of slack so she won't bolt and run. You love her, don't you? And you want her?"

Matthew started rubbing at his chest. "Sure I do, but I just didn't . . . dammit, Jimmy, I never knew somethin' like that could hurt so bad. Her turnin' me down, I mean. It ain't like I'd be all that thrilled to go through it again."

"Well, I declare," James said in amazement. "Never thought I'd live to see the day when Matthew Kagan got so scared of a little pain that he'd give up on somethin' he really wanted. If he *really* wanted it, he'd go after it, and that's that. You must not want Mrs. Call as bad as you say you do. That's all I can think."

"I do want her!" Matthew shot back. "You got no idea how bad."

James met his older brother's angry, still red eyes directly. "Then prove it," he challenged. "You prove it, Matt, or I won't have no choice but to believe you're either a coward"—he noted the tightening of Matthew's jaw with satisfaction—"or that when you talk about wantin' Mariette Call, you aren't doin' nothin' but makin' hot air."

20

Mariette had spent much of the night before, after Matthew had left, alternating between anger at Matthew's behavior—all of his behavior, from the moment she'd met him to the moment he'd slammed her door—and tears for what they had both lost. Being a sensible woman, however, and realizing that giving way to a fit of melancholy would neither make Matthew a federal marshal again nor make her the recipient of his love, she had at last sought her bed and fallen into a restless, unhappy sleep.

Before the sun had risen in the sky, her child had awakened her and had given her good reason to believe that, regardless of the baby's sex, he or she was already taking after his or her father. Only *Matthew's* child could be so perverse, so misbehaving, so utterly thoughtless as to keep her on her knees in front of the commode for more than an hour, repeatedly emptying an already empty stomach.

Now, lying once more on her bed, she felt as sick as she could ever before remember being. Her head throbbed, every inch of her body ached, and if anyone had asked her at this moment whether she would ever eat food again, she would have readily vowed with one hand on a Bible that she most definitely would *not.*

"Mrs. Call?"

Mariette groaned beneath the cool cloth Mrs. Keeler had laid upon her forehead half an hour earlier.

"I'm so sorry, ma'am," Mrs. Keeler said gently, tiptoeing into the room, "but Marshal Kagan is— oh, dear, I imagine I should say *Sheriff* Kagan, because he's our sheriff now, or so he's just told me. Sheriff Kagan is downstairs, ma'am, and he insists that he'll see you, whether you'll come down or whether he has to come up. I told him you weren't well, but he's being quite stubborn. I'm terribly sorry."

"Bother," Mariette muttered, wondering how she could face Matthew again so soon when everything she felt about him was still so muddled. "Drat the man."

"Shall I tell him to go away?" Mrs. Keeler asked.

"It won't help," Mariette replied, dragging herself into a sitting position. "He won't go. He is a beastly, stubborn man." Anchoring herself upright with both hands clutching the mattress, Mariette fought down the wave of nausea that washed over her.

"You're really not well enough to have visitors," Mrs. Keeler argued. "Why, you're pale as a ghost and that's just what I'm going to tell him."

"No," Mariette said, slowly and carefully standing.

She didn't want to delay speaking with Matthew; she would only worry about what it was he wanted if she put the matter off. "Please tell Marshal Kagan that I shall be down to speak with him shortly, just as soon as I've dressed."

Matthew wandered agitatedly around the living area, looking with only half an interest at all the little knickknacks Mariette had put out to make the place homey. Over half an hour had passed since Mrs. Keeler told him that Mariette would be down shortly, but Matthew was beginning to wonder if he and Mariette didn't have two different ideas of just what that word—*shortly*—meant.

"Women," he muttered to a smiling porcelain cat. "What was God thinkin' when He—"

"Marshal Kagan?"

Matthew looked up and saw Mariette slowly descending the stairs, one hand clutching the railing as if she must steady herself or fall headlong. He moved toward her without making a conscious decision to do so.

"I'm sorry to have made you wait so long," she said in a politely formal tone that was at odds with her pasty skin and puffy, exhausted eyes.

"My God, Ettie, you look like death warmed over. What are you doing out of bed!"

Her pale face took on an expression of surprise as he bounded up the stairs and promptly swung her off her feet and into his arms.

"Marshal Kagan!"

"Don't go actin' silly," he warned curtly, carrying her down to the floor and over to a divan. Setting her upon it, he said, "Mrs. Keeler said you wasn't feelin' well, but last night you looked fine as feathers and I just figured you was tryin' to avoid me."

"That," Mariette replied coolly, "would have been a vain attempt on my part, I believe. Matthew, please stop that," she added, pushing at his hands. "I don't wish to lie down."

Straightening, Matthew inspected her with disapproval. "Well, you sure look like you need to lie down. You look like you been scrubbed good and wrung out real thorough. What's wrong with you?"

The look she gave him was so chilly it actually made Matthew shiver, and her voice, when she answered him, was even icier. "It is quite common, I believe, considering the circumstances."

He gazed at her for a bewildered moment before he remembered what Justice had said the day before about her having some difficulty adjusting. "Oh, that's right," he said, filled with relief. "It's one of those woman things." Smiling, he sat beside her. "Thank God. For a minute there I was scared it was somethin' serious."

"Oh!" she cried furiously. "You—you unfeeling beast!" She looked like she was going to hit him and, startled, Matthew leaned away.

"Now, honey, there's no reason to get upset. All I said was—"

"No reason!" She jabbed an angry finger at him. "It's *your* fault I'm unwell in the first place, you wretched, miserable brute!"

Matthew was thoroughly confused. All he could think was that she was still upset from the night before, because of the way he'd handled everything.

"I guess that's true, Ettie," he admitted with honest regret, "and I'm sorry. I wish you could know just how sorry I am. I sure never meant for things to turn out this way, but I can't take back what's been done. All I can do is try to make it right."

All the fire in her died away. "I don't want you to make it right. I told you last night that I won't marry you, Matthew, and if that's what you've come for, then I'm afraid you have wasted your time."

"That ain't what I came for," he returned stiffly, angry that she wasn't even willing to give him a chance. "At least, it ain't all of it. I came to tell you some things I never got around to yesterday, about your father and Elliot Chambers."

"My father?" she repeated, surprised.

"I meant to tell you yesterday," he said again. "Prob'ly should've ridden here to tell you first thing I got into town, but what with tryin' to get settled in at Los Robles and all—"

She set a hand on his knee. "Matthew, what about my father?"

He took her hand and squeezed it. "Honey"—he met her worried gaze—"I know you and your daddy had some pretty bad times this last year since your husband died, and I know you been hurt 'cause you felt he didn't care for you the way a daddy should care for his daughter but, the thing is, he's decided to give evidence against Elliot Chambers."

The words shocked Mariette so completely that, for a moment, she felt dizzy, as if she might faint. Matthew rubbed his rough thumb over the back of her hand, and touched her cheek with the fingers of his other hand. "Are you all right, Ettie?" he asked, worry in his voice. "My Lord, you're cold as an Eskimo. I'm sendin' Jus to fetch Doc Hedlow."

"No!" she gripped his hand to keep him from

standing. "Please, no, Matthew." She drew in a deep breath. "It's just . . . Is this true? About my father?"

"It's true, honey."

"Why?" she asked, disbelieving. "Why would he agree to do such a thing? Was he forced into it because he knew Quinn would tell about his involvement?"

Matthew smiled at her. "Nah, that's not why. He said when he agreed to give evidence that he figured I'd kill Quinn and his boys. That didn't have nothin' to do with it."

"But—"

"The day after we left Sacramento," Matthew went on, "he showed up at the federal marshal's office in 'Frisco and turned himself in. Between your husband's journal and your daddy's and Quinn's evidence, Chambers doesn't have a prayer of escapin' justice. He's probably already been tracked down and arrested, or will be soon."

Mariette's hands began to tremble and Matthew held both of them tightly.

"But why?" she demanded. *"Why?"*

"Don't you know, honey?"

Mariette shook her head.

"I reckon it's 'cause he loves you. And 'cause he cared for your husband and felt so bad for what happened to him."

"But that can't be why!"

"Well, I sure can't think of too many other reasons why a man like John Hardesty would willingly hand himself over to spendin' the rest of his life in prison, can you? And I'll tell you somethin' else. He said he'd only give his evidence about Chambers on one condition and that was that the government promise to keep *you* safe at any cost."

She stared at him and her lips parted as if she would speak, though she said nothing. Matthew touched her cheek with his fingers once more.

"He loves you, Ettie. That's why he did it. Maybe it took him some time to get around to showin' you, but he's done it."

She swallowed and closed her eyes, trying to gain some semblance of control. Matthew cradled her cheek in his palm, and the heat of his hand against her chilled skin felt more than good.

"You don't cry like other women," he said wonderingly, as if he were speaking to himself. "You feel things so strong, Ettie. I sure wish I knew how to keep you from feelin' things that hurt you."

"I'm sorry, Matthew," she managed, sniffling and drawing in a breath. "It's just that I think so often of the way he and I parted. I've regretted it."

" 'Course you do," he murmured, bending to kiss the corner of one eye, to take away the tears there. "It don't take much smarts to figure out how bad you was hurtin' that day, how much it hurt you to leave your daddy the way you did. Look here, honey." Sitting up, he pulled a piece of paper out of his vest pocket. "I got somethin' to show you. This is—"

"Matthew." The touch of her hand on the badge pinned to his vest stopped him. She was gazing mournfully at the silver star. "What is this?"

"That's my new badge," he said, strangely embarrassed.

"Sheriff," she whispered, running a finger along the engraved letters.

"Hank was pretty glad to give it up this mornin'," he said quickly, pulling her hand away and pushing

the paper into it, "especially after last night. This is
where you can write your daddy, if you want."

She turned her unhappy gaze to the crumpled
paper. "Where I can write him?"

"He's under federal protection until Chambers is
caught," Matthew clarified, "and he didn't want to
get you all upset by tryin' to write you first, if you
didn't want him to."

"I see," she said, still gazing at the paper. "Thank
you, Matthew."

"You're welcome," he replied gruffly, then suddenly stood. "Now I'm takin' you back up to your
bed. You look like you're just about ready to drop."

"Matthew!" she protested when he bent and
scooped her up.

"Don't fuss at me, woman." He started for the
stairs. "You know full well it won't do any good. And
if you don't know it, you'd better learn it quick."
Then, admiring the flowery pattern of the day wrapper she was wearing as well as the softness of it, he
added, "This is a pretty thing you got on. Sure beats
that black dress you had on yesterday."

As her hands wrapped around his shoulders, she
reminded him, not unkindly, "I'm still in mourning,
Matthew."

He set her on her bed as if she were some kind of
snowflake, just as delicate and just as easily lost. "Not
for long, Mariette Call." He moved to take off her
soft, French kid slippers, which he tossed without
care to the floor before covering her up to the chin
with a blanket and sitting beside her.

"I shall wear mourning for as long as I please," she
said as he bent over her, stroking her hair gently.
"You haven't anything to say in the matter."

"I have a say in what my wife wears," he told her. "And you're going to be my wife." He stopped the words of denial on her lips by kissing her, and when he lifted his head and found her looking sleepy and content he kissed her again. She seemed too weary to participate, so he lifted his head once more and said, "I love you, honey."

"Oh, Matthew," she murmured, "you don't."

"I don't?"

She closed her eyes. "You don't and please don't lie about it. I won't know what to say if you lie about it. It's too much, after everything else."

"Is that what you think?" His hand moved over her hair in a soothing rhythm. Strangely enough, he felt so relieved he almost laughed. "Is *that* all I'm up against? My Lord, that ain't hardly nothin'."

She opened her eyes and looked at him. "Isn't it?"

"Less than nothin'," he said, smiling. "You're a stubborn gal, Ettie Call, but I've always liked a good challenge. Now, I admit I made a mistake in Mariposa, but now that we're courtin' proper I don't plan on makin' any more."

"We are not courting, Marshal Kagan."

"Sheriff Kagan," he corrected. "And as for last night, I just want you to forget it ever happened. I never asked a woman to marry me before. Stands to reason I need a little practice to do it right."

"Matthew," Mariette said wearily, "I am not going to marry you. There isn't any reason for you to make such a sacrifice, not when you never wanted this. I'll be perfectly all right on my own. I'm going to move to where no one knows me or my father, and I'll let everyone believe it's David's."

David's what? he wondered, thinking that she was

so tired she couldn't even finish her sentences. David's fault that she'd ended up where she was, and with him, and having to suffer this adjustment that was making her so ill?

"You ain't going nowhere," he stated, tucking her in. "'Specially not when you're feelin' so poorly."

"And I'd like to give it David's name," she went on as if he'd never spoken. "I realize what I'm asking of you, but it would be best for everyone concerned. Surely you must see that."

Could she do something like that? he thought with some amazement. He'd never heard of people giving their ailments names before.

"Well, sure, honey," he replied slowly, not wanting to say the wrong thing and get her upset. "If you want to give it your husband's name, that's fine. I'm sure that would have made Professor Call real, uh, happy. But that don't mean I won't take responsibility for my part in what you're going through."

"But I don't want you to feel responsible," she insisted. "For anything. I want you to be happy, Matthew. I want you to be a federal marshal again for as long as you want to be. You never made me any promises or any guarantees. This is as much my fault as yours. I'm the one who should pay for what's happened."

"Now, that's just not true, Ettie," he told her firmly. "I won't have you sayin' such things."

"It *is* true," she said miserably, pressing the fingers of one hand against her throbbing temple. "You told me you never wanted to marry, and I led you to believe that I—that David and I had never been able to—oh, you know what I mean."

He didn't, but he was sure it didn't matter.

Nothing she'd said over the past couple of minutes made any sense, anyway, and he was afraid she was becoming a little delirious.

"We'll talk about it later," he said gently. "Right now you're going to rest while I fetch Doc Hedlow."

"I don't wish to see Dr. Hedlow. He is already well aware of my condition."

"Just the same, I'm bringin' him to have a look at you."

"Matthew Kagan! I will not be treated like a child."

Chuckling, Matthew smoothed the covers over her once more, suggestively using both hands. "And I sure don't want to treat you like one, either." Kissing the set line of her mouth, he stood.

"You stay in that bed until I get back." When she glared at him, he added, "Now don't give me any more arguments, 'cause it won't make any difference. You're just going to have to learn, honey, especially once we're married, that when I got my heart set on somethin', I keep on till I get it."

21

    Propping his legs up on his desk, Matthew leaned back in his chair and read the poem aloud once more, very slowly, working to make the words sound just right.

    "How do I love thee, let me count the ways.
I love thee to the depth and breadth and height
My soul can reach, when feeling out of sight
For the ends of Being and ideal Grace.
I love thee to the level of each day's
Most quiet need, by sun and candlelight.
I love thee freely, as men strive for Right.
I love thee purely, as they turn from praise.
I love thee with the passion put to use
In my old griefs, and with my childhood's faith.
I love thee with a love I seem to lose
With my lost saints.—I love thee with the breath,
Smiles, tears, of all my life.—And, if God choose,
I shall but love thee better after death."

Closing his eyes, he rested his head on the back of the chair, let out a "whew," then muttered, "I can't believe I'm doin' this. Might as well try talkin' Hindu. It'd prob'ly make more sense if I did." Pulling his feet from the desk and letting them fall to the wooden floor with a *thunk*, he sighed. "If she don't know I love her after this, then there ain't nothin' more I can do to prove it. This is just about as bad as things can get."

Matthew had learned a lot about courting women over the past few weeks, and he'd discovered that it wasn't all that different from learning how to track down a criminal. There were ways and means in catching a criminal, and there were ways and means in catching a woman. If some of those ways and means seemed downright stupid to Matthew, well, so be it. His need for Mariette grew worse every time he saw her, and he figured he'd do just about anything to make her his wife, including looking like a fool on a regular basis and putting up with the Drohans' teasing every time he so much as glanced in Ettie's direction.

There was an awful lot a man had to know about courting. There were flowers and little gifts, and more flowers, and making sure Ettie didn't go anywhere with Nate Kirkland. Asking her to go out to dinner every day of the week, and more flowers, and trying to sit next to her at church before Nate Kirkland got there first, and keeping up a conversation with her when she wouldn't speak to him, and, after all that, more flowers.

A fella could wear himself right into the grave chasing the woman he wanted, if he didn't go broke first, of course.

And Ettie didn't make things any easier, being so stubborn. The only words he heard out of her mouth, mostly, were "No," "No, thank you," "I am not going to marry you," and "Will you *please* go away?"

Matthew didn't let any of that get him down, though, because like old Lang Tines used to say, a thing worth having is a thing worth fighting for, and Matthew was certain that once he actually got Ettie as his wife she'd more than make up for all the misery she was putting him through now. Her mouth said no but her eyes said something altogether different. Her eyes, when they looked his way, said things that made him hot as a pig in a smokehouse . . . things about what she was wanting, and needing, and maybe even dreaming about, though polite women weren't supposed to want or need or dream such things.

And he'd had a few successes with her, enough to give him hope, at least. She'd stopped slamming the door in his face when he showed up every morning with his daily offering of flowers, and she'd stopped pretending that he wasn't there whenever he tried to talk to her in town or at church. And twice she'd actually let him take her over to the hotel for dinner, though she'd spent both evenings telling him why she wouldn't marry him and talking about him not needing to feel responsible for anything. But he'd been enjoying himself too much to waste time listening to such nonsense. Just sitting across from her, watching her, made him happy. He didn't think he'd ever get tired of the graceful way she cut her food, or of how her long fingers wrapped gently around the stem of a delicate wineglass, or of the way she sat in a chair, stately and gracious, like she was some kind of royalty sitting on a throne.

One night, two weeks back, he'd wangled an invitation out of Virgil Kirkland to one of the fund-raising events for the new school that Ettie had been giving lately. Although she was angry to see him at first, he'd managed to get around her stiff words and rigidly polite behavior. By the end of the evening they'd danced together twice and he'd even made her laugh some. He'd asked her three times that night if she'd marry him, and when the third refusal came he'd detected a note of weariness in her tone, which encouraged him, because if she wouldn't believe that he loved her, maybe he could wear her down until she just gave in.

And last Sunday, Elizabeth had managed to get Ettie to come out to Los Robles for dinner after church. She'd pretty much ignored him, though she was friendly to everyone else, but in the middle of the meal Elizabeth had asked Jimmy if Grandma Kagan hadn't been a little German. Before Jimmy could answer, Matthew had joked, "No, she was a big German." Everybody sitting at the table had groaned, except for Ettie, who had laughed out loud in that amused, unexpected manner that never failed to make Matthew's heart throb. Jimmy had leaned over and whispered, "You'd better marry her, Matt. She's the only woman I know who laughs at your jokes."

When the meal was over, Nate Kirkland, whom Elizabeth had invited against all of Matthew's arguments, had offered to drive Ettie home, but Matthew wasn't having any of that. She almost made a scene when he picked her up and carried her all the way out to the stables, but she didn't. She'd waited until he hitched the buggy and drove her half a mile away from the house before giving him a piece of her mind.

"Your behavior toward Nathan Kirkland borders on madness," she said tightly. "It is absolutely, completely, and entirely uncalled for."

"Huh!" Matthew returned, slapping the reins. "You

don't know a thing about Nate Kirkland. He's a woman stealer. Whoever came up with that sayin' about the fox in the henhouse had Nate Kirkland in mind."

"Oh! That's unfair!" she cried. "Nathan Kirkland is a perfect gentleman in every way and he's been more than kind to me since I've come to Santa Ines."

"I'll just *bet* he has."

"He has!"

"He ever kissed you?" Matthew demanded.

"How dare you! You have no right to ask such things of me!"

"Dammit, Ettie." He brought the horses to a halt. "If he's done so much as set a finger on you, I'm going to break every bone in his body!"

"Matthew Kagan! You're—"

He had kissed her, and kept kissing until she was pliant in his arms. Until she was more than pliant, actually—until she was just the way he wanted her to be, *his,* and wanting him. Until her hands were around his neck and he could feel the heat of them. She was wearing black again that day, just as she'd worn it every day since he'd seen her in Santa Ines, and the material of her dress felt thick and stiff and unnatural against his hands as he moved to caress her breasts.

As soon as his fingers touched her, she'd lifted her head and pushed his hands away, then sat up and tried to calm her breathing. After a moment, straightening her jacket and hat, she said, primly, as if nothing had passed between them, "If you had any sense at all, you would realize that Nathan is already in love with someone else."

Matthew had fallen back on the bench seat, drawn in a shaking breath, and in spite of his frustration, admired her.

She was good, by God. So damned good. What a partner she would have made all these past years. He could just envision her acting as coolly as this with some of the bandits and thieves he'd had to track down. She would have undone them as easily as she'd undone Drew Quinn, as easily as she'd undone *him*.

"If you mean he's still in love with Elizabeth," he had said when his breathing slowed, "then I do know it. Why Jimmy still lets that Judas into his home, knowin' that, I'll never understand. But just 'cause he's still got feelin's for sister Elizabeth don't mean he won't go after some other man's woman. And it sure don't mean I'd ever let him set his sights on *my* woman."

"I am not your woman," she said. "I am my own woman."

"You're *mine*," he'd told her, setting the horses in motion once more. "Mine, Ettie. And my manners aren't like what you're used to from back east, so you'd better keep a watch out. If I catch Nate Kirkland makin' eyes at you, touchin' you, anything, I swear to God I won't care if he was the pope givin' you his blessin', he's going to get just what any man who touches you will get. And that's a lesson he'll never forget."

It had probably been a mistake to talk to her that way, he thought now, rising to his feet, setting the poetry book aside, and wandering over to the window to gaze out at the folks passing along the boardwalk in the heat of the late summer afternoon. Ettie had been plenty mad with him since then.

Of course, he wasn't so foolish as not to realize what he was up against. She was determined not to believe that he loved her, and Matthew couldn't really blame her for that, not after the way he'd left her in Mariposa. They'd never gotten around to discussing that, and he supposed he should try again to explain why he'd done what he did, how seeing her kissing David Call's photograph had hurt him so bad and that he'd just reacted. The trouble was, he was too afraid of what she'd say if he admitted that to her. He was afraid she'd tell him that he'd never be able to live up to David Call and that she'd never be able to love him the way she loved her dead husband. Those were the only words that would stop him cold in his pursuit of her, and he wasn't going to be the one to give her any reason to say them.

The jailhouse's front door swung suddenly open and Matthew's deputy sheriff, Teddy Stanfield, stuck his head inside.

"There's a drunk shooting up Miss Beverly's, Marshal."

"Hellfire and damnation." Matthew grabbed his hat off the desk and started for the door. "Third time this week. You wouldn't think a quiet town like Santa Ines would have so many troublemakers."

Teddy laughed as Matthew marched past him and out the door. "We don't have half as many as we used to," he said. "Not since you been the sheriff, anyhow. Folks are learning to behave themselves real good."

"They'd better start learnin' it *faster*," Matthew told him. "'Cause I'm all out of patience with this kinda nonsense. I got better things to do than waste time roustin' drunks outta whorehouses."

Half an hour later, as he and Matthew dragged a staggering young man toward the jail, Teddy was filled with admiration.

"Miss Beverly sure seems to like you, Marshal. That was some kiss."

"She knows how to do it right, that's for certain," Matthew said, grinning. "Reckon she was grateful that

I didn't get any blood on her carpet this time. And stop callin' me Marshal. I ain't a marshal anymore."

"Yes, sir, Sheriff," Teddy replied obediently, nudging their obstinate charge forward. "Come on, you. Stay on your feet."

As they neared the jail, Matthew looked up and saw Mariette coming out of Dr. Hedlow's office. She saw him, too, and stood where she was, her eyes fixed on the drunken man between Matthew and Teddy. Her expression was solemn as she watched them progress, and when she at last lifted her eyes to meet Matthew's, the sadness in them was clear.

"You can manage this boy the rest of the way, can't you, Teddy?" Matthew thrust his half of the drunk's weight onto his deputy.

"Sure thing," Teddy said, nearly falling off the boardwalk when the young man slumped against him. "No problem."

"Good." Matthew started in Mariette's direction.

He expected her to turn and walk away, but she stayed where she was, watching him. Nearing her, Matthew remembered the first time he'd ever seen her, in Sacramento, fighting off Drew Quinn and his boys. Had that only been three months ago? he wondered. It seemed like years, instead.

She looked very much today the way she had then, like the wealthy woman he knew she was, dressed elegantly in black in what Matthew figured was the latest style from back east. She wore all the usual female knickknacks—dangling onyx ear drops, a fancy ladies' watch fixed to her jacket with an onyx Victoria chain, a multiflowered black brooch— all black. Even her jewelry was in mourning, he thought with mild amusement. Her beautiful blond hair was swept up smoothly and topped by a black hat that was swimming with black ribbons and black lace that made her gray eyes look bigger and darker than usual.

"Afternoon, Mrs. Call," he greeted when he was close enough.

"Good afternoon, Marshal," she returned evenly.

"What're you doin' here by your lonesome? Where's Bertie?"

She nodded in the direction he'd come from and Matthew turned to see Liberty walking out of a saloon. Seeing Matthew, he stopped in his tracks, smiled and tipped his hat, then turned around and walked back inside.

"The Drohan brothers are faithful guardians, Marshal Kagan," Mariette said. "Except when you're present, of course."

Matthew turned back to her, grinning. "You don't need protectin' from me, honey. And it's 'Sheriff,'" he reminded her, as he'd been constantly reminding her since he returned to town. "I'm not a marshal anymore."

She unlatched her chatelaine bag and pulled out a pristine white handkerchief that was embroidered with a large *M*. "You should be." Lifting the silk cloth to his mouth, she wiped vigorously. When she pulled it back, it was stained with a bright pink blotch that they both stared at.

"Uh . . . ahh . . . " Matthew uttered, stupefied.

"Very pretty," Mariette commented, stuffing the handkerchief into her bag again. "Such a lovely shade of pink."

"Now, honey, there's a good explanation for that and no need for you to get upset."

Mariette responded as politely as if he were one of her high-society acquaintances. "I'm sure there is, Marshal Kagan. However, I fear I must be on my way and cannot stay to listen. Good day."

She turned to go but Matthew hooked his hand around her elbow and held her fast. "Don't be like that," he said in a low voice, pulling her close even as she struggled to be free. "There ain't no reason for it. Miss Beverly gave me a kiss 'cause I got rid of that drunk you saw Teddy take on down to the jail. She was just grateful that I got him out of her place without too much fuss. There wasn't nothin' else to it, I swear. Come on, honey." He grew persuasive. "You know I ain't even looked at another woman since I met you."

Stilling, she gazed at him with lifted eyebrows.

"Oh, all right. So maybe I've looked. But I damned well haven't touched. At least," he added quickly as she started yanking her arm again, "I ain't been the one who's *started* anything and I'll swear that on my mama's grave, if you want me to."

"Really, Marshal Kagan."

"I'm tellin' you the truth," he insisted.

"Very well, sir, I believe you," she said unconvincingly. "Though it really doesn't matter, because I don't care."

"Sure you don't."

"I don't!"

"Good. Then we don't have to talk about it anymore." He nodded at the door she'd just come out of. "You been to see Doc Hedlow? Everything okay?"

"Yes." A faint line of color threaded her cheeks. "The worst of my condition is almost over now, he says. The nausea should stop altogether in another month or so."

"Thank God," Matthew said with heartfelt relief. He'd never heard of anybody having such a hard time adjusting to a new town before, and he hoped Mariette would get over it soon. "You've lost so much weight lately I can almost see through you."

"That's common, or so I'm given to understand." She lowered her eyes. "And, of course, it won't be too much longer before I'll be gaining quite a lot of weight."

"Yeah?" Matthew couldn't keep the surprise out of his voice. She sure needed to gain some weight, but how was she supposed to do it when she ate less than a bird did?

Her eyes flew up to his, angry now. "I won't let myself get heavy as a cow, if that's what you're thinking. I intend to gain only the amount Dr. Hedlow thinks wise and nothing more."

"Well, that's prob'ly best," he agreed placatingly, not wanting to upset her. "Doc Hedlow knows more about this thing than you and me do. I had a talk with him last week, you know. About your condition, I mean."

She looked surprised. "You did? He said nothing to me about it."

"He almost didn't say nothin' to me, either," Matthew admitted, "but I told him how I was the one responsible for you bein' sick in the first place and he gave in."

"Oh, Matthew," she chided. "I wish you hadn't. I told you that I wanted to say it was David's."

"Honey, I already told you that I don't care what you call it, but I ain't the kind of man who won't admit when he's done somethin' wrong."

"I know," she said more quietly. "What did Dr. Hedlow say? I imagine he must have been rather surprised."

"He was a little, at first, but then he settled down

and told me all about how you're doing. He said it would only last a few more months, and that you're healthy and sound and will be good as new after it's all over." Matthew shook his head. "I'll tell you, honey, women sure have things hard. I never knew a man to go through anything like this."

She laughed. "Of course you haven't. Oh, Matthew, you ridiculous man." She laughed again.

He liked that, making her laugh, even when he didn't know how he'd done it. "You going home now?" he asked. When she nodded he took her hand and set it on his arm. "I'll walk you, then."

"It isn't necessary. Don't you need to get back to the jail?"

"I will, soon as I get you home." He smiled at her as they walked along. "Hey, I haven't asked yet today. Will you marry me, Ettie?"

"No, thank you, Marshal Kagan."

"Sheriff Kagan," he reminded her. "Don't you ever get tired of sayin' no?"

"Clearly not," she said with a smile.

They walked in silence for the space of a minute, then Mariette said, quietly, "I'll be leaving Santa Ines soon, Matthew. Probably in another two weeks."

He set a hand over hers and squeezed. They'd had this talk before and it was time she understood what was what. "You ain't leavin', Ettie. You get that in your head. You ain't going nowhere."

"I've had a letter from my father," she said. "I've told him everything, and he's asked me to come back to Sacramento to be near him while he awaits his trial. Afterward . . . well, he seems to think that in exchange for the information he's giving, he might be able to choose where he'll serve his prison term."

"That's prob'ly true," Matthew admitted. "He could go just about anywhere he wants, long as it's a federal prison."

"Yes, that's what he wrote. He's going to ask to be placed where it would be easy for me to live nearby without anyone knowing who I am, where I can simply say that David died and not have to worry about anyone knowing *when* he died, or how. So, you see, everything will be perfectly all right. There isn't any need for you to worry or to keep on as you have. There isn't any reason why you can't go back to being a federal marshal again."

"Sure there is. I resigned, remember?"

"But they never wanted you to," she argued. "Elizabeth told me all about what happened. She said that the federal marshal in Los Angeles would be thrilled to have you back, on any terms you'd care to name."

"Oh, I reckon he would," Matthew said, sounding wistful. He ran a thumb over the back of her hand. "But that's all gone now. Even if I went back, it'd never be the same. 'Sides," he added, grinning, "I'd miss you too much all the time. Wouldn't hardly get nothin' done for missin' you."

"Oh, Matthew," she whispered, her voice filled with pain, "you only think you would. Even if you did miss me, it wouldn't last very long. There are so many women who—" She drew in a breath and fell silent.

"Damn!" he muttered, stopping to open her garden gate. "I told you that kiss from Miss Beverly didn't mean nothin'. She was just sayin' thank you, and that's all."

"It doesn't matter," she said, moving past him toward the porch.

Matthew followed. "It does too matter. I ain't going

to be the kind of husband who's always lookin' for more'n what he's got at home. For Pete's sake, I'd have to be a dadburned fool to do somethin' like that after all the work it's takin' just to get you down the aisle."

"It doesn't matter, Matthew!" she insisted, climbing the porch steps.

When they reached the top Matthew took her arm and swung her around to face him. "What even makes you think I'd be that kinda man? I'll admit I ain't exactly no bud on the vine when it comes to women, but that's all over with now. Or is that what ol' Dave used to do? Leave you home alone to go out with other women? Is that why you don't want to get married again?"

She jerked free and glared at him. "David was a wonderful, faithful husband in every way. He hasn't got anything to do with this. Why can't you understand? I won't marry a man who doesn't love me and I won't marry a man who never wanted a wife. I won't make you miserable for the rest of your life because of something you never meant to happen. I want you to be happy, and you'll only be truly happy if you can go back to the way you were, free and doing the work you loved."

"That won't make me happy now," he insisted. "Bein' with you is the only thing I want."

"No," she said. "That's not true. When I saw you today—you—handling that wretched drunk! Oh, Matthew, it's unbearable to think that I'm the reason you've been reduced to such as that. To giving out licenses and collecting fees and dealing with drunkards." Her voice rose, filling with emotion. "You've become like Samson fallen, weak and chained, and *I'm* the one who's taken all your strength away." She drew in a sharp breath. "I can't—I won't—oh, *damn*!"

She strode to her front door and went inside, closing the door behind her without looking at him again.

Matthew didn't go after her. He was too bewildered to talk anymore, to anyone, so he sat in one of the porch chairs and waited for either Justice or Liberty to show up and take over watching her. It was important that she be kept an eye on until Chambers was caught, and the fact that he hadn't been caught yet gave Matthew plenty of reason for concern. The last wire he'd had from Harry Brown said that Chambers had disappeared; no one knew where he was or if he was even in the country any longer.

Trying to relax, he laced his hands behind his head and leaned back in the chair.

She wanted to leave Santa Ines.

He wasn't going to let her go, of course, but for the life of him, he couldn't understand why she wanted to leave in the first place. She'd only just got here, and after all the sickness she'd been suffering from settling in, he couldn't believe she'd want to move off and go through it all over again. Besides that, he knew she enjoyed the work she was doing for the school, making plans for the upcoming school year and holding fund-raisers for the new building. He was glad, of course, that she was mending her bridges with her daddy, but he sure didn't see why she needed to move just to be near him. He'd be more than glad to take her for visits when they were married, anytime she wanted to go.

The whole situation was getting out of hand, he decided. He wanted Ettie, but he couldn't keep courting her forever. He had to do something, and he had to do it soon.

22

"Are you sure about this?" James asked for the fifth time that night, dismounting his horse. "I mean, flowers and all is one thing, but *this*?"

"I know you think it's stupid, but she likes poems," Matthew told him, tying an unhappy Ugly to a stout tree trunk. "Her husband used to say 'em to her all the time, and she loved it."

"Beth likes that, too," James said, "but she likes it in private. If I ever tried somethin' like this she'd probably scold me good and send for Doc Hedlow to see if I had brain fever."

"Well, Ettie ain't like Beth and she won't do anything like that." Matthew turned a steady gaze on his younger brother. "You ain't going to back out on me now, are you? I got to have someone there to keep Jus and Bertie quiet."

James frowned. "I said I'd help you and I will. But I just don't know if this is the way to go about courtin'

Mrs. Call. I never figured her as the kind of woman who'd like this sort of thing."

Matthew shrugged. "There's all kinds, Jimmy. There's your kind and there's my kind and every other man's kind, and all I can figure is God's sittin' up in heaven laughin' His head off. Now, come on, before I lose my nerve."

Mariette pulled the silver brush through her unbound hair one last time, then set it down on her dressing table beside a handkerchief that bore a large, pink stain.

"That man is making you crazy," she told herself, touching the handkerchief with her fingertips. "More than crazy," she admitted more softly. Pursing her lips, she lifted her eyes and gazed thoughtfully at her reflection. "Is it possible?" she whispered. "*Could* it be?"

But it couldn't, she thought, accepting with honesty the plainness of her features, her too-wide mouth and undistinguished eyes and dull-colored hair. Her father had always said that she had a face filled with integrity, which was, she supposed, as kind a way of putting it as possible. David had generally avoided speaking of her in a physical sense, though he'd been lavish in his praise of her intelligence, her common sense, and what he had called her "great depths of understanding."

It couldn't be true that Matthew saw anything else in her, not when she knew full well there wasn't anything else to see.

But he'd called her beautiful. Many times, he had. And he'd made her feel beautiful, every time he kissed her, every time he looked at her with wanting in his eyes, and that night in Mariposa when he'd made love to her. She'd felt beautiful then. The way he touched her, held her, all of the things he said. He'd made her feel it so strongly. He'd made her *believe* it, until the morning came and she opened her eyes and found him gone.

"Oh, Mariette, you great fool. It's just because he's been so persistent. That's what's making you weaken. A man's never told you he loves you before, and you've let the nonsense go straight to your head. You are a great, foolish fool."

She began to braid her lengthy hair, nimbly separating the thick mass into three equal sections and twining them quickly and expertly.

"What would you do with such a husband, anyhow?" she asked. "With every woman he'd meet throwing herself in his way? You wouldn't know the first thing about keeping a handsome man like Matthew Kagan happy. Oh, he'd do his best, I know that. He's too good a man not to. And he'd be a wonderful father. Wonderful." She tied the end of the long braid with a section of cream-colored ribbon that matched the elegant silk sacque and nightgown she wore.

When it was done, she sighed and met her reflection once more. "But what would you do when you first saw regret in his eyes? When he came home after another day of dragging drunks out of saloons? Drunks." She shut her eyes briefly, trying to push away her memory of that afternoon. "It isn't right," she said softly. "Not for him. Not for Matthew Kagan. He might as well be herding cattle again as to be married to me."

She stood and moved to the lamp stand beside her bed. "And you, young lady or sir"—she patted her slightly increased stomach with one hand as she turned the wick down on the lamp with the other—"must allow me a good night's sleep tonight, if you please. Your father has already given me enough trouble for one day, and although Elizabeth has warned me that Kagans are quite stubborn and hardheaded, I wish you would remember that you are also half Hardesty, and Hardestys, as you will discover one day when you've met your grandfather, are highly diplomatic. Tonight, I think it might be wisely diplomatic of you to—"

"Ettie!"

She straightened and looked toward the open window from which the urgent yet softly spoken word had sounded.

"Ettie!"

She closed her eyes and groaned out loud. "Oh, my heavens," she said, her voice filled with disbelief and aggravation. "It's the middle of the night." Holding the collar of her sacque shut, she strode to the window and looked into the garden below.

He was standing there, gazing up at her, his hat in his hands and a strange look on his face.

"Matthew Kagan!" she whispered loudly, leaning out a little. "What on earth are you doing here?"

"Hi, honey. I'm sorry it's so late, but I just came by to—"

A rustling in a nearby lilac bush, followed by masculine laughter and a loud "hush!" drew Mariette's attention.

"Who is that?"

Matthew glanced at the wiggling bush. "Oh, that's only Jus and Bertie and Jimmy. I tried to make 'em stay on the front porch, but, you know, they got to come and see me make a fool of myself. It'll give 'em somethin' to tease me about for the rest of my natural born days, long as they don't mind losin' a few teeth every time they mention it. Right, boys?" he asked the bush pointedly, and the bush answered, "Right!"

"But what . . . ?" Mariette began, confused. "Did you need to speak with me? Can't it wait until morning?"

"Oh, no, it's nothin' like that."

"Shall I come down, then?" she asked.

He gazed at her thoughtfully. "No, I recollect Romeo did it this way with Juliet, so you stay put and I'll stay put and that'll prob'ly be the most romantic thing." He looked at the bush. "Is that right, Jimmy, or not?"

A voice that was clearly Liberty's called out dramatically, "But, soft! What light through yonder window—oof!"

"Will you be quiet!" James Kagan whispered. "Just get it over with, Matt. Do you want to wake up all the neighbors?"

"What's he going to do?" Liberty asked, chortling. "Arrest himself for disturbing the peace?"

"You're a real nuisance, Slow Bear," Justice muttered.

"Go on, Matt," James encouraged.

"Oh, no," Mariette murmured, suddenly understanding. "Oh, no, Matthew."

"It won't take long," he told her. "Is it the boys? They're upsettin' you. Should I get rid of 'em?" He glanced at the bush again, more anxiously.

"No, it isn't them, Matthew," she said quickly, "but it's so late, and the neighbors, and . . . Wouldn't you rather come and do this tomorrow afternoon?" she suggested hopefully. "In the parlor?"

His expression grew irate. "Like ol' Dave used to

do? Forget it. Now you just be quiet and listen. And
you boys keep quiet, too," he told the bush, "or I'll
come over there and make you wish you had."

Mariette and the bush fell silent. Matthew cleared
his throat a couple of times, then began.

"How do I love thee, let me count the ways. I love
thee to the death and breath and height my soul can
read, when . . . uh . . . feeling out of sorts at the end
of bein' ideal and . . . uh . . . sayin' grace."

Someone in the bush began to snicker, and Matthew
glared in that direction before starting up again.

"Ahem! I love thee at the end of each day, with . . .
uh . . . quiet need and by sun and . . . er . . . candlelight, too. I love thee. . . ."

"Mrs. Call? Are you all right?" Nathan Kirkland
interrupted loudly, calling over the garden gate. "Is
there someone here? Justice?"

Mariette set her face in both hands. "Oh, dear
God," she said.

Nathan unlatched the gate and walked through.
"Liberty? Mrs. Call?"

Mariette peeked through her fingers just in time to
see a long arm reaching out from the lilac bush to pull
Nathan inside of it.

"What the—! *Jim?* Dammit, you almost broke
my—"

"Hush up, Nate!"

The men in the bush fell to whispering and laughing, while Matthew turned an accusing face to
Mariette.

"What's he doing here?" he demanded.

"I don't know," she answered weakly, almost ready
to laugh herself at the comedy this night was turning
out to be. "I promise, Matthew. I really don't know."

When Matthew spoke next, his voice was as rigid as his expression. "Don't you think it's a little late at night for you to be havin' gentlemen callers, Ettie? 'Specially when you're dressed for *bed*?"

"You're here, sir," she reminded him, stifling the giggle that tried to worm its way past her meager attempt at feminine indignity.

"I was just passin' by on my way to Virgil's house." Nathan's voice drifted out of the bush. "I heard voices in the garden and wanted to make sure everything was all right."

Matthew stood there, twisting his hat as if it were Nathan Kirkland's handsome neck and glaring up at Mariette, obviously undecided. Loving him, Mariette couldn't help but take pity. She knew what it had cost him to do this thing tonight, what it meant for him, such a proud man, to open himself to humiliation.

"I didn't invite him," she said. "Please, Matthew, won't you go on?"

Scowling, he looked away.

"It's so lovely," she said softly. "One of my favorite poems. David never did anything so lovely for me, like this."

He looked up at her. "He didn't?"

"Never," she said honestly. "Never."

"Well, I—I forgot where I was."

"I love thee to the level of each day's most quiet need," she told him, "by sun and candlelight. I love thee freely, as men strive for right."

"That's right," he said, nodding. He glanced severely at the bush before starting again, sounding less certain than he had before. "I love thee purely, as they turn from praise. I love thee with the passion I used up in my old grief, and with all my childhood days."

Laughter from the bush stopped him briefly, but Mariette said, "Matthew," and he turned his eyes back to her and went on.

"I love thee with the love I had for all those old saints. I love thee with my breath, and with all the smiles and tears I had in my whole life. And if God decides, I'll love thee better after death."

Done, he let out a tense breath, as if he'd just finished a nerve-racking task, and tentatively grinned at her. The next moment the audience in the bush burst into whistles and loud clapping.

"Hell," Matthew muttered. "I can't do the rest of it with them makin' such a fuss. Can I come in for a minute?"

Mariette glanced down at her flimsy silk garments and pulled the front of her sacque tightly shut.

"Of course. I shall meet you at the front."

As she moved away from the window she heard Liberty say, "Show's over," and Justice yell, "Go get her, Matty-boy!"

He looked out of breath when she opened the door to him; he looked exultant. Smiling widely, he stepped over the threshold and closed the door behind him.

"I'm sorry 'bout the boys, honey." His voice was filled with happiness. "I don't think I could've paid 'em to go away."

"Matthew—"

"I'm sure glad that's over," he said, turning the lock. "I wanted to do that Romeo and Juliet speech, you know, but it was bad enough doing this one. I wasn't about to try somethin' that ain't even written in regular English." He laughed.

"Matthew—"

"You sure wear the nicest things I ever saw." He tossed his hat on the hall tree while his gaze wandered appreciatively over her silk-clad form. "Reminds me of that thing you was wearin' back at John Drohan's house. Remember?"

"Matthew—"

Reaching out, he folded her in his arms and bent to kiss her. His lips were cold from the outside air, as were his skin and clothes, but his mouth was warm as it opened and moved over hers. Her hands fisted in the thick sleeves of his jacket and all her senses took him in: the sinfully pleasant taste of him, the hardness and bigness of him, all the good, masculine smells that she would forever associate with him, leather and wool and gun oil.

"Mmmmm." He lifted his head and smiled. "Feels good as it looks. Will you marry me, Ettie?"

Yes, she thought, smiling back at him. Yes, yes, *yes.*

She opened her mouth to say the word, to give herself over to happiness, when the four men standing on the front porch suddenly burst into song.

"I dreeeeam of Jeeeeeanie with the liiiight broooown haiiiir, boooorne liiiiike a vapor on the suuuummeeeer aiiiiir."

Matthew and Mariette started laughing at the same moment.

"Oh, my goodness," she said. "They're *awful.*"

Matthew chuckled. "Sound just like a bunch of drunks. I oughta arrest *them* for disturbin' the peace."

He kept laughing, but Mariette's smile died. "Drunks," she whispered, pushing away from him.

He let her go, but kept the fingers of one hand wrapped gently around her elbow.

"Ettie?" His gaze was filled with tenderness. "You haven't answered my question, honey."

She couldn't meet his eyes; after what he'd done for her tonight, no matter how misguided his motives might have been, she couldn't bear to hurt him.

"I sent a letter to the attorney general today," she said, trying to speak over the loudness of the men singing on her porch. "After I saw you. I had Mrs. Keeler post it."

"To the attorney general?" he repeated with bewilderment.

She swallowed, and stared at the flowery carpet beneath her feet. "To the United States attorney general. I knew him in Washington. He was a particular friend of my father's."

Matthew's fingers tightened on Mariette's elbow, but she forced the rest of the words out. "I sent a letter asking him to have Marshal Brown reinstate you as a federal marshal as soon as possible."

"What?"

"I want you to go back to what you loved," she managed, agitated, struggling to keep her voice from breaking. "I want you to be free. I keep telling you that, but you never understand. You never listen to me!"

His fingers dropped from her arm.

"Why?" he asked.

"Because I want you to be happy." She lifted her eyes to his at last. "Matthew, I want you to be *happy*."

"I want to marry you. That's the only thing—" He stopped, drew in a harsh breath, and turned away.

She put out a hand to touch him. "Matthew, please understand."

He shrugged free and moved to the hall tree, where he picked up his hat. Fingering it, he murmured in a thick, angry voice, "That's the end of it. I ain't such a fool as to go on when there's no place to go."

"Matthew!"

"Good night, Mrs. Call." He put his hat on and unlocked the door. In another moment he was out of it.

The men on the porch stopped their romantic song abruptly and as the door swung shut, she heard snatches of words spoken by four simultaneous voices.

"Were we off-key?"

"How'd it go?"

"What'd she say?"

"Matt, what's wrong?"

23

"Matthew?"

Pushing open the swinging door, Elizabeth peered into the kitchen and saw her burly brother-in-law sitting at the table, a dimly glowing lamp and an untouched bottle of whiskey his only companions.

With a frown of disapproval, and pulling her thick wool shawl more securely about her shoulders, she walked into the chilly room.

"You ought to be in bed," she told him, first turning the light of the lamp up, then moving to take the big coffeepot off the stove. "It's almost four o'clock in the morning."

"Elizabeth, I ain't exactly in the mood for a talk, so if you came down here to tell me what's on your mind, I wish you'd forget about it and go on back to bed yourself."

"I didn't come down to talk," she replied, filling the pot with water from the sink pump and setting it on the stove once more. "I came to make a pot of coffee."

He laughed humorlessly. "At four in the mornin'?"

"Certainly," she said, turning the crank on the coffee grinder. "It's as good a time as any to make coffee."

"Oh, Lord." He made a miserable groaning sound. "I don't need this. I told Jimmy I wanted to be alone for a while."

"And so you have been," she said, carefully measuring the coffee out. "Three hours of sitting in the dark and feeling sorry for oneself is more than enough, if you ask me."

"I didn't ask you."

"Such behavior is quite foolish and really, I must say I greatly disapprove of grown men wallowing in self-pity as if they were children." She lit the stove with quick expertise, then made certain the coffeepot was where she wished it to be. A large range kettle that she'd filled with water the night before already sat on the stove, and she placed it over a burner as well. "Why, one would think the world had come to an end, to see you sitting here with that look on your face, when all that's really happened is that you've gone and made a great mess of things, as men generally do, and have needlessly upset poor Mariette with your thoughtless actions."

He turned a startled gaze on her. "*I* upset *her*!"

"Yes, I'm sure you did, if what James told me when he came to bed is true." Elizabeth moved to the bread box and took out a loaf she'd baked the day before. "You are a typical Kagan, Matthew, and more stubborn than's right. Mariette has enough to deal with without you standing under her window at night and giving her more. To be truthful, I'm rather put out with you for doing such a thing."

"Dammit, Beth, I was tryin' to be romantic! I was

tryin' to show her how I love her by makin' a fool of myself. What do you females want, anyway? Men are damned if we do and damned if we don't!"

"Matthew Hezekiah Kagan," she said sternly, vigorously slicing the bread into neat, thick slices, "you know very well I don't allow that kind of language in this house. And what Mariette needs isn't romance, it's consideration and kindness. And for the man she loves to be honest with her."

This remark filled Matthew with so much indignation that he could hardly speak. "Honest! I've been . . . she's been . . ." He suddenly sat up straight. "What man are you talkin' about, that she's in love with?"

"Merciful heavens," Elizabeth said irately, lifting a covered dish of butter and a jar of plum preserves out of a cupboard. "I mean you, of course. How can you be so ridiculous? Mariette's in love with you, as if you didn't already know it, and if you didn't," she added before he could deny it, "then you are more foolish than I ever knew, sir."

"Oh, well, of course," Matthew returned sarcastically, waving a hand in the air, "she loves me so much she's just dyin' to walk down the weddin' aisle with me. Didn't Jimmy tell you? She turned me down for about the hundredth time tonight. That's how much she loves me."

"Please do not exaggerate. Of course she turned you down. She doesn't think you love her."

Matthew pretended amazement. "Is that right? Well, my God, you could just knock me over with a feather, sister Elizabeth." He slapped his forehead dramatically. "Why didn't I think of that before?"

"Don't be absurd," she chided, setting a clean coffee cup in front of him, along with a pitcher of cream from the icebox. "How is Mariette to know you love her when you told her so much nonsense about never wanting to marry and about always wanting to be a federal marshal."

"But I already explained all that to her, that it don't mean nothin' to me anymore."

"Have you? From what Mariette's said, you haven't done a very good job of it." Leaning against the sink, Elizabeth folded her arms across her chest. "Matthew, tell me something. Have you noticed anything unusual about Mariette lately? That she hasn't been well?"

"Sure I have." He gave a slight shrug. "I even talked with Doc Hedlow about it, but he told me everything'd be all right. He didn't seem to think she'd suffer from her adjustin' too much longer."

"Adjusting?"

"Doc Hedlow didn't use that exact word, but I knew what he meant, 'cause that's what you told Jus—that it's one of those woman things, some kind of adjustment because of her movin' to Santa Ines. I'll confess I never heard of it before, but there's no doubt she's been feelin' poorly."

"I knew it," Elizabeth said, shaking her head. "She told me you knew, but I couldn't believe you did. No Kagan would ever sit by so mildly in a situation like that."

"What are you talkin' about?"

"I am talking about a man who's too thickheaded to take a good look at the woman he says he loves and understand what it is that she needs from him, and I'm talking about a woman who's so stubborn that she won't accept the fact that any man, or any person, for that matter, can truly love her.

"Now, you listen to me, brother Matthew." Elizabeth

shook the butter knife she held in one hand at him. "At some time during your journey from Sacramento, you did a good job of convincing Mariette that what you desire more than anything else is to remain a federal marshal, because whatever words you said, you spoke them from your heart and she knew it. Now, when you want to convince her that you feel otherwise, you go about it by doing all the same things her husband might have done for her, that any man might do for her. It isn't that she doesn't understand how difficult it's been for you to do those things, for I'm sure she does. The trouble is, she knows you might do the same thing for any woman you were determined to have."

"But I don't want no other woman!" he protested.

"I know that," Elizabeth told him, taking the coffeepot from the stove and filling his cup, "but she doesn't. If you're going to convince her of your feelings, you must speak to her from your heart once more. You must give her something that you've never given anyone else."

"All I got to give her is my love," he said angrily. "I never gave that to no other woman, but Ettie don't seem to want it."

"Oh, she does. She wants it very much. I won't say Mariette hasn't behaved foolishly in this matter, but there's a great deal more to all of this than meets the eye, and if you knew what it was, I'm sure you'd understand why she keeps refusing you."

He looked doubtful. "So how'm I s'posed to figure out what I can give her to make her change her mind? Whatever it was you said—somethin' I never gave anybody else."

"Words from the heart," she said. "Something you've never shared with anyone else."

"Don't seem like much of a gift."

"Words can be the most precious gift of all, when they're from the heart. And they can be the hardest gift to give, too, because you must give so much of yourself along with them."

"Well," he said with a weary-sounding sigh. "Don't reckon I can get hurt any more than I already have. Can't be any worse than quotin' poetry outside a woman's window in the middle of the night. But what do you think I should tell her?"

Elizabeth shook her head and gave him a sad smile. "I can't help you there, brother Matthew, though I wish I could." She bent to kiss his cheek. "You'll have to think of something on your own."

"Great," he muttered.

Lifting the range kettle off the stove, Elizabeth headed for the kitchen door. Pausing, she looked back at him. "I'll fill the shaving basin in your room with hot water. It should have cooled sufficiently for use by the time you've finished eating." Then she left.

"After I've finished . . . ?"

Matthew stared at the table, seeing for the first time everything Elizabeth had put in front of him. Bread with butter and jam, coffee, cream, sugar.

"I am kinda hungry," he admitted, taking up a piece of bread and scooting closer to the welcome warmth of the stove.

He was half finished with the small meal before he realized that his still full bottle of whiskey was missing.

"Elizabeth Kagan," he said aloud, smiling and shaking his head and realizing he would never see that whiskey again. "You sneaky critter. You sneaky, *female* critter."

24

Mariette had just come down the stairs, a small black hat in one hand and a black jacket in another, when a knock fell on her door.

"How wretched!" she muttered, wishing she hadn't sent Mrs. Keeler away quite so quickly that morning. "I don't have time for visitors." She wondered if she might be able to slip out the back door undetected. She'd done it before, a couple of times, but Liberty and Justice had found out rather quickly and had given her quite a scolding after tracking her down.

She was still standing at the foot of the steps in indecision when the knocking came again and Matthew called out loudly, "Ettie?"

The hat and the jacket dropped to the floor and in another moment she'd flung the door open.

"Matthew! I was just on my way to Los Robles to see you. Oh, Matthew, last night, I was so—"

"I know." He stopped her, taking her arm and pulling her into the house before shutting the door on the curious faces of Justice and Liberty. "I came because of that, too. I've got to talk to you for a few minutes."

"Of course," she said, feeling breathless and suddenly unsure of herself. She'd spent every minute since Matthew left the night before deciding what she was going to say to him and practicing how she should say it; but now that he stood there in front of her she almost couldn't remember her name. "Will you come into the kitchen and have a cup of coffee? Mrs. Keeler made some fresh just before she left."

He nodded. "That'd be all right." He followed her into the kitchen, taking his hat off. "You said Mrs. Keeler left?"

"I sent her home," Mariette said as he sat at the table. "I was planning on driving out to Los Robles at once, as I told you, and I couldn't see any reason for her to be here all day by herself when the house is already perfectly clean and there's nothing to be done."

"You were comin' out to Los Robles?" He poured cream in the coffee cup she set before him. "To talk to me?"

She sat in the chair beside him and spoke earnestly. "Oh, yes, Matthew, because I felt so badly after last night, and because I wanted to apologize for the way I behaved and for everything I said. I have never wished more that I could go back and do something over as I have wished that I could relive last night."

He made a sound of self-disgust. "You ain't the only one who's sorry," he said bitterly. "That's one of the dumbest things I ever did. I humiliated you and made a fool of myself. If I could go back, I never would've done it in the first place."

Reaching out, she gripped his hand. "Please don't say that, Matthew. I meant it when I said that David, no one, has ever done anything so wonderful for me before. It was the most perfect, the most romantic gesture I've ever known, and I shall cherish the memory of it forever."

He reddened and stared at his coffee cup. "Well, I'm glad if you liked it."

"Matthew, there's something I must tell you," she said. "I wish I'd said it last night. I wish I'd said it a month ago when you first asked me to marry you."

He pulled his hand from hers. "I know what you're going to say, but there's somethin' I got to tell you first. I ain't going to ask you to marry me again, so you don't have to worry about that."

"But, Matthew, that's what I—"

"But there's somethin' else and it's hard—honey, this is hard for me to talk about, so I wish you'd just stay quiet for a few minutes and let me do it. After, you can go ahead and say what you want, if you still want to."

"Very well, Matthew," Mariette whispered. "Just as you wish."

He still wouldn't look at her but gazed at the tabletop, his brow furrowed as if his head ached.

"Never thought I'd talk about this," he said after a quiet moment. "Never thought I'd even be thinkin' about it. After today, I don't want to talk about it again." He lifted his eyes. "Okay?"

His expression made her draw in a sharp breath, and she nodded.

He lowered his eyes to the table again. "I told you about Langley Tines. Ol' Lang Tines." He smiled. "Good old Lang. He took care of me those two years I was with him. He fed me, kept me out of trouble, taught me just about everything I know about bein' a lawman. A *good* lawman," he emphasized, glancing at her briefly.

"He was a stickler for doing things right. My Lord, he surely was. Everything I did had to be perfect. Had to shoot perfect, had to be able to recite the law perfect, had to ride my horse perfect." He shook his head. "'Cause that's how a man who enforces the law keeps himself alive. Lang knew that and he taught me that. There's rules you follow, rules you know the way you know how to breathe, and if you don't, you end up dead. I told you one of those rules that night when I showed you how to shoot a gun in Knights Ferry. You remember that, honey?"

"Yes," she said softly. "I remember. You said that if I found myself in a position where I had to shoot, then I must aim steady—"

"And shoot to kill," he finished approvingly. "That's right. That's one of the first things Lang taught me. You don't never point a gun at nobody unless you're prepared to kill him, and if you do have to kill, you *do it.* There's no second chances. You do it right the first time or you won't never do nothing else again."

"I understand," she said, tentatively touching his hand with her fingertips, feeling the tension in him.

"I saw Lang kill men," he said. "He was full of patience, never drew on a man unless he had to, but once he did, the matter was over. I never saw a man draw faster or shoot cleaner until I saw Drew Quinn handling his gun that day in Hetch Hetchy. Lordy, but Lang used to put the fear of God into me. I got sick to my stomach the first time I saw him kill somebody, it scared me so bad. But Lang, he said, 'The law was broken, the penalty was just.' He said that all the time. He always talked about the law like it was the Ten Commandments, just as sacred, and like he was Moses, in charge of makin' sure the rest of us followed the rules."

"I wish I could have known him," Mariette murmured. "He sounds like an interesting man."

"Oh, he was." Matthew let out a breath. "He surely was. He taught me lots of things. So much. I . . . I never told him how I—" He swallowed. "I never told him thank you, or what he meant to me, or any of that. I was just a dumb kid. I didn't think anything would happen to make things change. He was so damned good at everything, Ettie, I swear he was." His fingers curled around her hand, holding tight. "He was just what I wanted to be. He was so damned good. I thought he'd live forever, that's how good he was."

"You loved him," she whispered, squeezing his hand. "Like a son loves a father."

He nodded. "Yes, I did. Like that, I did. I was just this damned, *dumb* kid, but he understood. Lang understood. I never had to tell him, never had to explain nothin' to him. He just knew, and I loved him." He shut his eyes and crushed Mariette's hand.

"Oh, Matthew." She pressed her other hand against his, letting him crush it, too.

"He was from Abilene. Real Texas, he called it, 'cause it was in the heart of Texas. He'd always say whenever we finished up a job, 'Come on, boy, let's get us home to Real Texas.'" Matthew smiled in memory. "Abilene didn't look like much to me, 'specially compared to Santa Ines, but he sure loved it and he'd head in that direction every chance he got.

"We were on our way there after a month of chasin' some fellas who'd robbed a bank in Lubbock. It'd been a hard job, and Lang was lookin' forward to gettin' home. He was startin' to get some age on him and had been talkin' about maybe retiring soon. That's one of the reasons he'd written his friend, the federal marshal in Houston, about me, so I'd have someplace to go when he finally took off his badge.

"Anyhow, we were on our way to Abilene, and about a day's ride from there we stopped to rest our horses in this tiny little town. It was one of those places that comes and goes, you know what I mean?" He looked up at her. "Didn't really have no name to it. There was a rickety old saloon, and Lang and I went in to have a few drinks. We hadn't but sat down when the fella who ran the place came over and said, 'You Langley Tines?' which didn't surprise Lang or me 'cause he was pretty well known all around the Abilene area.

"Well, Lang says he is and all of a sudden the other men in the place start crowdin' around and tellin' us about this family that's got a homestead on the other side of the river. Young family, name of McHenry. Carl and Becky McHenry. They got three little kids and a brand-new baby that was just born a few weeks back. Nice family, good neighbors and all. Trouble is, no one's seen Carl McHenry for a couple weeks, and when their nearest neighbors went over to see the new baby, Becky McHenry met 'em at the door with a shotgun and actually fired a few rounds to make 'em go away. They said Mrs. McHenry was clear out of her head, shoutin' all kinds of crazy nonsense and real agitated. No sign of Mr. McHenry anywhere, no sign of the kids. Everybody in the little town is all upset about it, and nobody knows what to do.

"Lang tells everybody to just calm down. Says we'll go on out to the McHenry homestead and have a look, see if we can't find out what's going on. He says it's prob'ly nothin', prob'ly these folks had a little spat, you know, just havin' had the baby and all that. So"—Matthew let out another breath—"we rode out there."

He stopped long enough to drink some of the cold coffee in his cup, and Mariette noticed the fine trembling of his hand when he set it back on its saucer. He gathered up both her hands in his and held them tightly before he started talking again.

"First thing we noticed was the way the place smelled. It was a bad, strong odor, and it was comin' from this small barn on the property a little bit away from the house. We went in there first, though I swear I just about passed out from the stink. Never smelled anything that bad in my life, either before or since.

"Carl McHenry was in there . . . what was left of him, I mean. He'd been out there so long we couldn't tell how it was he'd died. About all we could make out was that he'd been either tryin' to hitch up his wagon or unhitch it, 'cause he was there on the ground with the harness reins in his hand, and there was two horses that'd been dead just as long as him lyin' there, still hitched to the wagon."

"Oh, dear heavens," Mariette murmured.

"Whole place was shot up," he said. "Everything in

that barn was dead . . . two milkin' cows, an old mule.
There was holes in all the walls, like who'ever'd done
it had just gone crazy and shot the whole place to
hell."

He held their clasped hands on the table, his head
bowed over them, as if he were praying.

"We got outta there pretty quick. Lang said somethin' like, 'We got to see what she's done with the
children,' and he told me to take the horses back
down the road a ways, 'cause we couldn't take no
chances of her doing anything to them." Matthew
shook his lowered head, and his voice was tight when
he spoke again. "I didn't want to leave him. I didn't
want to leave him, Ettie. But he—he told me to go on
and take the horses, and I did what he said. By the
time I got back . . . my Lord, I think I ran all the way
back, 'cause I was all out of breath when I saw them
standing out there by the house. Lang and Mrs.
McHenry. She didn't have no gun, she was just outside her door, shoutin' at Lang and tellin' him to go
away, and Lang was standin' a little away from the
house tryin' to reason with her. There was these three
young kids in the doorway behind her, watchin', as
scared as could be. Two boys and a girl. They were all
ragged and thin, and their hair had been chopped off
so they almost looked bald.

"Mrs. McHenry didn't look any better. She was
young, prob'ly not even thirty yet, and she was real
pretty. That's the first thing I remember thinkin'
when I saw her, how pretty she was, but she was thin
as a rail, and shakin' like a leaf. It wasn't normal, the
way she shook, like she was about to fall down and
take to havin' fits. Her eyes, Ettie—blue eyes, I'll
never forget them—her eyes were so scared. She was

just like a terrified kid, all grown up, scared right down to her bones of every little thing. But there was this madness, too. You could see it in her face. She was mad as a rabid dog.

"Lang was talkin' to her real slow, and she started to calm down a little. I moved up slow, too, and kept my hands out from my guns so she could see them. I was just a couple yards away from Lang when he told me to stay put and be still. He said, 'Don't make any wrong moves, boy. Keep your wits.'

"He'd calmed her down by then. Lang was good that way. He told her he just wanted to talk, that was all. She could do things any way she pleased, anywhere she pleased. He'd be happy to come in and have a cup of coffee, or they could stay right there and talk, it didn't matter to him. It didn't matter. . . ."

Matthew squeezed her hands harder, and his head dropped lower. Mariette bit her lips to keep from speaking.

"I don't know what all happened next," he said, his voice higher than before, and forced. "There was a wood pile by the door. A hatchet. She leaned back and grabbed it and then she started screaming."

"Matthew."

He struggled to speak, his voice thick. "I just stood there. I just . . . stood there."

With a strangled sound he pressed his closed eyes against their clasped hands.

"It's all right," she murmured. "It's all right."

"He didn't do *anything*," Matthew uttered suddenly, furiously. "He never even pulled his gun, he just . . . watched . . . with his back so straight. He just watched her come."

He struggled to draw in enough breath, and all

Mariette could do was hold his hands and cry, tears pouring down her face.

"It happened so fast," he managed. "Lang fell on the ground, and then she looked at me. She didn't move or scream or do anything else but look at me. I didn't even know I had my gun in my hand."

He couldn't say any more. Mariette felt his hot tears wetting her hands and she pressed her face against his bowed head, whispering, "Matthew . . . Matthew . . ."

A long time passed, she couldn't think how long, before he calmed and began to breathe evenly. "Rebecca McHenry," he whispered. "That's the first person I ever killed. With her little children watching, I killed her. There was a baby in the house. A tiny little baby, so weak and starved she couldn't even cry. I couldn't never get her brothers and sister to tell me what her name was." Sniffling, he lifted his head. "She died the next day, in the town. Wasn't nothin' nobody could do for her."

He let out a long, shaky breath. "You can prob'ly figure out what all happened after that," he said, unclasping their hands and wiping the moisture from his face. "Somebody in the town knew how to get in touch with Becky McHenry's family, and they took care of the children until her folks were able to get there and take 'em back to their home in Kentucky. The McHenrys and their baby were given a proper burial and I took Lang's body on to Abilene." Pushing back his chair, Matthew stood stiffly and went to the sink. Pumping out fresh water, he washed his hands and face, then he wet a clean dishcloth and took it to Mariette. "Here, honey, this'll make you feel a little better."

As she took the cool cloth and wiped her tear-stained face, Matthew sat down in his chair again. "The folks in Abilene gave Lang a real big funeral. Just about the whole town turned out, seemed like. He prob'ly would've laughed over it, if he'd known, 'specially if he could've seen the great big stone marker they set over his grave."

"What did you do after that?" she asked.

He toyed absently with the delicate bone china handle of his coffee cup. "Oh, I went sort of crazy for a while, I think. I wandered around, through New Mexico and Arizona, keepin' away from folks and stayin' drunk most of the time. I don't guess I knew that I was headin' for home until I actually got there, and even then I didn't know where I was. When I saw Daddy and Jimmy and a whole bunch of the ranch hands riding toward me all of a sudden, I looked at them and couldn't figure out what they were doing there, wherever I thought I was." He smiled. "Ah, Lord, I must've been some sight. Hadn't bathed or shaved for a couple months or more, and I was skin and bones, pretty much. My horse wasn't in any better condition. But they were glad to see me, I recall. Daddy actually cried. And Jimmy just about crushed my bones to dust, he held on to me so hard." He chuckled. "He sure had grown up while I was gone. He looked so different. Daddy did, too, and Mama and Grandmama and everybody. You know, until I met you, Ettie, I don't think I ever felt anything so good as that, as bein' home with my family. They took me right in again, like nothin' had ever gone wrong, and they never asked what had happened to me. Just gave me plenty of time and space to heal up."

He lifted his eyes to hers. "I never talked about this

to anyone before. It's supposed to be some kind of gift, Elizabeth says, but it sure isn't very romantic, is it?"

Reaching up, she gently touched his face. "It's the most precious gift I've ever been given. Thank you, Matthew, for trusting me with so much."

Setting his own hand over hers, he turned and pressed his mouth against her palm. "I love you, Ettie."

"And I love you, Matthew Kagan."

The kiss on her palm stilled. Matthew stared at her in complete surprise, his eyes wide.

"I love you," she repeated, moving off her chair to kneel on the floor before him. Her other hand lifted to press against his chest, where his heart was. "I've loved you for a very long time, and I love you as I've never loved anyone else before."

He blinked and pulled her hand away from his gaping mouth, and kept staring at her.

"P-Professor Call?" he said hoarsely.

"I loved David," she told him softly. "He was so good to me and I loved him deeply because he was my friend. But I didn't love him the way I love you, Matthew." Searching his eyes, she said, "The way I love you frightens me, it's so strong, so overwhelming."

"That's just how I feel about you," he said.

She smiled. "How can you? You're so handsome, and good, and fine, the best man I've ever known . . . and I'm so plain and ordinary."

She suddenly found herself sitting on his lap, crushed in a fierce embrace.

"Don't you ever say such things, Ettie. You're so beautiful it takes my breath away."

He spoke the words passionately, then kissed her with equal passion. When he lifted his head, he demanded, "Did you mean what you just said?"

"About you being handsome? Of course—"

He made a face. "Not *that.* The other. Did you mean it?"

She smiled. "That I love you? Yes, I did mean it. I love you, Matthew Hezekiah Kagan."

His expression was filled with complete amazement. "Was that what you was comin' out to Los Robles for? To tell me how you felt?"

"Yes," she admitted, flushing. "And to apologize and explain why I've been refusing to marry you and to tell you that I—"

His hand closed over her mouth, gently. "Let's leave it right there for now. Okay? I didn't sleep a wink all night, and I'll bet you didn't, neither, and what we both need before we have this talk is some sleep."

She pulled his hand away. "But—"

He put his hand back. "I already said I wasn't going to ask you to marry me today. It's just more than I can think about right now. Tomorrow I'm going to come back here and you know what I'm going to do then, don't you?"

She nodded.

"And after you're done tellin' me whatever you feel like you got to, and after I'm done askin' all the questions that've kept me awake for the past three weeks, you're going to give me an answer, aren't you?"

She smiled beneath his hand.

He smiled, too. "Aren't you, honey?"

She chuckled low in her throat, the sound muffled by his hand.

"Women," he declared, taking his hand away. "I'm going to get you back for that one of these days. Soon. But right now"—he stood and set her on her feet—"I'm so worn out I feel like I could just about sleep on your livin' room floor."

"You can sleep here, if you like," she offered.

The look he gave her was decidedly warm. "Honey, you don't know what you're sayin'. That's just about the most dangerous proposition I ever got in my life." He took his hat up from the table and set it on his head. "I'm going over to the jail to sleep. It's quiet there, and I don't think I could make it all the way back to Los Robles. But I'll be back here tomorrow afternoon. Around three."

"I'll be here," she promised.

He bent to kiss her, and when he stood full height again, he yawned, then, embarrassed, laughed. "I guess I'm plumb worn out. Gettin' too old for this kind of thing. Funny, though," he said, touching her hair with his fingers as if he couldn't believe how soft it was. "I never felt so good in all my life as I do right now. Bet I'll have good dreams."

"I hope so," she said, putting her arms about him and hugging him tight. "I love you, Matthew."

"I love you," he told her, and kissed her again. When he started for the back door he said, "Just make sure you give me the right answer tomorrow." Then he stopped, when he opened the door, and looked back at her. Rubbing his chin, he said, "Handsome, huh?"

She laughed.

"I like that," he told her, walking out the door. "Yeah, I like that real well."

25

"*Lovely,*" *Mariette murmured,* pushing the lid of the crate all the way back and pulling a large, heavy book out from the depths of the shredded packing paper inside. "Perfectly lovely." Setting the book in her lap, she ran her fingers over the green silk cloth of volume number one of the newest edition of the *Encyclopaedia Britannica.*

"The children will find this most useful," she said approvingly, then set the book next to where she knelt on the floor and started digging through the crate for another one. "Yes, indeed." She piled the second book on top of the first and began the search for a third. "New and completely up-to-date. Just as everything will be this year."

She glanced at the two other crates that needed to be opened and emptied, both of them filled with books for the school, and wondered whether she would be able to complete the task today. It was already past noon and she couldn't take the chance of not being ready to receive Matthew when he arrived at Hanlan House for his appointed visit. Aside from that, she knew very well that every extra hour she spent away from home would add that much more to the lecture Liberty and Justice would give her when they discovered she'd snuck out of the house without them knowing. As soon as they did know she was gone, they would shortly after show up at the schoolhouse and drag her home at once. Then the books wouldn't get put away and she wouldn't have the few hours alone that she needed to think things through.

Setting the last heavy volume down with the others, Mariette rested for a moment, letting her mind wander again through the maze she kept trying to find her way out of.

He loved her. He *loved* her. As impossible as that seemed, she believed it. More than that, she *knew* it, deeply and surely. From the moment she'd understood what he was telling her the day before, she had known.

Matthew Kagan loved her. It was nothing short of miraculous, and Mariette was still shaking her head in absolute amazement. She didn't know how it had ever happened, or what she had ever done to deserve such a wonderful thing. But one thing she did know: she would never again question the matter or take Matthew's love for granted. It was precious, and she would cherish it accordingly until she last drew breath.

Even if she didn't marry him.

With a sigh, she closed the lid on the empty crate and was just beginning to shove it beyond a row of desks when she heard the sound of a horse coming up through the schoolhouse yard.

"There they are," she told herself. "Or one of them, at any rate. How very vexatious." She gazed at the other crates first with regret, then with a look of increasing speculation. "Hmmm," she intoned thoughtfully. "I wonder . . ."

Matthew rode Ugly right up to Mariette's gate before stopping.

"Why don't you just bring him up on the porch?" Liberty teased as Matthew tied the angry, snorting horse to the fence.

"Hold your tongue," Matthew warned. "He may hear you and start gettin' ideas about tearin' the fence down." To Ugly he said, "You just behave yourself. I'm not going to be gone all day."

He strode to the porch and climbed the steps, nodding at the Drohan brothers who were relaxing, as usual, in the comfortable porch chairs.

"Afternoon, boys."

"Afternoon, yourself," Justice said, pulling his feet off the porch railing and sitting up straight. "What's wrong? You look like you've got bad news."

His mouth set in a grim line, Matthew rubbed tiredly at his eyes before saying, "Yeah, it's bad, I'm afraid. I just got a wire in at the jailhouse. Elliot Chambers and some of his boys killed Ettie's father five days ago."

Liberty sat up, too. "My God."

"How?" Justice asked. "He must have had protection."

"Four federal marshals," Matthew said. "All dead, killed along with Hardesty. Chambers is long gone, of course. God only knows where."

"Five days," Justice said. "That's a good lead if they haven't caught him yet. He could be just about anywhere by now, even out of the country."

"I can't think why it took anybody so long to let me know about it," Matthew said angrily, lifting his hat and running a hand agitatedly through his hair. "I s'pose they were tryin' to think up some kind of excuse before lettin' Ettie know, but dammit, if Chambers was crazy enough to kill Hardesty, then he's damned well crazy enough to try anything. I want Ettie under constant watch until he's caught and jailed. I don't want her leavin' this house for any reason."

Both brothers nodded.

"All right, Matt," Justice said.

"I'm going to bring some of my necessities and stay here at nights, too. We'll set up some kind of schedule and take turns watchin' the place."

"I'll take bedroom duty," Liberty offered.

Justice laughed and Matthew glared.

"I ain't in the mood for none of that," Matthew told him, sticking his hat back on his head. "Lordy," he muttered, "I've got to tell Ettie her daddy is dead."

"I'm sorry, Matt," Liberty apologized sincerely.

"She was just talkin' about him a few days ago," Matthew said. "She'd had a letter from him and they'd made up all their troubles. Lord."

The three men kept a momentary silence, none of them knowing what to say. At last Matthew started for the door.

"Better get it over with," he said with resignation, lifting his hand to knock.

She could hear him walking up the schoolhouse steps and quickly pried open the last of the two crates, tossing the lid back. Smiling triumphantly and lifting up the box chisel and hammer, Mariette stood to greet whichever of the Drohan brothers had come to fetch her.

"I know you're very angry, but I'm not going to listen to a word you have to say unless you first help me to unpack these books and put . . . them . . ."

Standing inside the open door, Elliot Chambers pulled the elegant black fedora from his head and smiled. "Good afternoon, Mrs. Call."

Shock paralyzed her and she stood where she was, staring. He was not a large or distinguished-looking man, but there was an air of sureness and ease about him. Dressed in an expensive suit of the finest fashion, he looked like an ordinary businessman, a trusted banker, perhaps, and just as harmless. She had always thought Elliot Chambers the greatest contradiction possible. He exuded gentleness and civility—it was nearly impossible to imagine him causing anyone harm or even unhappiness—yet he was evil and corrupt and, as she knew very well, heartlessly cruel.

"It's marvelous to see you again," he said, just as if they'd met at a social function in Washington, D.C., and he was about to ask her to dance. "It's been such a long time. You look very well."

Mariette swallowed, and her fingers tightened around the instruments in her hands, the chisel and the hammer.

"Wh-what are you doing here?"

He took a step toward her, casual and relaxed. "I was disappointed when you declined all my invitations in Sacramento, as it was you I had especially gone there to see. I was confident Mr. Quinn would be able to persuade you to change your mind, but unfortunately, Marshal Kagan intervened." He stepped closer, even as Mariette backed away, and laid his hat gently on a desktop. "Marshal Kagan has been unfortunate for me in many ways, as I'm sure you know. My, what a good many books there are on the floor."

Books? Mariette's mind whirled. Trembling with fear and anger, she said, "You have been unfortunate in the lives of many people, sir, as I'm sure *you* know."

He smiled benignly. "To those who have stood in the way between myself and my goals, yes. But for many more I have been a positive influence. An exceedingly positive and profitable influence."

"For men like my father," she said bitterly. "Not for those whose lives you traded for money and certainly not for my husband."

A stack of dictionaries sat on another desk and Elliot Chambers fingered them consideringly.

"Professor Call was a fine man," he said softly. "I admired and liked him and respected him in no small degree. His foolishness regarding myself was regrettable and I did all I could to make him see reason. Really, I can't ever remember having been so patient with another as I was with your husband. I was deeply sorry when it became necessary to silence him."

Her heart seemed to drop right into her feet. "Silence him? You *killed* him!"

Elliot Chambers lifted sad eyes to gaze at her. "There was no other choice, but I wish you will believe that I was sorry for it. I am an admirer of mathematics, though you may not be aware of it, and have read all your husband's writings many times over. He was—"

"How dare you!" Mariette cried, enraged to hear David's murderer speak of him in such a way.

"—brilliant," Chambers concluded. "Absolutely brilliant. It pained me to kill him, just as it shall pain me to kill you, Mrs. Call."

Mariette took another step away.

Elliot Chambers lifted an elegantly manicured hand and slipped it inside his jacket. "You may take it as a compliment, madam, that I regret doing this to you." A small gun, such as the one Matthew had given her to use when he left her alone at Knights Ferry, was in his hand when he pulled it into the light again. "There have been perhaps five people in my life whom I've disliked killing. Your husband was one, and you are another. Your father, on the other hand, was not. He was a constant thorn in my side these many years, always worrying, always complaining. I took great pleasure in watching him die."

The words struck Mariette like stones, and she gasped. "That isn't—that's not true!"

"I'm sorry," he apologized politely. "I didn't mean to distress you, Mrs. Call. I shouldn't have mentioned the matter." He took another step closer, tilting his head as he regarded her. "I have always liked you. You are not a beautiful woman, but you've a wonderful, clever mind and such an air of femininity. The combination is most effective. There have been not a few moments when I've contemplated the pleasure it would be to enjoy your charms in the physical sense, Mrs. Call, and when I've envied Professor Call his marriage rights."

"You haven't killed my father," she said, feeling, with wretched humiliation, her bottom lip trembling and her eyes filling with tears. "You haven't done that."

"I'm sorry," he apologized again, following as she

kept backing away. "I've hurt you, but you'll not suffer long, my dear, I promise. I wish I could say that you will soon be joined again with your father, but I can't believe that's true. You will join your husband in heaven, I'm sure, while your father, well, I don't think I can put it more kindly than to say that he is most likely not in that place."

"You're . . . you . . ."

"I'm afraid we can't converse any longer, Mrs. Call," he said, lifting the gun with a steady hand. "Your father made it impossible for me to stay in this country and now I must make my way to Mexico as soon as possible. I only stopped here, in Santa Ines, long enough to silence you." He laughed lightly, pulling back the hammer. "It's my conscience, I fear. A truly wretched device, but it does bend me to its will and so I give way to it. It will never let me rest, otherwise. I must kill those who betray me, those who lie constantly awake on the edges of my thoughts. I must put them to rest, else I must kill myself. You see the difficulty, don't you, my dear?"

David's face passed through Mariette's mind—David alive, and as he was when she'd found him dead. The memory weakened her, made her so afraid that she couldn't move. And then she thought of Matthew.

Mariette didn't know what she'd done until she heard Elliot Chambers's sharp cry and saw him pressing both hands against his face, near his left eye. Blood seeped fast through the fingers that still held the gun and Mariette realized that she'd thrown the hammer and chisel at him.

Uttering a savage curse, he swung the gun toward her once more, but Mariette was already moving, springing away just as the schoolhouse reverberated with the gun's loud report. She didn't have time to think; she started wildly throwing and shoving everything she could set hands on at him—desks, books, slates—as fast as she possibly could.

Another shot rang out, flying past Mariette with a rush of air. Screaming wrathfully, she hefted a volume of the new *Encyclopaedia Britannica* and tossed it with all her might. The heavy book caught him in the neck, upsetting his balance and sending him to the floor where he landed flat on his back with a loud boom. The gun slid away, clattering when it came to rest against a crate.

Mariette raced for the door, past Elliot Chambers's briefly winded body, but was jerked roughly back when his outstretched hand gripped her flying skirts.

"There!" he said victoriously as he sat, took hold of her skirt with both hands, and, with one strong tug, tumbled her down to the floor beside him.

Hands fisted, Mariette tried to strike him, but he easily deflected her blows. She saw him rising over her, his face dripping with blood from a long gash beneath his eye, and then a sharp pain flashed across her cheek, stunning her, and again, on the other side of her face, another blow of his fist. Dazed, she blinked, trying without success to clear her mind, to focus her suddenly foggy eyes. Elliot Chambers was crawling away from her . . . toward the gun.

With a groan of pain, she wrapped her arms about his legs.

He tried to kick free, to keep crawling, but she held him fast, gritting her teeth against the throbbing ache in her head.

"Bitch!" He reached down to grip her hair, yanking until he pulled a fistful of it free.

Mariette sank her teeth into his leg until he screamed. He took hold of her hair again, lifting her head off the floor and smashing it into the wood. Once, twice . . . pain and blackness flooded her. With only a thread of consciousness left, Mariette heard an inhuman roar, then felt Elliot Chambers being lifted from her as though he were a light, fluttering blanket instead of a man.

The furious roaring went on, and a loud, sickening pounding sound thundered in her ears.

Moaning, she opened her eyes.

"Matt, that's enough!"

Justice Twelve Moons? Mariette slowly pushed herself up, shaking her head, trying to clear it.

"You're going to kill him!"

Lifting her eyes at last, she saw them, only a few feet away. Matthew was pounding something into the floor, over and over. Justice gripped him, tried to pull him away, but Matthew only stopped long enough to shove him aside, then, emitting a feral growl, started pounding the object of his fury into the floor again. Elliot Chambers, she realized as her eyes focused. Or what was left of Elliot Chambers.

"Matthew," she murmured with effort. "Don't."

He didn't hear her. She tried to make her voice louder. "Matthew!"

A terrible cramp welled in her stomach, making her gasp. She pressed a hand over her belly and cried, *"Don't!"*

Still he wouldn't stop, not until Justice took his shoulders and shook him and shouted at him, turning him toward Mariette. She saw Elliot Chambers's bloodied body for only a brief moment, and then another cramp struck, making her squeeze her eyes tight.

"Ettie! Oh, my God." Matthew was kneeling beside her, putting his arms around her. "Oh, God," he said again, his voice filled with agony. "He hurt you, but it looks . . . it looks like it's not too . . ." Gentle hands touched her face. "Dammit, I'm going to *kill* him!"

She started to cry. "Matthew!"

"It's all right, honey." His voice was shaking almost as badly as his body. "It's over now. It's all over now."

Another spasm gripped her belly, and she cried out with pain.

"What is it?"

"The baby," she gasped. "The baby."

"The baby?"

"Oh, Matthew, don't let me lose the baby." Tears streamed down her face.

Stunned, he stared at her. "Baby? Ettie . . . what are you . . ."

The darkness began to flood her once more, and she couldn't hear what he was saying. His face, filled with concern and fear, blurred. She tried to grip him, to hold him and keep him with her, but he went away, just as the room went away, just as everything went away.

26

The first time Mariette woke, she found herself in her own bed, with Liberty sitting beside her reading "The Fall of the House of Usher," by Edgar Allan Poe, with wide-eyed intensity.

"Mr. Drohan," she whispered.

He made a sound like "whuh," bolted upright in the chair, dropped the book on the floor, and set both hands over his heart.

"Mrs. Call," he said after a moment, breathing harshly, "you just took ten years off my life." Looking at her then, his expression filled with concern, and he leaned closer and took her hand. "How are you feeling?"

She squeezed his hand weakly. "The baby . . ."

"Baby?" Liberty repeated, then said with sudden understanding, "Oh, the *baby*. The baby's fine, ma'am. Just fine." He blushed all the way up to the roots of his hair. "Matt wanted to be the one to tell you. I'm sorry he's not here. He was, until Dr. Hedlow assured him you'd be fine, but then he had to go round up the rest of Elliot Chambers's men at the place they were waiting and arrest them. Justice went to give him a hand and make sure he didn't kill anybody while he's still in such a bad mood."

"The baby's fine?" she repeated, wanting to make certain she understood.

"Yes, ma'am. Dr. Hedlow said you'll need to be careful for a few days and to rest, but that there isn't any sign of trouble. With the baby, I mean. Chambers bruised your face pretty good. I'll bet it hurts something fierce."

Gingerly, she touched her puffy face with her free hand. "Yes, it does."

"Dr. Hedlow will be coming back to see you again as soon as he's finished patching up Chambers, and then he can give you something for the pain. You got off pretty light compared to Chambers. He doesn't have hardly any face left at all. Matt sure can get crazy when he loses his temper. I imagine he would have killed Chambers if he hadn't been so worried about you, and he threatened to make Dr. Hedlow a eunuch if he didn't take care of you first before he went to have a look at Chambers. Never seen him so upset before. You sure gave him a scare, ma'am. Gave all of us a scare." His expression grew stern. "And I don't even want to repeat what Matt said he was going to do to Twelve Moons and me for letting you slip out unnoticed."

"I'm sorry," she said. "I never thought—"

"Oh, it's all right," he said quickly, patting her hand. "I shouldn't have said anything. You've been through plenty today without me making you feel badly. Why don't you try to get some more rest? Matt will be back soon, and you won't want to be too tired to talk to him."

The second time Mariette woke, Dr. Hedlow was sitting on the bed, poking at her. He confirmed what Liberty had told her, that as far as he could see, the baby was fine and unharmed, no thanks to Matthew.

"That man hasn't got a brain to call his own," Dr. Hedlow declared as he listened to her heart. "I must've dropped him on his head when I delivered him. Bad enough that Chambers fellow tossed you all over the place, but for Matthew Kagan to get you up on that demon horse of his and gallop you all the way back into town . . ." He shook his head with disgust and packed away his stethoscope. "I just hope you'll be patient with the man when you're wed to him, my dear, and always bear in mind that he's mentally deficient."

The third time Mariette woke it was dark, and her bedroom was dimly lit by lamplight. Matthew was there, sitting in the chair Liberty had been in, close by her bed, and he was gazing at his knees and scowling.

She weakly pushed a hand across the covers toward him.

"Matthew."

"Ettie!" He moved quickly to sit on the bed beside her. "Honey, how're you doing?" He stroked her hair gently.

"I'm fine," she murmured. "How are you?"

He bent to kiss her forehead. "Better now. Not so good before." Pressing his cheek against her hair, he said in a thick voice, "Thank God you're all right. Thank God." For the space of a minute he simply held her, not speaking, but when he at last straightened, his gaze was solemn. "You gave me the scare of my life, Ettie Call. I don't never want to go through that again."

"I'm sorry, Matthew," she whispered.

He started scowling again. "Sorry," he muttered, standing. "I don't want apologies outta you, Ettie. I want *answers*."

He was scowling at *her,* she realized, and Mariette swallowed.

"Why didn't you tell me you was pregnant?" he demanded. "And what do you mean by going all over town—*anywhere*—when you got my baby in you?"

Whatever she'd been expecting him to say, it certainly hadn't been that. "But you knew!" she protested. "I mean, you know. We've spoken of the baby often. You said you'd talked to Dr. Hedlow about it, even."

He was moving around the room, agitated. "I *didn't* know," he told her. "Damnation!" He ran his hands through his hair, then glared at her. "Do you think I'd've spent so much time messin' around and courtin' you and all if I'd known you was carryin' my child? I feel like a dadburned *fool*."

Mariette didn't feel that great, herself, all of a sudden. "But, Matthew—"

"I thought you was adjustin'," he said angrily. "I thought you were sick because you was adjustin' to movin' here, to Santa Ines."

"Adjusting?" she repeated, bewildered.

He waved a hand in the air and made a sound of disgust. "It's what Elizabeth told Jus and Bertie to keep 'em from knowin' you was pregnant, and what Jus told me when I came callin' that first day and Mrs. Keeler said you wasn't well. I know it sounds crazy," he admitted when she opened her mouth to speak, "but you told me you couldn't have kids, and it never entered my mind that you might be pregnant. If it had, I sure wouldn't've taken none of your no's for an answer, and we'd be an old married couple by now."

She stared at him, pacing back and forth at the foot of her bed, and was thoroughly amazed. "I didn't think I could bear children," she said honestly. "I didn't lie to you in Mariposa. The first time you asked me to marry you, you said I could give my wedding ring to our daughter, if we had one. I thought you meant this time. I thought you meant this baby, if it was a girl."

"I didn't know what all I was sayin' that night," he said irately. "I was half out of my head. But that reminds me." Resolutely, he moved back to the bed and took hold of her left hand, sliding off her wedding band. "There." He slapped the gold band on the bed stand and dug the engagement ring he'd bought her out of his vest pocket. "We're gettin' married as soon as possible."

She tried to pull her hand free. "Matthew, we need to talk about that."

"No, we don't," he said firmly, sliding his ring on her finger. "We're gettin' married and that's that. I ain't puttin' up with any more nonsense outta you, Ettie. That's my baby you got in there"—he pointed at her stomach—"and we're gettin' married. Besides, you love me."

"I do, Matthew. I love you very much and I want nothing more than to be your wife—"

"Good!"

"But I can't. Not unless you'll promise to go back to being a federal marshal."

"Lord." He sat on the bed again. "You got the hardest head God ever made. Bet I could crack rocks on it. *Why* do you keep bringin' all that up after I already told you I ain't going back to it?"

"Because I won't have you giving up the thing you love most just because of me," she told him tearfully, wanting so much for him to understand. "Because I can't bear to see Matthew Kagan spending the rest of his life dragging drunks out of saloons."

"*You're* the thing I love most," he said, placing a hand lightly on her belly, over the covers. "You and this little one here."

"But you loved being a marshal," she whispered.

"I was proud of it," he corrected. "I enjoyed it, and I didn't see no other thing for me to do in this life, but, honey, I'm just plain tired of it. I don't guess I knew that till I got a taste of somethin' different, but it's the truth. I'm tired of huntin' people down, tired of sendin' folks to their deaths."

Mariette bit her lip, feeling anew the pain of what he'd told her the day before, of Rebecca McHenry and of a young, frightened man watching his hero die.

Matthew touched her face, carefully, moving his fingers around the edges of the bruised places. "I'm tired of not havin' a regular home, and sleepin' on the ground, and eatin' cold food. I'm gettin' too old for all that, too." His fingers slid beneath her chin, lifting her eyes to his. "I got a hankerin' to have a more settled kind of life now. Like maybe being a sheriff in a small, quiet town and doing real easy things like handin' out licenses and draggin' drunks outta saloons. And havin' a wife and kids and regular meals."

Unwanted tears slid out of her eyes and Mariette gave a watery sob. "I can't cook," she confessed. "I almost burned the house down one day, and if Elizabeth hadn't been visiting and known what to do, I would have."

"Can't cook?" he said, pretending amazement as he wiped her tears away. "Oh, well. Guess we'll just have to keep Mrs. Keeler on."

"I guess so," Mariette managed. "Oh, Matthew, I've been an idiot. I don't know how you could love me."

He kissed her tenderly. "Don't cry, honey. You're worn out and feelin' poorly, but I swear everything's going to be okay. I'm going to take good care of you, and I'm going to be the best husband God ever made. I swear it. And the best daddy, too."

Her arms closed about his neck, hugging him tight while she cried.

"I love you, Ettie," he murmured, wanting to soothe her, wanting to make sure he didn't hurt her by holding her too close. "Are you going to marry me, now?"

She started crying harder, but nodded against his shoulder.

"Thank the Lord," he said. "That sure took plenty of doing, gettin' you to say yes." Pulling back to look at her, he asked, "You ain't going to change your mind on me, are you?"

"No," she promised. "Never."

He nodded. "Good," he said, sitting up and pulling his boots off, "'cause I am plumb worn out. The last thing I want to do right now is argue with the most stubborn woman I ever knew." He tossed his left boot on the floor. "You're too smart to argue with, anyhow," he declared. "Which is a lesson I'm glad I learned before we got wed, otherwise I'd prob'ly have wasted a lot of time tryin' to talk around you." His right boot fell beside its brother and was shortly joined by Matthew's coat. The next moment Matthew was lying beside Mariette, on top of the covers underneath which she lay, one arm carefully about her waist and his face pressed into the warmth of her neck. "Lordy," he said, groaning, "that's better."

Mariette didn't question the propriety of his obvious intent to sleep beside her; she lifted a hand and stroked his stubbly cheek.

"Matthew, before Chambers attacked me, he said something about my father. He said he had killed him."

Matthew's hand came up and closed over hers, squeezing gently.

"I'm sorry, honey," he murmured, and went on to tell her that Chambers had been telling the truth. He told her how her father had died and about the other men Chambers had killed along with him, and then, when he was finished, he said once more, "I'm so sorry."

"I'm sorry, too," she whispered, strangely calm. "I loved my father, though he did much harm and brought a great many people unhappiness. Still, I wish I could have seen him one more time. I did love him," she said more insistently. "I don't know why I can't cry for him."

"You will, in time," he told her. "You been doing so much grievin' lately, it'll just take awhile before you can do any more."

"Maybe you're right," she said softly. "It's still difficult for me to think of my father without remembering the part he played in David's death. Perhaps that's what the trouble is."

"Maybe," Matthew said, then fell quiet.

After a moment, Mariette asked, "What will happen to Chambers now?"

"He'll be sent back east for his trial, soon as he mends up enough to travel. If he lives, of course."

A tremor of shock ran through Mariette, but Matthew was unperturbed.

"Doc Hedlow said he'll prob'ly make it. Not that it'll do him much good. There's no way he'll get around bein' hanged or shot for his crimes, and I sure ain't going to lose any sleep over the likes of Elliot Chambers. The man's as rotten as spoiled meat. I'm more upset about gettin' all that blood on the school-house floor. That'll take some hard scrubbin' to get rid of."

He yawned again and snuggled to get closer, and Mariette, saying nothing, began to stroke his cheek again.

"I love you, Matthew," she said quietly.

"As much as Professor Call?"

She heard the need for reassurance in his voice and smiled, though it hurt her face to do so. "Yes, and much more. I never knew such a love existed."

Matthew hugged her. "Professor Call did," he said. "He loved you somethin' fierce, I reckon."

"No, we were friends," she said. "I told you that. He was kind to me, but our marriage wasn't made out of love."

"Maybe not on your end of it," Matthew replied, "but ol' Dave loved you, Ettie. I'd bet my horse on that. Why do you think he was tryin' so hard to turn Chambers in?"

"Because he felt it was the right thing to do."

Matthew made a *tsk*ing sound. "It's 'cause he was tryin' to impress *you*. That's what it was. Do you know why I left so quick that mornin' in Mariposa?"

"Because you regretted making love with me?" she ventured.

"Good Lord," he said, his breath hot against her

neck. "That's the dumbest thing anybody ever said. Makin' love with you that night was the sweetest thing that ever happened to me, and I been dreamin' about doing it again every night since. I left 'cause I saw you kissin' that photograph, that one of you and him on your weddin' day. After you came back to bed and fell asleep, I got up and went to have a look at it and you know what I saw?"

"What?"

"I saw a fella who looked like he'd just struck gold, that's what. If you can look at that photograph and not see the way David Call loved you, then you need to get yourself some specs, Ettie."

"I was saying good-bye to David that morning," she whispered.

Matthew's body stiffened. "Huh?"

"I was saying good-bye to him, because I had fallen in love with you and meant to tell you when you woke. That's why I kissed the photograph. I was saying good-bye."

"Well, for Pete's sake," he said. "I figured you was kissin' him 'cause *you* were sorry. About us."

"Never," she said. "I'll never be sorry. I'm going to spend the rest of my life being amazed that a man like Matthew Kagan could ever want a woman like me, and I'm going to do everything I can to make you glad for marrying me."

Chuckling huskily, he said, "Yeah? That sounds real promisin'. Soon as we get married, honey, I'm going to spend a whole lot of time showin' you just exactly how I like to be kept glad."

27

Two weeks later, in his bedroom at Los Robles, Matthew was impatiently, and against his will, being helped to dress for his wedding.

"Keep still, Matt, will you? I'm almost done."

"You're puttin' it on too tight," Matthew insisted, slipping a finger beneath the silk neck scarf his brother was tying. "Don't know why a man has to get so dressed up at a time like this, anyway."

"It's not too tight," James told him, finishing the knot before Matthew could ruin it for the third time in a row. "You're just so nervous your neck's swelled."

"Well, it's your fault if I am," Matthew grumbled, stalking around the room and tugging at the tie. "Yours and sister Elizabeth's. What'd I ever do to the two of you, anyway?"

James laughed. "Calm down, Matt. It's just a weddin'. Nobody's going to bite you."

Matthew didn't look entirely convinced of that. He shrugged uncomfortably in the fancy suit he'd worn to court Mariette, trying to make it fit his large body and savoring the thought of burning it after the day was over. "All I wanted was a quiet little weddin' out in Ettie's garden," he said. "That too much to ask? But, no, you and Elizabeth got to go all out, got to invite half the town out to Los Robles to watch me and Ettie tie the knot and turn the thing into a spectacle."

Following his restless brother's pacing, James brushed a bit of lint from one of Matthew's broad shoulders. "We invited the whole town," he corrected, "and it's only right for you to get married at Los Robles. This is your home."

"Not for long, it ain't. Hanlan House is where Ettie and I are going to live. It's where my children are going to be born and raised."

"You can go live on the other side of the moon, for all I care," James replied. "You're a Kagan, and your children will be Kagans, and Mariette's going to be a Kagan in about half an hour here, and Los Robles is the place *all* Kagans call home. Here." He walked over to the dresser and filled two large glasses with whiskey from a decanter set there. "You'd better have a swallow of this to settle your nerves."

Tugging again at his collar, Matthew accepted the drink James handed him. "What I need is to get this thing off so I can breathe again."

"Here's to Mariette," James said, lifting his glass.

"To Ettie," Matthew agreed.

Sipping his drink, James took his older brother in from head to toe. "You look good, Matt. Never thought I'd see the day when Matthew Kagan would be dressed up to get married, but I'm real glad I have. Sure wish Mama and Daddy could see you."

"Me, too," Matthew said solemnly.

"They'd sure be happy," James went on, "and they'd love Mariette."

"Yeah, they'd prob'ly ask her why such a nice gal like her was marryin' a crazy old coot like me."

"You aren't old. You're only forty this last June."

"Don't remind me," Matthew said sourly, taking a big swallow of whiskey. "Can you believe I'm going to be a daddy? Forty years old and I'm going to have a baby."

"That worries you?"

"Well, some," Matthew admitted, tugging at his collar again. "But I talked it out with Ettie these past couple weeks and she says I'll be all right. She's so happy, you know, to be havin' a baby after all this time. She just got over feelin' poorly from being pregnant, and all she can talk about is havin' another one, already, soon as this one's born and diapered."

James laughed. "Sounds like she's going to keep you busy, Matt. Being such an old man, you'd better keep your strength up."

Matthew grinned. "You're one to talk, little brother. Sister Elizabeth told me this mornin' what you been up to, not like you're ever up to anything else, of course. Congratulations."

Reddening, James accepted the hand his brother extended. "Well, this one wasn't planned, but, you know . . . these things happen, and Beth is happy to be havin' another baby."

"That's what she said," Matthew told him. "And it'll be nice for my baby to have a cousin close to his age. Or her age."

"I'd like a girl, this time," James said, his smile growing dreamy. "A pretty little girl with black hair and big black eyes, just like her mama."

Matthew set his empty glass aside. "I'll take anything I can get. I don't care what it is."

A knock came on the door, and James went to open it. He turned back into the room carrying a package wrapped in white paper and tied with silver ribbons.

"For you," he said, handing the package to Matthew. "From your bride, I'll bet."

"Well, my word," Matthew said, amazed. "What's this, I wonder."

It was a watch, as he discovered when he sat down to open his present, a man's watch with a twenty-jewel Hampden movement and a solid gold case ornamented in a simple design with large diamonds and a matching fourteen-karat gold vest chain.

"Good Lord," James said, much impressed, leaning over his brother's shoulder to gaze at the expensive gift. "That sure beats the little watch I gave Beth a few years back. Good thing your wife's got plenty of money. I wouldn't even want to guess what that thing costs."

Wordlessly, Matthew opened the hinged front. The clock's elegant face stared back at him, and on the inside of the case's smooth gold surface the words *Happy am I* were engraved in a large, rolling script, along with his name and Mariette's.

"There's a note," James said, but Matthew had already set the watch aside and was unfolding the single piece of paper that had been in the box.

Then he read what was there, written in Mariette's hand.

I know, not, love, when first you found me,
What instinct led you here:
I know the world has changed around me
Since once you came so near.
I yield a thousand claims to nourish this,
At last the dearest hope; the nearest tie;
And looking but to you for happiness,
Happy am I.

—"Your Coming"
by Dora Read Goodale

Swallowing, he set the paper aside and took the watch up again, blinking rapidly.

"Well," he said.

"That's nice," James said, squeezing his shoulder. "You got yourself a good woman, Matt."

Matthew nodded and swallowed again and kept blinking. "I sure have, Jimmy." He let out a breath. "Did I ever tell you 'bout the time she faced down Drew Quinn?"

James chuckled. "Only about a hundred times."

"Oh, well, then, when the heck is this weddin' gettin' started?"

Forty-five minutes later, exactly when Elizabeth had said the wedding would begin, Justice Twelve Moons Drohan and Liberty Slow Bear Walking Drohan walked the bride down the aisle to her anxious and fidgety groom.

When they got there, Justice leaned over to Matthew and whispered, "You take good care of her or I'll have my Cherokee grandmother put a curse on you that you'll carry beyond the grave," and Liberty leaned over and whispered, "If you ever make her cry I'll spend the rest of my life on your front porch," both of which promises made Matthew's eyes widen. Then the brothers grudgingly gave Mariette over to Matthew's care.

"What's wrong," she whispered as he took her hands. "What did they say?"

"Nothin'," Matthew lied, shaking his head to clear it of horrible visions of being stuck with Liberty for the rest of his life.

She smiled at him, then, looking so beautiful and perfect in her flowing white gown that he felt like he might get all emotional and make a fool of himself.

"Ettie," he whispered, full of awe that she was going to be his at last, "after all my years, after all my wandering . . . honey . . ."

He couldn't go on, and tears shone in Mariette's eyes.

"Yes," she said, squeezing his hands, understanding. "Oh, yes, Matthew."

He squeezed back, swallowed, and said, not caring how loud he was or who heard it:

"Happy am I."

Epilogue

Matthew Kagan wasn't a man who shed tears often in his life. The number of times, in fact, could be counted on less than ten fingers.

He cried when he told Mariette of how Langley Tines had died. He cried again when Mariette gave birth to his twin sons, when he held them for the first time in his arms, and yet again three years later when she presented him with a daughter.

In 1901, when the first motorcar made its way over the San Marcos Pass and into the Santa Ines valley, Sheriff Matthew Kagan, in the middle of his workday, heard the news as he stood outside of Simonson's Dry Goods, then sat down on a nearby bench and cried as if a member of his family had died. In 1913, when the local paper reported that President Wilson had signed into law a bill allowing the damming of the Hetch Hetchy valley so that it could be turned into a reservoir for the city of San

Francisco, Matthew sat in his garden, with his wife holding his hand, and wept mournfully.

But his life and Mariette's were filled much more with laughter—and plenty of broken beds—than with tears.

In spite of his fears, Matthew was a good father and his children proved to be the joy of his life. He taught his sons, and his daughter, how to fish and hunt, how to shoot a gun properly, how to start a decent fire. He taught them, as Langley Tines had taught him, to respect the law, weapons, and the lives of others. And each spring, long before it was dammed, when he was certain the snow had melted, he took his family camping in the Hetch Hetchy valley.

He tried to learn poetry and then tried to recite what he'd learned to his wife, who always kissed him and put him in a chair and sat on his lap and asked him instead to tell her stories about his days as a federal marshal, which Matthew was glad to do, because he never was sure that he had got the poetry memorized the way it was supposed to be.

In the evenings, when they were young, Matthew would arrange his children comfortably on his lap in a big chair before the fire and tell them a story. It was the story of the man whose photograph held the place of honor on their mantel, a man who had been good and intelligent and very brave. It was the story of a man who had once loved their mother so much that he had risked and lost his life because of her.

It was the story of David Call, whom Matthew taught his children to respect and admire, just as he had grown to respect and admire the man who had given him the most precious gift he had ever received.

Evensong by Candace Camp

A tale of love and deception in medieval England from the incomparable Candace Camp. When Aline was offered a fortune to impersonate a noble lady, the beautiful dancing girl thought it worth the risk. Then, in the arms of the handsome knight she was to deceive, she realized she chanced not just her life, but her heart.

Once Upon a Pirate by Nancy Block

When Zoe Dunham inadvertently plunged into the past, landing on the deck of a pirate ship, she thought her ex-husband had finally gone insane and kidnapped her under the persona of his infamous pirate ancestor, to whom he bore a strong resemblance. But sexy Black Jack Alexander was all too real, and Zoe would have to come to terms with the heartbreak of her divorce *and* her curious romp through time.

Angel's Aura by Brenda Jernigan

In the sleepy town of Martinsboro, North Carolina, local health club hunk Manly Richards turns up dead, and all fingers point to Angel Larue, the married muscleman's latest love-on-the-side. Of course, housewife and part-time reporter Barbara Upchurch knows her sister is no killer, but she must convince the police of Angel's innocence while the real culprit is out there making sure Barbara's snooping days are numbered!

The Lost Goddess by Patricia Simpson

Cursed by an ancient Egyptian cult, Asheris was doomed to immortal torment until Karissa's fiery desire freed him. Now they must put their love to the ultimate test and challenge dark forces to save the life of their young daughter Julia. A spellbinding novel from "one of the premier writers of supernatural romance." —*Romantic Times*

Fire and Water by Mary Spencer

On the run in the Sierra Nevadas, Mariette Call tried to figure out why her murdered husband's journals were so important to a politician back East. Along the way she and dashing Federal Marshal Matthew Kagan, sent to protect her, managed to elude their pursuers and also discovered a deep passion for each other.

Hearts of the Storm by Pamela Willis

Josie Campbell could put a bullet through a man's hat at a hundred yards with as much skill as she could nurse a fugitive slave baby back to health. She vowed never to belong to any man—until magnetic Clint McCarter rode into town. But the black clouds of the Civil War were gathering, and there was little time for love unless Clint and Josie could find happiness at the heart of the storm.

COMING SOON

Say You Love Me by **Patricia Hagan**

Beautiful Iris Sammons always turned heads and was doted upon by her parents, whereas her fraternal twin sister Violet was the quiet one. An attack on their caravan by Comanche separated them irrevocably, but their legacies were forever entwined through their children, and through the love that ultimately bound them.

Promises to Keep by **Liz Osborne**

Cassie McMahon had always dreamed of a reunion with the father she hadn't seen since she was a child. When her hopes were dashed by his distant manner, she found consolation in the arms of a mysterious but seductive stranger. But Alec Stevens was a man with a secret mission. Could he trust his heart to this irresistible woman?

Cooking Up Trouble by **Joanne Pence**

In their third outrageous outing, professional cook Angelina Amalfi and San Francisco police inspector Paavo Smith team up at the soon-to-be-opened Hill Haven Inn. Soon they encounter mischief in the form of murders and strange, ghostly events, convincing Angie that the only recipe in this inn's kitchen is the one for disaster.

Sweet Deceiver by **Angie Ray**

Playing a risky game by spying for English and French intelligence at the same time, Hester Tredwell would do anything to keep her struggling family out of a debtor's prison. Her inventive duplicity was no match, however, for the boldly seductive maneuvers of handsome Nicholas, Marquess of Dartford.

Lucky by **Sharon Sala**

If Lucky Houston knows anything, it's dealing cards. So when she and her two sisters split up, the gambler's youngest daughter heads for Las Vegas. She is determined to make it on her own in that legendary city of tawdry glitter, but then she meets Nick Chenault, a handsome club owner with problems of his own.

Prairie Knight by **Donna Valentino**

A knight in shining armor suddenly appeared on the Kansas prairie in 1859! The last thing practical and hardworking Juliette needed was to fall in love with an armor-clad stranger claiming to be a thirteenth-century mercenary knight. Though his knight's honor and duty demanded that he return to his own era, Juliette and Geoffrey learned that true love transcends the bounds of time.

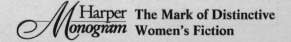

*M*onogram **Harper** The Mark of Distinctive Women's Fiction

Glory in the Splendor of Summer with *101 Days of Romance*

BUY 3 BOOKS — GET 1 FREE!

Take a book to the beach, relax by the pool, or read in the most quiet and romantic spot in your home. You can live through love all summer long when you redeem this exciting offer from HarperMonogram.

Buy any three HarperMonogram romances in June, July, or August, and get a fourth book sent to you FREE!

Look for details of this exciting promotion in the back of each HarperMonogram published from June through August—and fall in love again and again this summer!